Christina Rainville has been a successful lawyer for thirty years, including eight years as a Chief Deputy State's Attorney in Vermont, where she successfully argued a landmark criminal case before the United States Supreme Court, headed a Special Investigations Unit, and handled juvenile court proceedings.

She lives in Florida with her husband, Peter Greenberg, who is also a lawyer and author.

THE COURAGE TO TELL

A NOVEL ABOUT SECRETS

BY
CHRISTINA RAINVILLE

GREENVILLE PUBLISHING
DESTIN, FLORIDA

This is a work of fiction. All of the characters, organizations, and events portrayed in this novel are either products of the author's imagination or are used fictitiously.

ISBN 978-1-7354680-4-4 (paperback)
ISBN 978-1-7354680-3-7 (e-book)

First published by Greenville Publishing
April 2021

To my law school friend and sister-in-law, Gay Parks Rainville, for giving me the courage to write this book.

Prologue

A warm spring night on the South Side of Chicago. Driving his squad car outside the most dangerous public housing project in the city, the cop is waiting for something to happen. Usually if he's patient, he'll find someone he can nail, for something. He's sick of this shift, sick of dealing with the shootings, the junkies and gangbangers -- scared that one day he'll get hit in the cross-fire. He should have been transferred to Rogers Park, like he'd been asking for years, but his boss was a jerk. Across the street he sees a woman in a car parked with the windows down. Waiting for something. He wonders what law she's about to break. He doesn't recognize her, she's not one of the usual sex workers or dealers. She's still sitting there in her car even after he pulls up. Pretty brazen to be selling her wares across the street from a squad car.

A kid comes out of the building. Him, he recognizes, this one has a record, he doesn't remember exactly for what. The kid is running toward the parked car. He has something dark and metal in his hand, it's glinting in the streetlights. If you're a cop, you need to think fast. He's been around, he knows how to read a situation. The kid has a gun, he's gonna carjack her, the bitch must have something worth stealing, drugs, who knows what. He calls for backup. The kid already is at the car, reaching in the open window with the gun. He's out of his own car, reaching for his service revolver. He shoots, then again and again. The kid drops the gun. He missed. The kid's off and running. But, bad news, the woman is slumped over the wheel.

She's hit, three times in the chest. If she isn't dead yet, she's about to be. There's a small camera sitting on the passenger seat. Not a gun. He picks up the camera and puts it in his pocket. Then he looks in the back for the drugs. There's a little kid in a booster seat, behind the driver, just staring into space. "You'd better keep your fucking mouth shut about what you just saw unless you want the same thing to happen to you," he snaps. He waits for backup.

Chapter One

"Bad guys win again, huh Mom," Cyndi said as Karen Harding walked in the front door.

"You're all over tv, 'family of teen girl who died after taking acne drug distraught after judge throws out case,'" Cyndi continued. "'High-priced Chicago lawyer gets German pharmaceutical giant off the hook on a technicality. Live at 6.' Proud of you, Mom."

Karen Harding, whose mother always told her she could be beautiful if she would only bother to wear makeup, heels, and do something with her hair, was, in her mid-forties, a partner and a litigator at Chicago's biggest and most prestigious firm, Christian and Johnson. Until now, she'd had a good day: getting a judge to toss a lawsuit against Wilkommen, GMBH, the firm's biggest client, on a technical argument she managed to spin out from the legislative background of an obscure drug labeling law from the 1960s; holding a televised press conference with the company's joyous CEO; and getting tv time that she could live without.

At 16, Cyndi was sure all her opinions were beyond dispute. Joey, her 11-year-old brother accepted them as gospel. "I hate when you're on tv," he added, "cause I get so much shit in school."

"Your mouth?" Karen scolded, with a smile.

They were good kids. Entitled, yes, expecting everything; grudgingly agreeing to do dishes in return for being chauffeured wherever; bought whatever they needed (wanted) on the family Amazon account but at least asking permission first; and living in a house on the Lake in the toniest of the North Shore suburbs. A modest house for the neighborhood, true, with dirty white vinyl siding, a '70s kitchen, bathrooms with nasty green tile, but it was better to save for their college than upgrade Karen thought, even though she made a lot of money as a partner.

"There's a new website, 'Justice for Kayley.com,'" Cyndi went on. "'Pimples aren't worth dying for, and they are better than kidney failure.' And don't start with everyone's entitled to a lawyer, blah, blah,

blah. Nothing says they're entitled to you. Did you hear that people are now calling your Wilkommen client, 'we'll come and kill you'?"

Karen has learned better than to engage with Cyndi when she's on a roll. "Dinner?" she asked. "Chinese? Thai? Korean? Pizza?" Cyndi once said that Karen's recipes consisted of a folder of takeout menus she kept in the drawer by the refrigerator.

"No time," Joey said. "Dad's picking us up soon. Just make pasta."

"Diablo sauce," said Cyndi."

"Way too spicy," said Joey. "Marinara."

Karen took the sauce jars out of the cabinet -- as usual, she'd heat up both -- and asked when their father had decided he was picking them up -- since it was her weekend.

This hadn't been a friendly divorce to begin with, and things hadn't improved. She and David communicated exclusively by text, and as little as possible. Mostly, they communicated through the kids.

"So Twisted Sister called into some radio show and got four tickets to some concert in Detroit, and I guess they don't have any friends, so we're going for the weekend," Cyndi said.

"Your father's going? Since when is he into music?"

"He does what Twisted Sister tells him," Joey said.

After the kids first met Judy, David's silicone-enhanced girlfriend who broke up their marriage and would never be forgiven, Judy told Cyndi that she would be like her sister. After all, she was only eight years older. Henceforth, Twisted Sister.

Cyndi pulled Joey into the next room, and Karen overheard them arguing.

"If you don't tell Mom, I will," said Cyndi.

Karen walked into the hallway. "What are you talking about?"

"Tell her, Joey."

"I can't believe you're doing this to me Cyndi. I had nothing to do with it!"

They both blurted it out at the same time: Twisted Sister had bought Joey a box of condoms.

They looked at Karen to see what her response would be.

4

"She said it was better to be safe than sorry," Joey weakly tried to defend his father's girlfriend.

"Excuse me, but you're 11." Karen was pissed. What kind of message does this send to an 11-year-old boy? She wanted to scream. She wanted to call her divorce lawyer and get an injunction to prevent Twisted Sister from having any input in decisions involving her children. She wanted David to pick up the fucking phone and telephone her if they were going to do something important and -- for once in his life -- maybe think about the consequences without just running forward like a bull in a china shop. She wanted to tell the kids that their father was a low-life scum-of-the-earth who couldn't keep his pants on; had given her not one but two sexually-transmitted diseases; and falsely convinced Karen she had gotten chlamydia and HPV from a toilet seat, which seems crazy to think of now (how could she be so stupid?) -- but that was back before you could google "chlamydia" and "HPV" on the internet. Above all, Karen wanted to tell her kids that she did not want them to grow up to be like their father or Twisted Sister or to date anyone like them.

But the kids' therapist had told Karen that it was important to not say bad things about their father to the children, and to not react with hostility when David pissed her off, so she tempered her voice and refrained from saying the things that she wanted to scream from the rooftops.

"Look, this is a very important discussion that we need to have, Joey, but you've got to eat quickly and get ready for your dad. In the meantime, leave the condoms in the house because you will certainly not be needing them in Detroit or at any time in the near future."

Cyndi snickered.

"Okay, Mom." The kids seemed relieved that she hadn't exploded. Karen was proud that she had gotten through tonight's events without screaming about their father. And now she would have the entire weekend to figure out how to have a calm discussion with her 11-year-old son about sex, relationships, consent. Consent? At 11?

Divorce sucks, thought Karen for the thousandth time, especially when you have kids and have to play nice about it. Playing nice wasn't how Karen litigated her cases. She was famous for ripping her opponents to shreds in the courtroom. She'd love to do that to David and Twisted Sister. At night, she fantasized about cross-examining them on live television to show the world how disgusting they were. She'd wanted to take the divorce to trial to shame them, but she had given in -- primarily for the kids, but also for her -- and settled it by consent decree. She'd so much wanted to destroy David.

After the kids quickly slurped down their pasta and collected their things for the weekend, Joey watched by the window for David to drive up. They knew that their mother wanted nothing to do with their father, so they always ran out to his car and got in. Not that he would ever bother getting out of the car anyway. He hadn't stepped foot in the house in three years, since the day he cleaned out his closet and left a note saying he wasn't coming back. On Valentine's Day.

It was pouring and very gusty as David drove up. Karen kissed the kids goodbye, then went inside and ordered Chinese food: three dishes so nobody would know she was home alone. The leftovers would last the weekend.

As she opened the door for the delivery person an hour later, the wind blew the door wide open. It was blowing so hard, and she could see by the streetlights that it was raining sideways. She could barely hold onto the door. She took her food, tipped the delivery man, and thanked him for venturing out in the terrible weather.

"Yeah," he said, "This is our last delivery. We're closing early due to the weather. I heard tornado warnings. One of our guys told me that a tornado hit on the Northwestern campus."

As the wind howled outside, she put the Chinese food on the kitchen table, opened a bottle of wine, and started to dig in the containers with the chopsticks from the bag. "Why dirty dishes if I'm the only one eating it?" She pulled up a weather app on her iPad to see if there were tornados -- she could get to the basement in a second, and, because she was paranoid about tornados, she had emergency water and other supplies all ready. She decided that staring nonstop at the weather radar was stupid, so she went back to reading the news.

The doorbell rang again. The delivery man in trouble? Something must have happened. She went quickly to the door and pulled it wide-open without even looking to see who was there.

A kid. Maybe late teens? Dripping wet. Wearing a bathing suit and nothing else. No shoes. He was holding a life jacket in one hand and a cell phone in the other. He looked exhausted, and his skin wasn't a normal color, on the blue side, like he had hypothermia. His lips were purple and he was shivering terribly. The wind was howling and whipping the life jacket as he held it at his side and the rain rattled inside the door.

Chapter Two

"I'm really sorry to bother you. I was windsurfing, and, when the wind picked up suddenly, my mast line broke. I got blown God knows where. I had to hand-paddle in, I ended up on your lawn. I don't even know where I am. My phone is supposed to be waterproof, and the screen is on, but I can't make a call." He pulled his phone out of his bathing suit pocket to show her. "Would you mind letting me use your phone so I can call a friend to pick me up?"

"Oh my God. Come in."

"No, that's okay. I really don't want to bother you. I just need to make a call."

There was a simultaneous flash of lightning with very loud thunder. They both startled.

"Maybe getting inside is a good idea," he smiled uncomfortably.

As he stepped inside, Karen had to push the door closed against the wind. A pool of water immediately formed at his feet.

"Are you alright? Let me get you some towels." Karen was concerned. He didn't look okay, not at all.

"Yeah, I'm fine. I'm really sorry about this," he said as he looked down at the pool of water on her wood floor. "A towel would be really nice. And something so I can get the water off your wood floor. But I don't want to trouble you. I really just need to call my roommate to come pick me up. And I don't even know where I am. Is this still Evanston?"

"No, Winnetka. You must have gotten blown pretty far north," Karen called out as she collected a handful of towels and her phone. He started drying himself off, as she put a towel over the puddle on the floor. He took her phone and began to dial.

"Shoot. I keep getting voicemail. My roommate was going out tonight. I'll try another number."

He wasn't having any success.

He made another call. "Hi, is this Northwestern sailing center? Good. It's Richard Adams. Yeah, I just want to let you guys know I'm okay. My mast line broke, but the board and everything else are fine.

9

Yeah, definitely call off the Coast Guard search. I ended up in Winnetka, but I'm fine. I'll return the board tomorrow. Okay? Thanks. See you tomorrow."

Karen realized that he must be a college student at Northwestern. She knew the sailing club well.

The kid was shivering terribly. As Karen watched him leave a voice message for his friend, she realized that his lips were completely purple. It really did look like he had hypothermia. Maybe he's older than she first thought. Mid-twenties? His trembling seemed to be getting worse.

"Look, the weather channel is urging everyone to stay inside," she pointed out. "Three tornados have hit the area already, and it's very dangerous out there. It's not really safe for your friends to pick you up now anyway."

"You really should get into a hot shower right away," she insisted. You look like you have hypothermia. Your lips are really purple and you're shivering terribly. You can't go anywhere right now in this weather. Please, let me show you where the shower is."

"Thank you, you're really kind, but I'm okay, I think." He was trembling so badly that his teeth were chattering now. "And I don't want to be a bother. I can just wait outside until I reach my roommate."

"I'm not going to let you wait outside in this weather. Please, get in the shower. Hypothermia can be really dangerous."

"Okay. I guess." He could barely get the words out as his teeth kept clicking together. "Thank you."

She walked him back to the bathroom. "I'll get you a robe. My husband's." Be smart, she thought to herself. Although he didn't look scary, it seemed safer if this stranger thought she had a husband.

She stepped aside, went in her bedroom, and grabbed the box with David's robe from his closet. The robe she had spent way too much money on for the last Valentine's Day gift -- the day when she came home to his empty closet and the note. Too distressed to return the robe to the store, she left the box on the dresser until she moved it into his empty closet. Now, the thought of another man wearing this robe gave her a perverse pleasure. She took it out of the box and took the tags off.

She handed him the robe and some clean towels. "Actually, you might be better to take a hot bath. Do whatever you want -- stay in the warm water as long as you need. Call me if you need anything."

"Thanks," he chattered. He went into the bathroom. Karen heard him turn the bath on.

She texted her friend Denise from work. Unlike Karen, Denise was happily married, with grown kids.

"There's a naked man in my house."

"Are you okay? Should I call the police?"

Karen was kind of insulted that Denise knew immediately that it wasn't like she'd had a date and was now happily naked with some guy.

"It's fine. A kid was windsurfing and got stuck in the storm. He has hypothermia, so I told him to take a hot bath."

"You have a naked stranger in your house? You need to get him the hell out."

"I know it sounds crazy, but I think he's fine. He's just a kid."

"Shouldn't you call his parents to pick him up?"

"Not that kind of a kid. A college student, maybe."

"Well, maybe, if he's of age and opportunity knocks. When was the last time you had sex? Three years?"

Karen had figured that Denise would turn this conversation into a discussion about how Karen never has sex. The truth was that Karen didn't like sex much. She had spent 18 years in a relationship with David and never once had an orgasm that she didn't give herself. Sex was often dry and painful, and David never cared. He was your classic "Wham, Bam, Thank you ma'am" kind of guy. Except he didn't even say thank you. She had had a boyfriend in college for a little while, and sex with him was no better. She'd read a story in the Tribune about a tv show that was joking about a vibrator. She bought one discretely and kept it hidden in her closet. That was way more pleasurable than being intimate with David.

After David left, her friends had tried to fix her up. There was the guy Denise had vouched for. When he came to the house to pick her up, Karen let him inside while she quickly went to the bathroom before they left on the date. Karen came out of the bathroom to find him lounging stark naked on the couch, in a "come fuck me" position.

"When a woman invites a man into her house, it sends a clear message!" he complained when she kicked him out. And then he yelled back at her as he got back into his car, for all the neighbors to hear, "What was I supposed to think when you went into the bathroom!" There was the guy who took her out to dinner and hit on the waitress the entire time. And the guy who insisted on ordering for her, and even insisted on ordering the lamb even after she told him she was allergic to lamb. He told her no one was allergic to lamb and she'd love it. Then, he had the nerve to be angry when she refused to eat it or anything that touched it. There was the guy she had a miserable lunch date with who then embarrassed her publicly the next day by sending the world's biggest bouquet of flowers to the office. Or the guy who insisted on repeatedly moving her water glass at dinner to the other side of her plate. The list of horrible dates was endless. By her age, the good men clearly were all taken. She didn't date anymore and she had no regrets about it.

It wasn't like she had given up. She just wasn't interested. Her work took so much of her energy, and everything else went to the kids. She had decided when the kids were born that she couldn't have it all. If she was going to work hard enough to be a good lawyer and make partner, something had to go, and it wasn't going to be the kids. She had eighteen years to do it right before they each left for college, so they got every minute that was left after work. While she had had an enriching group of close friends whom she loved to spend time with, she had to let them all go. Every vacation was focused on the kids, every minute of every weekend, every minute of every evening. She worked sixty hours a week or more: they got everything that was left. That was how it had to be. Karen was the first woman to ever work in her family after she had kids. Her dad was an engineer. Her three brothers had corporate jobs and none of their wives worked. They all viewed her work with unwelcome sympathy -- like maybe if David had been a better provider she would have somehow *chosen* to give up her law degree and stay home to change diapers. She had no role models for how to work and parent at the same time.

But the pressures were real. How can you be a mother when you drop little kids off at daycare at 7 a.m., pick them up at 6 p.m., and don't get home until 7 p.m.? Now that they were older, her time during the week with them was limited to rushing them off to school, feeding them when they got home, and encouraging them to go to bed at a reasonable hour. Weekends were the only real quality time she had for them, and even then, she often worked a few hours after they went to bed.

When Karen was a kid, Karen's mother greeted her when she got off the school bus. Her mom immediately asked her about her day, got her a snack, helped with homework. Karen's kids did their homework in the after-school club. Karen hardly even knew what they were learning. By the time they got home at 7 pm they were starving, exhausted, and grumpy. When Joey was little, he would simply scream, for hours.

And then there was the guilt over school events. Karen had never once been able to go on a field trip, and rarely could take the time off for school events that occurred during the day, like parent's day, the choir program, teacher meetings. Her mom had attended *everything*, but Karen attended basically nothing. She had planned, many times, to attend, only to be called for some emergency hearing scheduled by a court at the last minute. You can't get a court extension because you have a parent-teacher meeting scheduled that day. Judges don't care, opposing lawyers would object to your request, and clients would be livid if you postponed their case because you had to meet with your kid's teacher. A judge once called her into his chambers and reamed her out for sending a colleague to cover a hearing because she had to attend an emergency medical appointment for her daughter. Karen burst into tears in the judge's chambers, hoping he might be ashamed of his conduct. Fat chance.

So, finally, Karen gave up on the idea of attending school events because the kids were so disappointed when she inevitably failed to show up. The kids needed to know that they could rely on her when she said she would do something -- unlike their father. Not showing up when they expected you was far worse than never scheduling in the first place.

Of course, there were other mothers who worked and somehow had time to attend field trips and teacher meetings and everything else.

The kids were always supportive about her failure to attend school events. "Don't feel bad, Mom," Cyndi had said. "We don't want you there anyway." Cyndi was only part-joking. "The important thing,"

Cyndi said, "Is that we're really proud of you for how hard you work." That was pre-teen Cyndi, when she was the nicest kid in the world. "What would she say now?" Karen wondered.

Karen was terrible at socializing with the other parents and frankly hated most of them anyway for their entitled and judgmental attitudes. "Oh, you let your child eat candy?" one parent asked as she glared at the tiny pack of chocolate that seven-year-old Cindy was sharing with the woman's daughter. "Please don't give candy to my daughter," she complained, "sugar is really bad for a child's development." Or the mother who declared, "I don't let my boys play with video games, so please make sure that Joey does not bring them to our house." Every time her kids brought home perfect test scores, Karen couldn't wait to hear from her kids how poorly the kids who received "proper parenting skills" had performed. The parents ought to spend more time reading to their kids than hovering over their food choices and prohibiting video games, Karen thought. She got angry all over again.

Karen heard the bathroom door open. The kid must be out of the bath. She got up to make sure everything was alright.

Chapter Three

"Thanks a lot. I didn't realize how cold I was."

His color was better, and he was no longer shivering. Karen noticed the robe. To say that David's robe didn't fit him would be an understatement. The sleeves ended just below his elbows, and, while he had wrapped the robe around him as best he could, it wasn't exactly big enough to stay in place and it was way too short. Even with the belt tied, he needed to hold it together with his hands.

"Do you want me to put your wet bathing suit in the dryer?"

"That would be great. Thanks."

"Here," she said, handing him her phone. "Try your friends again, but the weather's still too terrible for anyone to come out."

He called a few numbers, but they all went to voicemail. He left messages, explaining what had happened, and asking his friends to call Karen's number.

"While we wait for the weather to clear up, are you hungry? I just had Chinese food delivered."

"I'm actually starving, but I don't want to be a bother. I can just wait in your garage or something."

"That's ridiculous. Sit down" -- she motioned toward the small table in the kitchen which was pressed up against the wall, with one seat on each of the three open sides -- "and have some Chinese food. I'll get you a plate. Would you like a glass of wine? Some water?"

She put the food in serving bowls, decided to put out two plates and utensils so she could join him, and poured them both a glass of wine.

She sat down at the end of the table as they ate.

"Wow, this is a lot of food. Were you expecting company?"

"No, my kids were supposed to be here, but they ended up having other plans," she kind-of lied.

"I'm really hungry. Am I eating too much? Are you sure this is okay?"

"Don't be ridiculous. Eating will help to get your strength back. Don't worry about it."

Together, they quickly finished the containers.

"So, I overheard on the phone. Your name is Richard?"

"Oh yeah, I'm sorry. Richard Adams."

He looked embarrassed. "It's really nice to meet you,"

"I'm Karen." She refilled their wine glasses.

"Yeah, I know. I know who you are. I've been following your career for years. I'm a law student at Northwestern. You're pretty famous there, as I'm sure you know. I also saw you talk at the Wigmore lecture last year. And, of course, I saw you on tv this afternoon."

"My alma mater! What year are you in?"

"I just finished my second year. Two down, one to go."

"Do you have a job this summer?" She was being polite to try to keep the conversation going, but she wasn't really interested.

"Yeah, I have a job at a law firm."

"That's great. Good luck with that." She refilled their wine glasses.

"Thanks."

Karen wondered how long she'd need to be entertaining him.

"Well, you're going to be here for a while. Want to watch tv or something?" she asked.

"Sure. I feel really, really bad about this. Are you sure I shouldn't just wait in your garage until the storm dies down?"

"Don't worry, it's a great story to tell our friends." He laughed too.

As they sat down on the couch, Karen tried very hard not to look at him as he clutched the robe. He was not her type -- who was? -- and he was way too young, but he was really good looking. Second year law student -- he must be around 24 years-old?

"You said you had been following my career? Are you interested in litigation?" Karen asked. Making conversation with this kid was painful, but she had to be polite.

"Yeah, what really got me interested in your career was the work you did when you worked for the U.S. Attorney's Office and prosecuted those police officers. That was when I became aware of who you were."

"The case where the cops were selling seized guns to the teenagers in the street gangs in the housing project?"

"Yeah. That one."

16

"What were you, like five years old when that happened?"

"I was ten. I've kind of followed your work ever since."

Karen remembered how, when she was ten, she had first decided that she wanted to be a lawyer. She had wanted to play little league baseball, because the option for girls was pathetic. The boys' baseball season lasted all summer, three games a week. They got cleats and full uniforms, and daily practices. In contrast, girls' softball was a joke: a six-week season, one game and one practice per week, then two weeks with a total of three playoff games. No uniforms. No cleats -- most girls slipped and slided around the bases in their treadless girlie sneakers, in jeans, wearing a hat and a crappy t-shirt that the girls had to pay for. They didn't even have any sponsors like "Joe's Garage." No one in the community supported their teams. Karen was way taller than every boy in her class, and better than some of the boys at sports. She didn't want to play in a girls' program that everyone dismissed as worthless. It was humiliating.

She wanted to sue. Her parents told her that nothing was to be done about it. The next year, a girl did sue. The case went to the state supreme court, and the girl won. Ever since, girls had been allowed to play little league boy sports because one girl's family had the courage and the resources to sue. Karen learned that law was the way to correct injustice through the courts. That's why she went to law school.

But, somewhere along the way, her sense of idealism lost out to making big dollars at the law firm. Someone had to support the family, and David's career had never been stable. It was a sacrifice, but worth it. She had near enough money in the bank to pay for the kids' college tuition. That was priceless.

There was a startling thunderous crack and then a series of loud creaks, cracks and crashes and thuds, and the power went out. Karen and Richard were sitting in total darkness.

Chapter Four

Karen used the light on her phone as she ran to the door to see if a tree had fallen on the house. The giant oak tree on the front lawn -- it was probably over 100 years old -- was uprooted, lying on its side across the lawn into the middle of the street and all the way to the yard on the other side, the root ball probably 15 feet in the air. Karen was relieved to see that it had not fallen on her house, but it was completely blocking the road. Another tree was also lying across the street down the block. It looked like a tornado had come through, but, by some miracle, missed all the houses. Karen and Richard were completely trapped in the house between the two fallen trees -- no one would be getting in or out until the town came and cleared the street. That would take hours, and the crews probably wouldn't even go out until after the tornado warnings were lifted and the lightning had passed.

The tree had taken down the power lines. Still sparking, they had provided moments of bright light, but the sparks were smaller now, and Karen and Richard looked on in darkness as she listened to the pouring rain and wind. As her eyes adjusted, she could see that the whole road was soaking wet from the downpour, little lakes were everywhere, and the downed lines dipped into the pools and wrapped around the tree limbs.

"Holy shit," Richard said as he stood behind her. "This is insanely dangerous. We'd better get back inside."

Good thinking kid, she thought as they ducked back in. David would have been out there with his cell phone, taking pictures to post on Instagram and Facebook. If he'd electrocuted himself back then, it would have solved lots of problems.

But all this meant that now, the kid was going to spend the night. She wasn't sure how she felt about that. What if he's a psychopath who has been following me since he was ten? He didn't say why he was interested in that case -- maybe he's friends with the defendants and wants to kill me. (She'd received death threats on and off for years when she had high-profile cases.) She'd make sure to lock her bedroom door when she went to bed. But that would be useless, she realized. He was so big and strong and muscular. That flimsy lock designed to keep out little children while you're having sex would never hold. She'd just have to stay awake, stay on guard. But how? She was exhausted and it wasn't even 9:00 p.m. Maybe she should take him up on his offer of staying in the garage.

He was obviously reading her mind. "I'm really sorry. It must be scary to have a stranger in your house like this. Really, I can stay in the garage."

But he did seem really nice. Or maybe really good at manipulation? She had long ago lost her trust in herself, after letting David get away with all his lies. "What are the odds that this guy, who has been following my career for fourteen years, ended up at my door by chance?" she asked herself. She didn't know what to think. She stood there, frozen.

"Do you have any flashlights or candles? You should probably try to save your phone battery, this could be a while," he pointed out.

He was right. Her phone battery was already at 50%. She didn't have any flashlights, and she didn't use candles because she had asthma. But she knew that David had kept candles -- they had had a huge row over it after she returned from a three-week jury trial in Salt Lake to find that he'd bought fancy silver candelabras for the dining table and had placed scented candles all over the place. Then she learned that he had sent the kids to his mother's for a week. She knew he must have had some lowlife woman in the house, but he denied it and she couldn't prove it. She wanted to throw the candles out, but he refused, and said he had a right to use them when she wasn't home. Where were those candles now?

"My husband kept candles, but I have no idea where. Can you hold the phone for me and help me look?"

"Of course. Whatever I can do to help."

He held the phone as she pulled open drawers and cabinets. It was hopeless. Now her phone was at 40%. As he handed her back the phone, his robe slid open. He quickly adjusted it, but Karen could not shake the image she had seen in the shadows from the phone light. She pretended like she hadn't seen, but it was now all she could think about.

He looked at her. He could tell what she was thinking. She was sure of it.

"Do you have kids? Maybe one of them has a flashlight? I always had a flashlight when I was a kid."

"Great idea. Let's go look." And then she remembered the condoms. What if Joey had left them out on his desk or something? What would Richard think of her giving condoms to her 11-year-old son?

"Actually, let me run in there quickly. My son's room is quite a mess."

"Okay . I guess I'll just stand here in the dark until you get back!" He laughed. Should she be worried?

No flashlight to be found. She didn't come across the condoms either. Did Joey take them to Detroit after all?

She went back to the living room. "No luck," she said. Karen guided them both with her phone light to the couch. They sat down on opposite sides, leaving the cushion between them empty.

They finished the bottle of wine. Karen got up, opened another bottle, and refilled their glasses using the light on her phone.

Richard smiled. "My Dad told me a story once -- I don't know if it was true. He said a long time ago, New York City had a total black-out, and that 9 months later, they had a record number of births."

Karen laughed. "That's definitely true. My parents were in New Jersey and they told me about it. It was bizarre. They had power, but all the television stations and radio stations went off the air because they were all of out in New York City. They honestly thought there was a nuclear war or something."

Karen's mind started racing. Was he coming on to her? If not, why bring that topic up? While Karen had plenty of friends who had one-night stands with people they met in bars, Karen had never had the slightest interest in having sex with a random stranger, who, for all you knew, might be a serial killer. And why would this law student want to have sex with her, unless there was something seriously wrong with him, like he was a total fool-around like David and surely was carrying multiple STDs all at once. Having sex with him would be really stupid. But still, it was a thought. Maybe even a possibility?

Richard looked at her phone and seemed concerned. "Do you think we should turn off your phone light? What if there is some emergency and you need to make a call, or if your kids need to call you? At least if you have a little battery left, you can turn it on to check."

More good thinking. Karen turned off the phone. The room was completely dark. "I can't even see you. This is kind of scary. Where are you?" She drunkenly reached out with her hand.

Richard's hand met hers. They both moved closer.

Richard pulled his hand away. "I'm sorry, but I'm uncomfortable with this. You're married, and I respect that."

"I'm actually not married. My husband and I divorced three years ago. The robe's a present I never gave him."

"But you must be in a relationship with someone now." Somehow, he seemed incredulous that she wasn't involved. If only he knew.

"No. After work, all of my time goes to my kids. How about you?"

"I had a girlfriend from college, but we broke up over a year ago. I haven't been with anyone since."

Okay, he was definitely not like David. And if he had any STDs, he'd probably treated them by now.

There was a sudden gust of wind that made the house shudder, and Karen jumped a little. Richard reached for her hand.

"Kind of scary sitting here in total darkness with the wind like that," he said.

"I agree"

Karen moved a little closer still. "I'm not a religious person, but it seems like there is some superior force that put us together on this couch in total darkness."

"Me too. In a lot of ways."

She held his hand, and he entwined his fingers with hers. His hand felt warm and reassuring. It was a simple touch, but it felt really good. Had she ever held hands with David? She didn't remember.

Soon, they were kissing and Karen's thoughts raced back to the handful of men she'd kissed in her life. Richard's kissing skills were in another league, and made her want more.

But could she go through with it? Denise had been harassing Karen since the divorce to get out and meet someone new, but Karen had zero interest. "Think about six degrees of separation, Denise," Karen explained. "Except that this time, imagine that your husband was a chronic womanizer, and think of all the places where your husband's dick has been, and all the dicks that have been in that same place. It's repulsive."

"The fact that your husband is scum doesn't mean that all men are scum," she said. "You can't live the rest of your life thinking about how things won't work out and use that as an excuse for doing nothing."

Denise had been unrelenting, but dating was a nightmare. Denise wanted her to keep trying – "Try those online dating sites everyone uses nowadays!" – but Karen had reacted viscerally.

"What are you nuts? Putting my face and name out there in public? You know how many psychopaths are still trolling me from the cases I handled at the U.S. Attorney's Office? I'll end up on a date with someone who wants to kill me."

Karen had decided that she would try again (maybe) when Joey was seventeen or so. You have eighteen years to raise your kids right. Joey was eight at the time. She could wait another nine or ten years without sex for her kids. She hadn't been with a man since. Why start now?

Chapter Five

All of a sudden, Richard pulled away.

"Karen, I'm sorry. I'm a bit drunk, I just don't do casual sex. But --"

"Me neither." That was the truth. She had slept with David on their sixth date. She had dated a prior boyfriend for a year. The only other person she had slept with was a partner at the law firm when she was a summer clerk, and not until they'd had lunch a couple of times -- back before David had "committed" to being monogamous with her -- which, in retrospect, never happened. Anyway, the sex with the partner was so bad, she figured she was being punished, and -- although they were now friendly-ish -- running into him in the hallways was a constant reminder of how bad casual sex can be. But now? At least she wouldn't have to see this kid again if she didn't want to.

"Maybe I'm too drunk, but I don't feel like this is a casual thing that we have going on here," he said as he started to kiss her again. A nice line he's handing her?

After a few more wonderful minutes, Karen said, "I think we should move to the bedroom,"

Richard stood up as he held her hand. It was pitch black. Karen turned her phone on and lit the way.

She had never been with anyone like Richard. He made it all about her pleasure -- not his. Within twenty minutes, she could have just as well died and gone to heaven as far as she was concerned.

When the beating of her heart slowed to something more normal and she was able to speak, she told Richard, "I want you desperately."

"Do you have any condoms?"

"What?"

"Do you have any condoms? I only do safe sex. For both of us, you know?"

Did he really just giggle?

"Wasn't expecting, you know, to be meeting you when I took off on a windsurfer in a bathing suit."

"Condoms?"

"Yeah, you know what condoms are right?" He teased.

How dumb do I sound? "Obviously."

JOEY. Joey had condoms. She had told Joey to leave them in his room. They had to be in the room somewhere. He wouldn't have defied her.

"I'll be back in a minute."

She grabbed the phone, turned on the light, and tried to walk nonchalantly to Joey's room.

God, he has to figure out that I live like a nun. She'd had her IUD taken out a year ago when it expired, figuring there was no reason to replace it, and why have condoms around if they had as much use to her as a boomerang and would expire long before she had the opportunity to use them. "Shit, I damn well better find those condoms," she thought to herself.

The phone light, at 15%, was getting dimmer. It was hard to see anything in Joey's room. And it's such a mess. She stumbled over his clothing and toys on the floor.

She checked on top of his desk, his dresser, his closet shelf, inside his desk drawer, full to the brim with 11-year-old boy stuff. Rubber bands galore, but no rubbers.

Almost no light left. She started just dumping everything out on the floor.

Dresser drawers.

Nothing.

Closet shelf.

Nothing.

Under the pillow on the top bunk, in with the bedding, under the mattress.

All nothing,

Same with the bottom bunk.

Still nothing. She was out of places to look. He must have taken the condoms with him. But would Joey really defy her without an argument? And what would he do with them anyway, have groupie sex with music fans? At 11?

Wait, she could see through the slats in the bottom bed frame. There was a ton of stuff shoved under his bed. She shined the phone light there.

She saw the box of condoms and grabbed it.

"Thank God," she muttered. And then she carefully composed herself to calmly walk back into the bedroom.

Chapter Six

"What took so long? I was starting to think that you were lost in the dark or had changed your mind."

He looked incredibly hot in the dim phone light.

"Took a while to find them." That didn't sound good. "Uh, I left them in a different place than usual."

Sex with Richard was a revelation. She realized for the first time that her disinterest in sex was because the men before Richard were only focused on themselves. Richard could not have been more different. She'd had no idea what she had been missing, and now she wanted more.

But when she woke up, the room was filled with sunlight, and she was filled with guilt.

"Good morning beautiful."

"Oh shit," Karen thought to herself. "What have I done? How drunk did I get last night? He's still here. What am I supposed to do with him?"

He moved a strand of hair away from her face.

"I had no idea how beautiful you were when we were doing things in the dark."

He needed to be on his way home. And out of her life.

The clock was still off.

"Still no power. How'd you sleep?"

"Really well."

"I need to pee." He got up and walked to the bathroom without putting on the robe. She hadn't imagined he would look that good naked in the daylight.

She got up and put her own robe on and sat by the side of the bed. When he came out of the bathroom, she went in. She looked at herself in the mirror. "He thinks this is beautiful? He's fucking nuts." Her hair was disheveled, the mascara she'd put on for the televised press conference was all over the place. Age lines everywhere. She drank some water, washed her face and cleaned up a bit. The urge to vomit subsided. She'd tell him that he had to leave because her kids would be there any minute.

She walked back into the bedroom. He was lying naked on the bed on top of the sheets.

She decided to get rid of him later.

It was almost noon before she got out of bed and looked out the window. Still no electricity, the street still blocked. But the sun was out, the wind had died, the Lake was blue-green like the Caribbean, the way it sometimes looks in the summer after a storm. She wanted to go out, but he declined windsurfing, said he wasn't sure he ever could again. You'll get over it, she told him and suggested paddle boarding near shore instead.

They stayed out for hours, on the boards or swimming when they got too hot, in unseasonably warm water so crystal clear you could see eight feet down. They were starving when they got back to the house, and scrounged up food that hadn't spoiled, peanut butter and jelly, Frosted Flakes without milk. "I love your cooking," he joked. There was still no way for him to leave, so she figured she might as well take him back to bed.

Lying together, they could see the lights from Chicago glowing orange in the distance through the windows, open since they had no air conditioning. Around them, all was completely dark. "Karen, this time together has been pretty amazing," he said. "What an awesome time in the lake today."

Yeah, she thought. It was a great time. Plus, the sex! But he was like 20 years her junior, she truly could be his mother. A second-year law student. The same age as Twisted Sister? The last thing the kids needed was a Twisted Brother. This wasn't going anywhere.

"Can I keep seeing you?" he asked, surfacing her worst fears.

Karen didn't say anything.

"Is that a no?"

"It's not a no and it's not a yes. I need to think about it." Did she? Hadn't she just decided?

"It's complicated. We're at different stages in life. I have children and I'm done. You'll want children."

"I don't. Definitely."

"Everyone says that at your age. Trust me. You'll want children."

"I promise. Never."

"And all the other reasons."

"Whatever reasons you're thinking of, it's like anything else," he argued. "Maybe it works out, maybe not. But don't NOT try something because it MIGHT not work out."

Karen said only, "We'll see." But they started to kiss again.

Chapter Seven

Karen woke up to bright sunlight streaming in the bedroom, and the sounds of chain saws, trucks, and workers yelling directions. It was Sunday morning. Finally, the power might go on.

She rolled over to reach for Richard. He wasn't there.

She panicked. Had he left? Maybe she shouldn't have been so honest last night about how she felt. Why did she always push men away? What was wrong with her? She worked herself into a frenzy. She'd blown it for sure. But wasn't that what she wanted? To be rid of him?

She got up and went to the bathroom to wash up, put on her robe and walked down the hallway to the living room. He wasn't there.

She found him in the kitchen, eating scrambled eggs.

"Are you crazy?" she nearly shouted. "You could die from eating rotten eggs. What about salmonella?"

He told her he'd seen a kitchen show, that back in the day, people couldn't refrigerate eggs, and that you can tell whether an egg is spoiled by putting it in a glass of water and if it floats, it's spoiled. These sank.

Karen grinned. "Yeah, I'll pass. I suspect that there are reasons why people refrigerate eggs regardless of whether they pass a swimming test."

The television suddenly came on, along with all the lights she'd left on Friday night. After the water heater kicked in and had sufficiently warmed the water, they each showered. Karen got dressed; Richard put on his dry bathing suit. They put his board and mast on top of Karen's car, with the sail, boom and rigging inside. He asked if she could drop him off right after they showered. He didn't say why he needed to get there early. After years of dealing with David, she was concerned and suspicious.

"Any reason why you need to get back early?" she asked hesitantly.

"Yeah, I have plans for today." He didn't provide any details, and that concerned Karen more.

"Something you don't want me to know about?"

"Can we not talk about it?"

A big red flag was going up.

"It's not another woman, if that's what you're thinking. I just don't want to talk about it."

Why believe him? A woman, that would be fine. One more excuse to get this over with.

Another beautiful day. The parking lot by the sailing club was full of cars. The Lake was full of boats, windsurfers and paddle boards.

"Can I kiss you goodbye?" Richard asked with a puppy dog look in his eyes again.

She looked around. No one was in sight. She leaned in to kiss him. She suddenly felt terribly conflicted. "Can you send me a text when you get home just to let me know you got back okay?"

Stupid. She sounded just like a mom.

He smiled. "Of course. I was planning to do that anyway."

He took her hand. "Maybe dinner one night?"

"I don't know. This was supposed to be my weekend with the kids, but now the schedule is all screwed up."

"Next weekend maybe?"

"I really don't know how the schedule with the kids is going to work out."

"Is this your way of saying no more?" He looked upset. Teary even, not the angry look that David made whenever there was a hint that he was not going to get his way.

"It's not my way of saying goodbye. I just don't know. I need to think about it, spend some time with my kids. Let's talk later this week, okay?"

They exchanged numbers.

"Sorry, about my writing" he said, smiling. "I have a disability with my hands. And what you're seeing is after years and years of occupational therapy. But think of my other skills." He smiled -- an amazing smile that lit up his whole face.

He fumbled with his seatbelt as he was about to get out of the car.

"Here, let me help you." Karen reached toward the belt.

Before she could help, Richard undid the seatbelt. "Got it. I really hate these things." He looked distracted. "Well, I hope to see you soon," he said as he got out of the car.

His "other skills" were exactly what she was thinking of as she watched him walk away, barefoot, in his bathing suit -- exactly as she'd met him some forty hours before. She made herself think of something else. She had a lot to do before the kids got home: replace Joey's condoms, and somehow put Joey's room back together.

She stopped at the grocery store on her way home to replace all the spoiled food and to stock up for the week. Then to the pharmacy, where she was relieved to find a box of condoms of the same brand and style -- and expiration date. Joey shared her attention to detail, and yes, he would have noticed. Hopefully he hadn't memorized the batch number. The wind had picked up a little bit. It was a perfect day for windsurfing. She'd take the board out if it was still light when she finished with Joey's room.

As she turned onto her street, she felt a little sad. The truth was she missed Richard already.

Down the block, she could see police cars. Lots of them. Lights flashing, but no sirens. She assumed that it had to do with the power outage -- maybe there was an electrical fire or something. And then, as she drove closer, she realized that six police cars were parked in front of her house, and the kids were standing outside, talking to Tim Reilly, the Director of the State Police. He was also David's best friend from high school, and Joey's beloved summer basketball coach. He'd also been her witness in a handful of criminal cases back before he was the head of the State Police, when she was a junior prosecutor at the U.S. Attorney's Office, before she left for the firm. The kids weren't supposed to be home until dinner time, and it was only 3:00 o'clock. Her heart started racing.

Chapter Eight

State Police cars blocked the driveway. Cyndi and Joey ran up, crying, as she parked two doors down.

"We were so scared," Cyndi said. "The cops thought you were kidnapped or something," Joey added as he hugged her.

"What's happened?" Karen asked. The neighbors were standing in their yards, watching and staring at her -- always loving a scandal, and long disproving of her small house with old siding and a teenager-mowed lawn. She had never liked her neighbors much.

Tim Reilly walked up. "Hey kids, can you hang out in your Dad's car while your mom and I have a little chat?" Tim motioned to David's car, which she now realized was parked across the street. It was hot and the car windows were open. David was in the driver's seat. She could see enough of the dyed platinum hair flowing in the slight breeze to know that Twisted Sister was in the passenger seat. The kids got in the back.

It was a Sunday, and Tim was dressed like he'd just left church. Other than that, he looked like your typical state trooper. Well over six-feet tall. His hair, to the extent that you could see it at all given that he kept it somewhere between shaved stubble and an extremely short crew cut, was sandy brown with an occasional wisp of gray. Like most people in the state police, he was in perfect physical shape. All troopers have to train throughout the year to meet the annual athletic test requirements deemed necessary to outrun criminals and the like, and the brass liked to keep up. Tim was probably 190 pounds of solid muscle. Not someone you would want to be resisting arrest against in a dark alley. But the truth was, Tim was the kindest and gentlest person Karen knew. She was proud to be his friend.

And this was despite the fact that Tim had been David's best friend since high school. Other than their love of sports and an occasional beer, it seemed to Karen that David and Tim had absolutely nothing in common. Tim was a devoted husband and father who gave all of his free time to his family and the community. In addition to coaching his kids' sports teams, he was at every community fundraiser, he ran in every charity race, he attended every funeral. He was beloved by everyone. And, like many police officers, he also served in the National Guard. And, like so many others, he'd never expected to go to war when he signed up, but he served honorably. He won so many awards for bravery in the Middle East -- Karen had read about them in the local paper -- but he came home a mess. He was working as a Detective Sergeant in a patrol car back then, and, in classic Tim form, he self-reported his own bad behavior and asked to be removed from the street. Tim had kind of lost it when he was called to a domestic assault, and he had grabbed the guy by the neck for a couple of seconds. Tim was so upset about it afterward that he first took a leave of absence, then asked to be removed from the community patrol and placed instead at the Police Academy, where he worked his way up to head the academy, and from there to the Director position, in charge of the State Police.

Tim had spoken to Karen privately about his Post Traumatic Stress Disorder diagnosis. As a former federal prosecutor of human trafficking cases, Karen was an expert in PTSD -- just about all of her trafficked witnesses had it, she had routinely used expert witnesses to explain their otherwise inexplicable behavior, and she had even conducted trainings for prosecutors on how to work with witnesses who had PTSD. One day, when Tim was feeling down about no longer being able to work on the street because of his fear that he might fly off the handle and be aggressive (or worse) with someone, Karen had said something about PTSD being the brain's natural response to trauma and that it was nothing to be ashamed of, especially after what Tim had undoubtedly experienced during his deployments. Tim had immediately opened up to her.

"You know, actually, my PTSD has nothing to do with the war. Of course, I tell people that's how I got it because it's socially acceptable to have PTSD from being a soldier. But the truth is that I got it from being a cop."

"Really?"

"Yeah, I saw worse things as a trooper than I ever saw in Iraq. Not that I didn't see bad things in Iraq, because I did, but seeing a convoy blown up a half-mile away, seeing guys not coming back at the end of their shift, or seeing a bunk mate who hanged himself -- don't get me wrong, it was terrible. But my job there wasn't as bad as the things other soldiers saw, and for me, it was nothing like the terror I felt every time I stopped at a car accident on the highway and had no idea what I might see that I could never *unsee,* every time I stopped a car for a traffic violation and didn't know whether there would be some lunatic inside who would shoot me or my guys, every domestic where I didn't know if the guy would kill the woman and his kids as I watched or turn the gun on us. It got to be where every time dispatch would send me somewhere -- anywhere really -- I'd go into a sweat and my heart would start pounding so loud that I couldn't think straight."

Karen had never thought about how being a police officer could be as bad as going to war, but what Tim was saying made sense.

"Do you know what I see every night when I can't sleep and I'm lying in bed for hours?" Tim paused. "Jimmy Watson's eyes, looking up at me from the bushes."

Jimmy Watson was the seventeen-year old driver of the most horrible crash anyone in the community could remember. Four teenagers were driving in an open jeep at excessive speed. No seat belts. The jeep rolled. All four boys were thrown from the car and killed -- three were killed instantly, the fourth died a few days later in the hospital. Jimmy was decapitated. They found Jimmy's body quickly, but it took hours of searching in the darkness before Tim had been the one to find Jimmy's head, lying in some bushes. Tim and the rest of the police had worked nonstop until they found the head because they didn't want some child to come upon it, or some dog to show up with a part of Jimmy. The accident was horrible enough for the family, so the police teams worked without complaint on the most horrible of tasks. Tim was the unlucky one; most of the others never stopped to look at what he had found. The senior troopers all knew the risks of seeing things you couldn't unsee.

"That was horrible. But you were such a hero."

"Thanks, but for a lot of us, playing a hero has permanently affected our brains. Of course, you can't tell anyone that. We're supposed to be strong and brave, you know? I think the way the state police across the country are all required to retire with benefits early, like at 55, is compensation, but it doesn't really make up for changing who you are -- who you were. My biggest fear -- maybe I shouldn't tell you this --"

"Go on Tim, I won't tell anyone."

"My biggest fear is that one day I'll get triggered and put my hands on Sally's neck, or hurt one of the kids. I think about that every single day."

"You're doing everything right Tim, so I'm sure that won't happen. You're in treatment at the VA, right? You're doing the counseling. You're talking about your struggle. You removed yourself from environments where you were likely to be triggered, like the patrol. I'm sure that won't happen. You've always worked to keep Sally and the kids safe, and that won't change."

"Yeah, I like to think that, but the truth is my brain is broken, and might never get fixed."

Now, standing outside her home, Tim took her out of the kids' earshot. "Karen, everyone has been worried sick about you. A bunch of the lawyers on your 'We'll Come and Kill You' case got emails with people threatening to kill you. We've all been trying to contact you. David hasn't been able to reach you, the kids haven't. David brought them home early because they were worried, and he wasn't comfortable having them go in when you didn't answer your phone or the doorbell. He called the police for a wellness check.

"Karen, your house has been ransacked. We need to talk about getting you and the kids to a safe place. Where have you been?"

"I just stepped out to do some errands and go to the grocery store." There was no way she was going to tell Tim about Richard. Despite whatever rules there might be for privacy in police investigations, Tim would tell David in about 30 seconds.

At that moment, one of the troopers walked up to Tim.

"Director Reilly, we searched the entire perimeter. There's no sign of forced entry."

Tim turned to Karen. "Did you leave the doors or windows unlocked?

"Definitely not. You know me and how I'm obsessive about locking doors and windows. We -- I mean, I had the windows open all weekend because the power was off and the AC wasn't working, but

40

when the power came back on today, I closed and locked every window. And the door to the garage locks automatically when you leave."

"Ugh." Tim sighed. "You know that makes this more concerning, don't you? I mean, I'm sure it's nothing, but, well, you know. . . ."

"Yeah."

Karen, like other lawyers, had been through this before. Over the years, she'd had a number of threats.

"Did you get threats Karen?" Tim asked.

"I don't know. I've had no power since Friday night. My cell phone died within a few hours. The landline is all cordless phones, so they were not working either. I have no idea."

"Sergeant Hooper found your phone inside the house. That really scared us. You should always have your phone with you, especially with your history of threats. What if the kids needed to reach you?"

"I know Tim. I'm sorry. The phone was totally dead and useless, so I left it charging when I went out after the power came on today."

"Can you unlock it for me so we can see if you got any threats?"

"Sure. Should I go in and get it?" Karen asked.

"It's been taken into evidence. We couldn't open it because David and the kids didn't know your password. You need to fix that." Tim gave her the look of "How could you be so stupid that your family doesn't know your password?"

"Sergeant Hooper, can you bring me the cell phone?" He called out to a trooper nearby.

Sergeant Hooper went to a squad car and returned with her phone in a sealed evidence bag.

"Well thank God we don't need to keep this as evidence," Tim said as he ripped the bag open and handed her the phone.

She turned the phone on and checked her texts. Seventeen text messages from David and the kids. One from a Chicago number she didn't know. One from Richard (she starting thinking about his special skills again). "Just got home. Had a really special time. Thanks again for everything. Later this week?" A bunch of texts from people on the

Wilkommen team telling her that they had received death threats about her and asking if she was okay. Nothing else.

She turned to email. She had two accounts. She checked her personal account first. Nothing new except a litany of emails from Amazon about the kids' latest purchases, and when they'd be arriving.

She looked at her work email. Fifty-two new messages. Even for her, that was a lot for a weekend. She skipped through all the names she knew and looked for something unknown.

"The threats were from an email address called 'Justice for Kayley.'" Tim was looking over her shoulder at the phone. "There," he said, pointing. "Try to get that first one in preview -- don't open it."

She got the email in a preview pane. It was bad. She read the first three words and stopped.

"Can you forward that to my work address," Tim said. Karen forwarded the email without reading it.

"Any others?" Tim asked, still looking over she shoulder. He was standing a little too close and making her uncomfortable.

"No, that's it."

A detective walked up to Tim. "Director Reilly, we've searched the whole house. The only room that was ransacked looks like it was the boy's room."

Karen felt immediate relief, but then became terrified.

Chapter Nine

Lying to the police in the course of a police investigation is a crime. In Illinois, it's a Class 4 felony which brings up to three years in prison. This investigation involved use of the wires (the internet) to send the threat, so it would also be a federal investigation. The federal statute is even harsher -- up to five or eight years, with a potential for an enhanced sentence if you are the subject of the investigation. And they can also charge you with conspiracy to add another five years. Not to mention permanent disbarment from practicing law, but if you're going to be in jail for years and never see your kids because the closest federal prison is hours away, who cares about disbarment, Karen thought.

Lying to the police about how Joey's room got ransacked was therefore not an option. On the other hand, if they ever arrested someone for the death threats, whatever Karen told the police now would become public. The police would write up a full report of their conversation today, and, after the person was arrested, a copy of that report would be given to the defendant's lawyer. Having been a prominent female prosecutor for years, there were a handful of good-old-boy criminal defense lawyers in Chicago who disliked her from the time that she handled child trafficking cases. She believed that serious jail time was warranted when someone trafficked or sexually abused a child, but some of the old men in the defense bar liked it the old way where victims were discredited regardless of the evidence and perpetrators who could afford to hire a pricey private lawyer ended up with a slap on the risk -- if they received any punishment at all. ("She was doing terribly in school and smoked marijuana! How can you find her credible!")

Karen had no doubt that a report detailing how she ransacked her own home in the midst of a sex romp with a law student, given to the wrong criminal lawyer, would become a viral story on the internet in about fifteen minutes. Plus, there was zero chance that Tim would not tell David about it. And David would immediately tell the kids to make him look like the better parent -- for once.

"Can I have a minute?" She asked Tim. "I'm feeling a little dizzy. I'd like to just sit in my car for a minute.

"Sure. I'll have Detective Harris sit with you," Tim responded.

"Well shit," thought Karen to herself. "That didn't work."

She sat in her car with Helen Harris. Karen had known Helen for years, from when Helen worked on the human trafficking joint task force. Helen could be a terrific cop, but she was known behind her back as "Sanctimonious Helen." She was very thorough, very honest, and she gave defendants a fair shot by always looking at the evidence from both sides. But Helen's strong religious views sometimes interfered with her work because she couldn't keep them to herself. Like telling a gay teenage boy who had been sexually trafficked for years that all gay sex was against God and a sin; or railing against safe bathrooms for transgender kids at a town school board meeting when the police were prosecuting a gang assault on a transgender student in a bathroom. People in the State Police work with vulnerable populations, and Helen's comments were alienating to the very people she needed to protect. She was removed from the task force -- which then started a huge commotion, with some of the church leaders in the community claiming the state had discriminated against her due to her religious views.

Karen could only imagine what Helen's view would be about Karen's tryst with Richard. Karen was sure that everyone at the East Presbyterian Church would know the exaggerated details within twenty minutes of Karen's signing the statement.

On the other hand, prison for making a false statement to a police officer was not very appealing.

"Look Helen, I want you to know that I ransacked Joey's room," she finally said. "It wasn't someone else. I don't think the house was broken into, unless you've got something else."

"Why did you ransack his room?" She was too good of a cop to take an answer that made no sense without investigating further.

"I'm not going to talk about that. I'm just telling you that I ransacked Joey's room." Karen's heart was pounding.

"There was something else, Karen." Helen looked concerned. "The guys found four used condoms in the garbage. Your husband and your daughter said that you aren't seeing anyone. The sanitation department said that your garbage pickup was on Friday at 4:00 p.m.

44

That's four condoms in less than 48 hours. We took the condoms into evidence. Do you have any explanation for that?"

Karen thought she was going to throw up. If Helen knew about the condoms, rest assured that everyone in the State Police knew too. It was only a matter of time until every lawyer in the City knew it as well.

Karen weighed her options. Prison or public humiliation? Honestly, which one would be worse? It was a challenging decision.

"Look Helen, I know about the condoms. There was no break in," Karen responded. She thought it was odd that they only found four, because Karen very clearly, and in great glorious detail, recalled there being five. Maybe Richard flushed one down the toilet.

Helen looked concerned. "Karen, you and I have known each other for years. What on earth is going on here? These threats are frightening and I'm very concerned. I don't feel like you're being forthcoming."

"Helen, yeah, we've known each other for years. But we lead different lives and my life is private. That's all I'm going to say." Karen responded.

"It seems like you're covering for someone or something."

"Trust me, I'm not. Yes, there was obviously a death threat that I didn't know about, and I'm incredibly grateful that you guys are giving that your full attention. But the house was not broken into. In terms of the house, and me and my children, we're fine."

"You know I'm going to have to write this up," Helen said. "And I feel like I have to add that you were not forthcoming."

"Look," Karen said, "I would be grateful if you kept this as private and as limited in detail as possible. I understand why you guys went in the house and why you searched it, but this stuff is private. And I'm not going to talk about it. I'm not going to tell you whether it was me, or my teenage daughter or whether I had company this weekend who might have engaged in sexual conduct with or without my knowledge. I'm just not going to talk about it because it's private, and frankly, it has nothing to do with police business. Period. Okay?"

Karen's heart was pounding. She felt every heartbeat in her neck and her eardrums. She realized that Helen's pocket camera was attached to her shirt and the light was on. Helen was recording everything on video. That was standard policy now. Karen thought the video would play well -- and present her in the best possible light -- if it ever became public.

"Can the kids and I please go in the house now?" Karen asked.

"Let me talk to Tim. Wait here." Helen got out of the car and Karen watched her talk to Tim. Tim looked over at Karen, sitting in her car. What was he thinking? Tim walked over and got in.

"Karen, are you sure you're okay?"

Karen looked down as she spoke to him. "Obviously, I'm upset about the death threat, but, as you know, I've been through that lots of times before. What I'd really like is to go back in the house with the kids and just move on from the rest of this, okay?"

"Okay. But will you promise to call me if you need anything or want to talk about this more?" he asked.

"Yes. I promise."

"I talked to Chief Smith, of the Winnetka Police. He's going to have one of his squad cars drive by your house every hour or so, staffing permitting. And I figured that, if one of our guys is driving through Winnetka, we would do the same."

That was classic Tim. Going above and beyond, even it if seemed like a wasted effort, since the chances of them driving by during the 45 seconds someone might be seen on the front of her lawn before they climbed in a window was next to zero. Still, she graciously accepted the offer.

At times like this, she often wished she could afford the security details that celebrities pay for. But, she concluded, even if you have all the money in the world, if someone is determined to get you, they will. She thought of a pop star whose home had been broken into three times by the same crazy guy. And who wants to live with all that security anyway?

"We've gotten calls from the press," Tim said. "I think one of your neighbors must have tipped them. I feel like I have to issue a statement. I need to run it by the detectives, but I'm thinking of something simple, like, 'a death threat was received, and, in an abundance of caution, we searched the house and the Winnetka Police and the State Police are providing increased security.' Okay with you?"

"Sounds perfect. Thanks Tim." Typical of Tim to add the "increased security" statement, even though it was largely not true. Maybe it would help to keep whoever was behind this away.

"And, um, on the rest, I told Helen not to put it in a report. It's not relevant. No crime was committed here, and, if it ever becomes relevant, she could always amend her report by viewing the video of your statement. And, unless you tell me differently, we're going to destroy the condoms."

"Thank you, Tim. I really appreciate how you're handling this. Can you please not tell David?" she asked. It seemed like a reasonable request.

Tim looked upset. "I'm sorry, Karen. I told him about the death threats your colleagues had received, and he also knows about the condoms. I had to ask him if he knew whether you were seeing anyone, or whether you and he. . . ." Tim's voice trailed off.

"Okay, I understand. Did the kids overhear that discussion?"

"Absolutely not. I talked to David in the back of a squad car."

"Thank you for that. Does David know that I ransacked Joey's room?" Karen asked.

"Not unless you tell him."

Running through her head was how all of this would play out in family court by the judge who signed the custody decree. If David found out that she had ransacked Joey's room, David could file a motion with the family court seeking custody -- claiming that she was unstable or mentally unfit. She wouldn't put it past him to do that. Not that he wanted the responsibility of having the kids, but if he had custody, she would have to pay him child support and David was always in need of money because he lived beyond his means. She pondered whether the court would give him custody because of the death threat. Probably not, unless the kids wanted out of the house for their safety, in which case she would want them to be with David anyway. The condoms would mean nothing to the family court -- you're allowed to have sex, especially when your children are off with the other parent.

"Are you good?" Tim asked. "Anything else we can do?"

"Does Joey know that his room was ransacked?" Karen asked.

"Yes. When the detectives saw the state of the room, they came out of the house and asked the kids whether they knew why Joey's room was such a mess. Joey said it was tidy other than a few clothes on the floor, and that he had to keep it clean to get his allowance. So, yeah, they know -- but not all the details."

"Do the kids know about the condoms?" Karen asked.

"We didn't tell them," Tim said. "But I don't know if David did."

"Thanks Tim. You're a good friend."

Karen wanted to throw up. David would absolutely have told the kids about the condoms already. He would be thrilled to use that information to attack what he regularly told them was her "sanctimonious attitude." David had not even known what that word meant until he had asked her what "Sanctimonious Helen" meant when Tim had used that nickname for Helen. Karen never should have told him. It was now the longest word in his vocabulary, and he used it often to attack Karen.

Tim was always the kind of guy who looked uncomfortable when you gave him a compliment. "No need to thank me. Okay, so we'll all head out now. If anything happens -- anything at all -- I don't care if it's just floors creaking at night -- you call 911, okay? And you can call my cell, but call 911 first. They'll get a squad car here quicker. We've informed dispatch of the situation, and special arrangements are in place."

"Thanks Tim." Karen gave him a hug, and he got out of the car.

Karen stayed in her car for a moment, thinking. About what she had said to Helen, about how traumatic this must be for the kids and how they needed her support. And about how she was going to explain ransacking Joey's room and the condoms.

Chapter Ten

Karen wasn't about to face Twisted Sister, so she texted David, asking him to come to her car.

She watched as David looked at his phone. He got out, crossed the street, and got in the passenger seat of her car. In the course of just a few hours, Richard had sat in that seat, the Director of the State Police, a detective with the State Police, and now her ex-husband. She preferred Richard.

"Are you okay?" he asked as he sat down and closed the door. "The kids were really worried. I was really worried," he added as an afterthought because it sounded bad otherwise. She reminded him that she'd had threats before that amounted to nothing.

"I know, but now someone has broken into our -- I mean your -- house."

"That's what I want to talk to you about. No one broke in. I'm struggling with how to tell the kids what really happened."

"No one broke in? Jesus, that's a relief. What can I do to help?" For once, he seemed like he really wanted to support her.

She decided to come clean. "I met someone Friday night and things moved faster than I anticipated. We were at the house, and I needed condoms. The power was out, I couldn't find a flashlight or even a candle (she threw that one in to make him feel guilty). My phone battery was dying. Cyndi and Joey told me that your girlfriend (she would never dignify that woman by using her real name) had given Joey a box of condoms, and I knew that he was going to leave them in his room over the weekend. I went into Joey's room to find the condoms. It was hard to see. I was afraid that the light would give out. So, I dumped out his drawers on the floor, dumped everything on his closet shelf, and looked under his pillows, blankets and mattresses before I found them hidden under the bed. You were supposed to bring the kids back at 10 p.m. I was planning on putting his room back together this afternoon before you brought the kids home."

Karen sighed. "I'm planning to tell the kids that I made a mess of Joey's room because I was looking for a flashlight as it was getting dark and I was afraid that I would have no light once my phone battery died." She also contemplated telling David that it was the best sex she had ever had in her life, but decided that wouldn't help things.

"How are you going to explain his missing condoms?"

"Did you tell the kids the police found used condoms?"

"No. They were upset enough already without thinking about you being raped."

"Thanks." A surprising exercise of good judgment.

"Can you take the kids out to dinner now while I put Joey's room back together, and replace the condoms where they were with the new ones I just bought? They're in a bag in the back."

"Okay."

"Thank you."

"Listen, I know I was a total shit, but what happened tonight and the thought of you being hurt, or worse, well, it changes things. I know you have every right to hate me, but I would really like it if we could be one of those ex-married couples who get along for the sake of the kids, that we can be polite to each other at drop offs, and maybe socialize sometimes with the kids, you know?"

"I agree. I think the kids would prefer that. I'll work on it."

"And maybe you could tell the kids to stop calling Judy 'Twisted Sister'? She's overheard them talking about her in the house. It's very hurtful."

"You need to talk to them about that. I can't stop them from hating her. She broke up their parent's marriage. That's not something that they'll necessarily ever get over."

"Come on, you know we were not happy for a very long time before that."

Back to normal, classic David blaming their failed marriage on anything but himself. But she was so relieved that he was going to help her with Joey, and she just wasn't up for the thousandth argument about his life-long problem of blaming everyone other than himself.

"Yeah, well. Thanks again for helping with the kids tonight. If they say anything concerning, or you think they need anything else from me, please let me know."

"Will do. Hey, if you need anything, I'm always there for you. I know how upsetting these threats are to you -- to me -- to all of us."

"Thanks."

They walked to his car across the street. Karen ignored Twisted Sister, put her hands on the back-window frame and stuck her head in to talk to the kids.

"The police have determined that there was no break-in. We're all safe. There was a threat by email, but you know, that happens all the time and those threats always amount to nothing. I made a mess of Joey's room when the power went out and I was searching for a flashlight. I'm going to clean it up now for you, kiddo -- she tossed Joey's hair -- so you don't have to deal with it, while Dad and Judy take you out to dinner. Ok?"

"Are you sure you don't need our help? You don't want us to stay with you?" Cyndi asked, looking concerned.

"No, I'm all set. Actually, the police are going to increase security a bit for a few days just to make sure all is well. No worries. You guys have a great time. I don't know for sure, but I bet you could talk your Dad into taking you to Walker's for an amazing pancake dinner."

She sighed as they pulled away. As many threats as she'd received over the years, you never get used to it. Her own little bit of PTSD.

It took Karen forever to get Joey's room back in order. Karen had a near-photographic memory -- which was a great gift to have as a litigator. She was famous for being able to point to a specific line of testimony, on a specific page in a 500-page transcript in an instant, and she remembered every case opinion she had ever read and could spout off the findings without any preparation when it helped her argue before a judge. This otherwise useless skill enabled her to know *exactly* where Joey had left everything in his drawers and in his closet and under his bed, and she took the time to make it right. She placed the new box of condoms under his bed in the same place, at the same angle, that the old box had been.

A few minutes after she finished, the kids got back.

"Shit," Cyndi said. (Karen wasn't able to enforce limits on her own swearing, so she didn't bother with the kids' language much.) "I totally forgot that summer book report was due today!"

"On no," Joey was equally upset. "Mom, my summer worksheet was due today too."

"Today ends at midnight, guys, unless the instructions say otherwise. Let's get to work."

By the time she finished helping Joey, and proofreading Cyndi's paper, Karen was completely exhausted and went straight to bed. As she put her head on her pillow, she realized that the sheets still smelled like Richard. She was sure she would never see him again, but the memory made her smile. She took a deep breath through her nose to take it all in and went to sleep.

Chapter Eleven

Karen slept fitfully. The next day, Joey had swim and sailing camp in Glencoe, due north, while Cyndi had tech camp in Northbrook, which was north and west. A lot of driving, but she felt safer taking them than putting them on the camp vans. At 3:00 a.m., she sent the texts cancelling the vans, and an email to her secretary to let her know she would be in around 9:45.

And then there was Richard, who her thoughts kept turning to. Ridiculous. Could never last. But he had made her happier in forty hours than anyone she'd ever been with. And why would a handsome law student like Richard stay interested in her for anything more than a fling? How could she possibly bring him to the already horrible firm formal in December? He would, she was sure, look very hot in a tux. But the looks she would get from the lawyers in the firm would be unbearable. How could he fit in with her friends, and she with his? Like going to a bar on his arm with a bunch of law students? Nope. Not happening. Everyone would assume she was his mother. She was definitely going to end it: the only thing she was wavering on was when. Maybe see him a couple times more for sex? The sex was amazing. No, the only thing -- and the right thing -- was to end it now. Never respond to his text and just let whatever they had die a natural death. He'd reach the same conclusion if he hadn't already.

When her alarm went off, she felt as though she hadn't slept at all.

She dropped off the kids and made it to the office without being shot at. Her morning drive, from Winnetka to Glencoe to Northbrook to her office downtown, all during rush hour, was endless but uneventful. When she got to her office building, Karen went through security and, as always, welcomed the security staff with a big smile and by name. "Shawn, you're up awfully early? Have you switched to the day shift?"

"Just temporary, Ms. Harding. We're switching around a bit, you know, summer vacations and all."

It offended Karen how so many lawyers and executives treated people who weren't lawyers or executives like shit or just ignored them altogether like they didn't exist. Whether it was the barista who made her coffee or the security guy who scanned her bags, Karen always tried to know their names, and acknowledge their work with gratitude and praise.

Karen got on the express elevator, which would take her to the 59th floor. The elevator trip from the 59th floor to the 83rd floor generally took five to ten times longer than the express to 59.

All lawyers, like doctors, know that you never talk about anything of substance in elevators. Big city elevators have cameras and microphones, and you never know who at security is listening in and watching. And anything you say in an elevator can be used against you or your client if you're a lawyer. Of course, people forget this rule on a daily basis, and juicy gossip was known to spread like wildfire through the firm.

So, when Karen's friend Denise got on the elevator at 60 and Denise asked Karen how her weekend was, Denise was careful not to mention the naked man text, and Karen subtly indicated that she couldn't talk about it in detail by giving a one-word response: "Amazing." Denise immediately knew Karen had a story to tell. After the elevator emptied on 72, Karen quickly said, "You won't believe the details about what the storm blew in. We need to talk."

Denise couldn't manage a response before two people got on at 73. Then people got on and off and the elevator was never empty. Denise was supposed to get off at 81.

"Do you have time for a quick meeting in your office right now about that topic we were discussing?"

"Yes, of course."

They walked toward Karen's office on 83. Because Karen was a prominent partner who brought millions of dollars in client fees to the firm, she had a corner office, with a spectacular view of the marina. Sometimes on weekends, or late at night when no one was around, she would sit by the window and look at all the tiny people and cars below and the sailboats in the distance. Her office was decorated in the latest high-end law-firm style -- with a big glass desk, and modern white furniture that cost way more than Karen thought possible, and three chairs and a small white leather sofa for her staff to sit on during meetings. The sofa was a sleeper, and she had spent many nights on it when she pulled all-nighters and could fit in at most an hour or two of sleep. The architect who designed the building space for the firm installed showers on every floor so the lawyers and paralegals could bill as many consecutive hours as possible without going home to bathe.

Denise closed Karen's office door behind them and took a seat on the couch, while Karen sat down behind her desk. "Okay. The naked man?"

"You're not going to believe this. I finally took your advice. I had sex with a total random stranger, and he was amazing."

"What, are you on drugs? This is not the Karen that I know." Denise was grinning.

Karen lowered her voice and described what happened in polite detail -- omitting, for example, his special skills she'd been thinking of all morning.

"You did this with the kids there?"

"No, they ended up with David for the weekend."

"Do you know anything about this guy? Sounds kind of creepy." Denise seemed concerned. "Are you sure he isn't a stalker? I heard about the threats."

Richard behind the threats? Well if he was going to kill her, he certainly had the opportunity. Instead, he showed off other talents.

"He's a second-year law student at Northwestern. He's working at a law firm this summer. That's pretty much all I know about him. Um, we didn't talk much."

"What's his name? Two-thirds of the class applied for jobs with us. I could find his resume for you if he applied."

"No need. It's over. It was just a fling."

"Are you worried that he might be a stalker? "Don't you want to know if he's even actually a law student?"

"I really don't think he's a stalker. But I'll think about it."

"Can you tell me his name so I can look him up?"

They both laughed. "Uh, no, because you're married Denise."

Chris, Karen's secretary, knocked and came in. "Hey, we need to go over your schedule for today. Your first meeting is in ten minutes."

Denise got up to leave. As she got to the door she said, "Can we continue this discussion later?"

"Sure," Karen smiled.

"Okay," Chris said as she sat down. "Let's get started."

Karen was dependent on Chris, who knew how Karen could get hyper-focused on her work and forget where she was supposed to be, and who therefore kept track of Karen and made sure she left on time for every appointment and met all the courts' deadlines. She helped Karen draft letters and briefs, spoke to dozens of people on Karen's behalf every week, and had terrific judgment. Karen routinely ran complex ideas by Chris for advice on everything from what to do about a crisis with her kids to how a jury would view a particular piece of evidence. Chris was extremely smart, and could have easily been a lawyer if she had grown up in a family with money for college and law school.

Karen thought about telling Chris about her weekend and asking her advice about what to do about Richard. Maybe later.

"Okay, so you have a crazy day. We have thirty-two summer clerks starting today, so there's a litany of dog and pony shows you have to be at."

The biggest law firms, like Christian and Johnson, still recruit summer clerks like they were the Lakers going after NBA free agents. The firm would only hire the top of the class from the best schools, competing against all the major law firms across the country for the same small pool of students. The firm needed an annual influx of brilliant young lawyers to do a large part of the work, and credentials matter to the firm and its clients. After nine or ten years, a few exceptional associates out of the dozens who had started in their class would make partner. Karen was one of eighteen summer clerks at the firm her second summer, and she was only one of two who had eventually made partner -- after first spending a few years with the U.S. Attorney's Office in Chicago.

The firm's thirty-two clerks would be getting star treatment despite their complete lack of legal experience. There would be daily free lunches at fancy restaurants, and endless parties, dinners and outings in the evenings and on weekends. Partners (or at least the partners who were deemed to have social skills or were famous) were encouraged, and not so subtly *required,* to attend many of these events.

Of course, Chris had everything organized. "Okay, so Denise told me that thirty of the thirty-two clerks asked to work with you. Obviously, we can't put all thirty on your cases, but she and I worked on it and you're taking six. We're putting two on the Wilkommen acne drug team, two on the Wilkommen pregnancy drug team, one on the cell phone patent infringement case, and one on the bank antitrust case. We've set up team meetings in all of those cases today so the clerks can meet you and the whole team and get started with real work right away.

"Lunch is at 12:30, at Aegean in Greektown. The weather's nice, so you can all walk there from here. All six of the clerks assigned to your cases are going, along with the partners on those cases. That's twelve of you altogether, I've reserved a table in your name.

"Make sure you get the receipt this time? If not, I'll call and get a copy.

"The first meeting is on the acne medicine cases. It's at 10:00, in conference room 83 D. I've ordered the catering for the meeting. There will be fresh fruit, bagels, lox, etc."

"Oh, yeah," Karen interrupted. "I'm feeling really lousy, like I have a bladder infection." Can you please call up for a really big container of cranberry juice?"

"Do you want me to call your doctor to make an appointment?"

"No, but thanks. Let's wait and see how I feel after I've sucked down a couple of gallons of cranberry juice."

"Okay. Let me know. I'll call catering and have them bring up a large bottle in a carafe." She looked at her watch. "I'll have to send them directly to the conference room."

Chris continued to outline the rest of the day for Karen. The most important thing was a conference call with Wilkommen's general counsel in between the clerk events. But there was one surprise.

"Oh yeah, I don't know if you checked your voicemail, but I checked it this morning. You have a message from Senator Williams' office. She left it on Friday afternoon. The Senator wants to meet with you, and they said that it's urgent, and that they want you to go to her office today or tomorrow. You're booked solid, but I think I can fit them in if the Senator can come here. What do you think?"

"That would be fine, but if you need to move things for me to go to Shondra's office, just move whatever you can to fit her schedule." Karen was surprised that Shondra Williams had an urgent need to see her. Karen had known Shondra since they had worked together as prosecutors in the U.S. Attorney's Office, and they were very friendly. Shondra was a genius -- she graduated first in her class from Yale Law School, left the U.S. Attorney's Office to run for District Attorney, where she did an outstanding job for six years, and now she was a very beloved and respected Senator. "Good God," Karen thought to herself, "I hope she doesn't want me to run for some kind of office." Karen and Shondra had a lot of respect for each other, but their lives were too busy -- they both had high-powered jobs and young children -- to develop anything more than a professional friendship over the years.

"Please explain to the Senator's staff that I was off the grid all weekend, and that's why I did not respond immediately."

"Got it. One more thing -- remember on Wednesday night you're signed up for the Cubs game with the summer clerks, in the Firm box. I don't know if you have the kids this week? Do you need to make arrangements?"

"Oh, right. Thanks for reminding me. I'll text David." Karen was eternally grateful for Chris' organizational ability.

"You need to get going, I'm going to call catering now about that cranberry juice. I put the resumes for the clerks on your to-do pile, but you don't have time to read them now. Denise gave you the best students, as always."

"Thanks, Chris. You are always so amazing."

"Just doing my job."

Karen walked down the hall and entered the conference room. The clerks weren't there yet, but the lawyers were. There was the mid-level partner, the junior partner, the senior associate, two junior associates, and two seats by the door were open for the summer clerks. They were all glowing in the success of Judge Stewart's opinion throwing out the acne medication case.

Han, the senior associate who also happened to be on the Recruitment Committee, told Karen that the summer clerks would be a few minutes late, because they were just finishing up learning how to do their time sheets.

"Well, since we're all billing Wilkommen for this time, we should get started," Karen said.

Julia, the mid-level partner, handed out the agenda, and started the meeting. As she began to talk, two summer clerks walked in and sat down. One was a brown-haired woman. The other was Richard. Karen was shocked and speechless. Richard looked down at his feet as he took a seat. He looked like he wanted to disappear.

As Han introduced the clerks to the group, catering came in with the cranberry juice. "Ms. Harding, we have some cranberry juice for you."

"Thank you very much, Stan." She hated that the staff was required to refer to the lawyers by their last names, but at least Karen made the effort to learn the names of the support people.

"Chris said you wanted a whole bottle." He put the bottle, a carafe, and ice next to her.

"Thank you." What Karen wanted most right now was to crawl under the table and disappear. An invisibility cloak would be nice.

Karen was so livid that she could not even look in Richard's direction. Honestly, even David had never done something so despicable. How could Richard not have told her that he was going to be working at her firm? And, he had obviously ASKED to work with her, so he KNEW that this would happen. She was so angry she could barely focus during the meeting, but she did a good job of acting.

They went around the room while Karen raged. "What the fuck am I supposed to say? Nice to meet you?" After all the intros were done, she said to them both, "Welcome to the Wilkommen team."

The team went through the agenda, discussed the pressing issues, set deadlines for work that needed to be done, and divvied out assignments to everyone.

At the end, Karen thought that she needed to address the death threats. While being reassuring -- and making eye contact with everyone except Richard -- she offered that if they were uncomfortable, just let us know, and they could get off the case, no questions asked.

She hoped Richard would take the hint. In fact, the decent thing would have been to stand up and excuse himself from the meeting to begin with. He did nothing. Karen only got angrier. And then her mind began to run wild, as she had a thought which sent a shiver down her spine. What if he *was* stalking her? What if *he* was behind the death threats? His whole story really made no sense. Why was he obsessed with her when he was ten years old? How exactly did he end up on her lawn? This wasn't some big coincidence. It was scary and creepy.

Meanwhile, it was clear that no one was leaving, including Richard.

Karen thought it was important to add: "And, if any of you decide to stay on today, that doesn't mean that you cannot change your mind tomorrow or at any later date. Everyone will understand if you would prefer to work on other cases, and you can make that decision at any time." Maybe he'd see the light.

With that, they adjourned at 11:30, which left plenty of time before lunch for Karen to blow her top at Richard. On the way back to her office, she asked Chris. "Can you please call that summer clerk, Richard Adams, and ask him if he can meet me in my office?

Chris picked up the phone.

A few minutes later, there was a knock on Karen's office door.

Chapter Twelve

"Close the door and have a seat."

She made sure to keep her voice down, but her anger was clear from her tone and body language. She stayed behind her desk. Richard took a seat in one of the chairs facing her.

He started apologizing right away. "I'm sorry. I'm really, really sorry. And I'll give you my explanation which will be woefully useless, but first, I need to ask you: are you feeling okay?"

"I'm incredibly angry, if that's what you mean."

"No, I mean the cranberry juice. Are you okay?" He was visibly upset. "Did I hurt you? Was I hurting you and you didn't tell me? I'm really upset that I might have caused you pain." He seemed genuinely concerned. If it was an act, he was a particularly good at it.

"No, I just feel like I have a bit of a bladder infection. You did not hurt me." Her tone was still very angry. Something between "angry-with-the-kids" and "I-Just-caught-David-cheating-again" hysterical.

"Are you sure?" He seemed only a little relieved.

"Yeah, it just happens sometimes, you know, with too much 'activity' – especially, I guess, when I hadn't done those things in a long time. But no, you definitely did not hurt me."

He once again looked like a sad puppy dog, with those big brown eyes and dilated pupils. He also looked incredibly hot in a suit and tie. She'd never seen him with clothes on before. He kind of looked like he might cry. How could he do this? She had started out being incredibly angry and ready to scream, and now she was utterly disarmed. She added, "Believe me, pain is not how I would describe it."

He smiled, just a little. "You never responded to my text. I assume that's because you decided it's over?"

"I'm sorry. I meant to, but it was crazy at home."

Richard looked at his watch. "So crazy for twenty-two hours straight that you couldn't take thirty seconds to respond with 'Glad to hear you got home okay?' Please, just be honest with me. I'm a big boy, I can take it.'"

"I was still on the fence," Karen said, "until you pulled this stunt. Talk about what you could have disclosed in thirty seconds. Like, 'I'm going to be a summer clerk at your firm, and I asked to work with you'? That would have been a nice touch Richard. You deliberately did not do that because you knew I wouldn't go to bed with you if you did." Karen was trying very hard to keep her voice down, but it was a real effort.

"That's not true. I didn't tell you because, well, I started to tell you, right in the beginning, but I didn't tell you because I was so ashamed. I recognized you immediately at the door. Here you were, this important partner at the firm, and what would you think of me as a lawyer for fucking up and going out on a windsurfer in that weather? What would you think of me for having to swim for hours, at risk of death, and show up at some stranger's door in the dark with hypothermia and wearing nothing but a bathing suit? I wasn't just embarrassed, I was mortified. I was worried that you would think I was a loser and a joke, and that you would tell everyone at the firm how badly I messed up and how I was obviously irresponsible and immature."

Karen had never considered that possibility.

"And, while it is true that I asked to work for you, Denise told me in April that the chance of anyone getting to work with you was next to nil because everyone had requested you. So, as I stood there inside your door, dripping wet with hypothermia, and I recognized who you were, I calculated my odds. Keep in mind that I am one of thirty-two summer clerks. The firm's Chicago office has 822 lawyers of which 287 are partners. Denise said that the firm was aiming for us to work with six partners over the course of the summer. Six divided by 287 is .0209. I had a two percent chance of working with you. Or maybe three of the thirty-two clerks might get to work with you -- that would still be less than a ten percent chance that I would ever see you. I calculated my risk, and I took it because I was ashamed. Not because I wanted to get you into bed. And, on that front, I clearly recall that you -- not me -- were the one who made the first moves. The way you looked at me when the robe accidentally slipped open? And you were the one who started with the touching. You held my hand. I never would have done anything if you hadn't made the first move. I respected you way too much to do

62

that. I'm not going to lie and say that I wasn't already thinking about it, a lot, but I would never have made that first move."

A brilliant argument, backed up with facts and statistics. And he seems so honest.

"The problem, now though, is infinitely bigger. Do you know that the Firm has a policy prohibiting sexual harassment and that whatever happened with us now puts us in that category? You cannot work for me. I cannot be your supervisor. I'm going to ask Denise to take you off the Wilkommen case."

"You can't do that to me."

"I have no choice."

"You just can't. It's actually against the law. Everyone at the firm will know that I got kicked off for some reason, and people won't know the truth, so they'll assume that I fucked something up. None of the partners will want to work with me, or they'll be hesitant about it. I might not get a permanent offer as a result. If you go forward with that, it will have real consequences for me, maybe even long-term consequences, all because we had sex both of us wanted, and I happen to be a subordinate now at work."

"That's crazy. You weren't a subordinate at the time. We'll just tell people that you had a conflict we didn't know about. Like you have a cousin who took the drug and suffered kidney failure or something."

"I'm not starting my career here with a lie. Lies come back to haunt you. I'm not doing it. I will have to tell people the truth, and the truth is that if you take me off this case, it is solely because we had sex. And the law explicitly prohibits you or the firm from taking retaliatory action against me because we had sex."

"Excuse me?"

"I'm sure you know it as well as I do. A supervisor cannot take an action against an employee because of a sexual relationship with that employee. I could file a complaint with the Attorney General's Office or the EEOC. It's a slam-dunk case."

"Well, it would be your word against mine."

"No, it wouldn't. I have evidence."

"What are you talking about?"

"I took a condom home. Your DNA on the outside, mine on the inside. It won't be my word against yours."

Karen was shocked and horrified. But very impressed. That explained the missing condom. Richard was brilliant. She was not capable of lying and would never do it anyway. She felt bad for even suggesting it.

"I would never have lied about what happened. But I'm impressed that you were smart enough to collect evidence to protect yourself if I were to turn out to be an evil shit." Karen was calming down.

"I knew you wouldn't lie about it. That's why I threw the condom in the trash the moment I got home. Well, that reason, plus it was really disgusting and starting to make my apartment smell."

They both laughed.

"But I guess I could still dig it out of the trash can, should you change your story."

They laughed some more about how disgusting that was.

"Seriously, though, you can't work on this case. The firm has a policy about that. Let me pull it up. Let's look at it together." She printed out two copies. They started reading the policy.

"Look right here, 'No supervisor shall engage in any sexual activity, nor discuss or propose any sexual activity, with any employee who works under that person's supervision. Violation of this policy will result in immediate sanctions which may include termination of the supervisor, including partners.'"

"Okay, that just means we have to stop while I'm working here."

Karen thought about it. "Do you want to get off the case because of the death threats? That would be convenient."

"No. I had offers from a dozen law firms. I came here because you are one of the best lawyers in the country, and I want to learn from you. I'm only here ten weeks. What do you think of just putting things on hold for ten weeks? You don't want to be involved with me anyway."

"I don't know. If you were to get off the case, now is the time to do it."

There was a knock at the door. "Come in," Karen called out.

Chris came in with some papers in her hand. "I'm sorry to bother you."

"Karen, we just received two emailed orders from Judge Stewart's Chambers. The first is that she has scheduled an emergency conference for tomorrow at noon -- she's obviously fitting us in in the midst of her jury trial, and we have to let her know whether you will be attending in person or by phone by 5:00 p.m. today. The second order is that, on the recommendation of the U.S. Marshals, she has ordered the Marshals to transport you and your staff to and from the court for security purposes." Chris handed the orders to Karen.

"Also, Director Reilly from the State Police is at the reception area on 62, along with someone from the U.S. Marshals Office and the FBI. They said that they do not have an appointment, but they hope you can make time to see them."

"Shit."

"I know." Chris had been through this drill before.

"Yeah, that's fine. Please bring them to my office?" Karen looked at her watch. "Please tell them that I can only meet with them for 10 minutes before my next appointment."

Chris left to get Director Reilly and the others.

"I'm sorry," Richard said. "What does this mean? I mean you downplayed the threats in the meeting like they were nothing. Is there reason to be worried?"

"Judge Stewart's order means that the U.S. Marshals have assessed the threat and think that there's reason to be worried."

"That's concerning." Richard looked very upset.

"I'm sure it will be fine. It's not the first time I've been under federal Marshal protection to and from court. I expect that I'll be getting details in a moment."

"I know that, but still. . . ." Richard hesitated. "Karen. Don't trust Director Reilly. I know him. He's a bad cop."

"What are you saying? I've known Tim for 20 years."

Richard was now starting to sweat. "I can't talk about it. Please, don't trust him. Don't trust him with anything. I've got to go. I have to do something in my office before the lunch."

Richard was now sweating profusely. He jumped up and quickly left the room.

Chapter Thirteen

If there had to be a threat, better in a federal case. The U.S. Marshals protect the federal judges and the litigants in court. Judges get threatened all the time, and the federal Marshals are terrific.

Tim Reilly came into her office, along with Ken Shapiro from the FBI and someone from the Marshal's Office whom Karen had never met before named Joe. She didn't catch his last name.

She knew Ken, both from law school and from her time at the U.S. Attorney's Office. Ken was a thorough and honest investigator who put together rock solid cases, and who opposed going forward unless he was confident that he had sufficient evidence not merely to get a jury to convict, but -- and this wasn't the same thing -- enough evidence to be confident that they had the right guy and guilt was certain. While the final decision to take a charge to the grand jury was always made by the lawyers in the U.S. Attorney's Office, Ken's views had a significant impact. Often, victims got angry with his approach; his colleagues in the FBI sometimes got angry; and people in the U.S. Attorney's Office had been known to take issue with his reluctance to charge someone when he wasn't confident the person was guilty. He was exactly the person Karen wanted on her investigations, and they always got along well -- with mutual respect between them.

"So, what's up?" she asked.

Tim started. "We're here on the threats, obviously. It's kind of bad news, Karen."

Ken picked it up from there. "There were four emails sent to lawyers at the firm. They were all from the same email address 'justice.for.Kayley@gmail.com.' Logically, 'Kayley' has to be the first named plaintiff in the Wilkommen acne case -- the fifteen-year-old who died of kidney failure last year. We tracked all of the emails. The emails appear to have been sent within a few minutes of each other, but from different IP addresses."

"Shit."

"Yeah, so, the only way for that to happen would be if four different people sent the emails simultaneously, or one person sent the emails from four different devices connected to different servers, or some combination of the two. So, we looked at the IP addresses. As you know from the cases we did together in the past, every device that connects to the internet has an IP address when it logs onto the internet. We found that there were four different devices sending emails within minutes of each other. We tracked the IP addresses to precise locations. Karen, they were all public wi-fi addresses that we can't trace to a specific person. Remember the case involving Judge Smith?"

"Ugh. I do." Karen had read about Judge Smith getting death threats from a fake email account over public wi-fi connections.

"And do you know about what happened to Judge Smith?" Ken asked.

"I remember vaguely reading that he got some threats and some guys confessed," Karen said.

Ken continued. "Joe can best explain the next piece."

Joe started speaking for the first time. "Karen, as you know, the U.S. Marshals, we keep the judges safe. We've never lost a judge in a federal building, but people don't know the details about the scare a few years back with Judge Smith, shortly after he was promoted to the federal bench.

"Your case has a lot of similarities to Judge Smith's threats. He received multiple threats over the internet from different locations, all within a matter of minutes. Your threats were all sent within minutes of 5 p.m. on Saturday."

"Here's where it gets particularly concerning," Ken added. "Where do you park your car when you're in the office?"

"Two blocks down, on Wacker."

"Wacker and what," Tim asked.

"Wacker and Madison. Why?"

"One threat was sent from the coffee shop across the street from this building. The other three threats were sent down the block on Wacker, from public spots between here and where you park your car on Madison," Ken said. Tim and Joe looked down.

Karen's head started to pound. She started to feel sweaty.

"There's more." Tim said, turning to Ken.

Ken continued. "Judge Smith's case involved four likely gang members in Chicago who got incensed after Judge Smith ordered a house seized after there were arrests at the house for drug dealing. As you know, federal judges have discretion to do that. These guys sent the judge threats and they used the same technique that we see here. We ended up getting four of them, but some of us felt we never found the ringleader. We debated that a lot in the office, but we did all we could. It was a joint investigation with the State Police, the FBI and the Marshals. We had to make the arrests when we did because the attack on Judge Smith seemed imminent. The four of them are serving sentences for conspiring to kill a federal judge. They all ended up confessing, and they all told the same story that there was no one else involved. Maybe that was all of them and this is just a copycat. We don't know. But we checked with the wardens in their different prisons and they have zero access to the internet. There was a cell phone that someone sneaked into one of the facilities a few years back, but that's it. I don't see how these guys could have done it, but it is exactly the same technique."

"The concern," Tim said, "is that these guys were the real deal. They had weapons, tons of ammunition, fake IDs, and they had a real plan that they took steps to implement."

Tim concluded, "Basically, if we had waited another day or two to arrest them, it would have been too late. It was that close."

Karen felt like she was going to throw up. She looked at her watch. Her kids would still be at camp.

She went to her desk and buzzed Chris on the intercom. "Chris, can you come in a sec?"

Chris opened the door and came into the office.

"This is pretty urgent. Please contact everyone who is going to the Wilkommen lunch and tell them not to go. They should stay in the building and not go outside. Call them, text them, make sure they each get the message, okay? Tell them I'll explain -- we need to set up a team meeting, for as soon as possible today."

Chris looked at her watch. "On it!" She ran out the door.

Karen turned her attention back to the men in the room. "Look, we really need to bring the Chairman of the firm and the Executive

Committee into this meeting. This involves the security of a lot of people beyond me. They need to be involved in any decisions that are going to be made, and they need to know the facts so they can assess the risk to employees and take precautions."

Tim said, "I think we all agree on that, but they get an abbreviated version of the facts, okay? This is a live investigation. We just tell them that we have concerns, and what we think needs to be done."

"Before we do that, Tim, I need help figuring out what to do with my kids. What do you guys recommend? They're at camp. Is my home safe? Should we move somewhere? What do we do?" Karen was terrified and barely holding it together.

"And you guys need to talk to building security about this risk," Karen added.

"Agreed," Tim responded. "We'll do that as soon as we leave here. This might be a good time for the kids to visit their grandparents, or they are welcome to stay with us until things blow over."

"Thanks Tim." She was glad to have a reliable friend who was the Director of the State Police, but Richard's words about Tim were stuck in the back of her head, and they troubled her.

There was a knock on the door. It was Chris. "I got everyone. They'll eat in the cafeteria on 82 and wait for further word from you. Maybe you can meet them there."

"Thanks Chris," Karen said. "Can you do me a favor and see if you can track down Jonathan and the rest of the Executive Committee? Whoever is around? This is urgent -- they should really be participating in this meeting."

"Will do." Chris left the office. Karen would give Chris the details as soon as the guys left.

"How secure is the cafeteria?" Ken asked.

"It's pretty secure. You have to have a firm key card to get on the floor, a key card to get beyond the elevators, and a key card to get into the cafeteria." Karen had no time to eat anything this morning, and she was now hungry and wanted to meet her team there.

"Yeah, but we know nothing about the people who work there," Ken said.

"I know all the people who work there," Karen said. "All long-term employees. I'm not concerned."

"Okay," Ken said, "but you need to be very careful."

"So, tell me what you know about these guys who planned the prior attack," Karen said.

Ken explained, "They were angry over a drug forfeiture case. A drug deal went down at a house. The homeowner was renting out rooms to make ends meet. There had been a prior drug sale at the property. We took the house under the forfeiture law; the homeowner lost everything, and the family was out on the street. Shortly after that, the threats started. One of the guys was the oldest son in that family -- his mom, little brother and sister were put out on the street -- and the other three were his friends."

"How old were they?" Karen asked.

"Early 20's. All black. All with troubled juvenile histories. You know, kids who spent time in custody as juveniles, either because they were out of control or abandoned by their families, I don't remember the details. They met as kids in a group home or something. One, the ringleader, was involved in a murder of an old lady when he was very young, like ten or something. These were really troubled and violent kids who graduated from the juvenile system and weren't out long before they went to adult prison."

"Can I get names? Photographs? What do I need to be on the lookout for?"

"I don't think that would help," Tim said. "They're all in jail and aren't behind this."

The others nodded in agreement, but Ken said, "I'll send you an email with their names, latest photos, and whatever I can provide you under the public access laws."

Tim disagreed. "I really don't think that's necessary. These four are in jail and they're not going anywhere."

Tim continued. "So, here's where we are. We're looking at security video to see if we can get any images from the four public wi-fi spots. Maybe we'll get a hit through facial recognition to someone who is in CODIS."

71

Tim didn't need to explain the CODIS system to Karen. She was familiar with the national crime data base.

"But this is going to take time. There's always a backlog when you need forensic work done, terrorism and homicides get priority of course, and there are never enough people doing facial recognition. We're also going to interview employees and witnesses and ask if they saw anything suspicious, you know, all the usual things you do in an investigation."

Chris knocked on the door. "The chairman can't make this meeting but will meet with you in his office at 1. We're lining up the executive committee members to join, either in person or live conference. Remember, we need to tell Judge Stewart about whether you are going to appear by phone?"

"Thanks Chris. Please inform Judge Stewart and the parties that we will be appearing in person." There was no way Karen was going to give in to threats, ever. It was a matter of principle for her.

Joe the U.S. Marshal seemed concerned by her decision. "Are you sure you want to do that Karen? Judge Stewart won't care if you appear by phone."

"Yes, I'm sure."

Chapter Fourteen

Tim, Ken and Joe got up and left. But less than a minute later, Tim knocked on the door and peeked in.

"Hey, sorry. I forgot something."

"Oh, sure. Come on in," Karen said.

"We forgot to tell you that we want to put a tracer on your phone and your computer. I have a USB drive to load the program onto your computer, and I'll need your phone and your password -- you can put in the password for me -- to download the phone app."

"What for?"

"We want to be live if you get another threat. We don't want to wait for hours or over the course of the weekend. We want to be on top of it, immediately, you know? Getting the threat and then the IP address seconds later makes it possible for us to get them before they leave wherever they are. We haven't divvied up the investigation yet in terms of what responsibilities the State Police and the FBI will have, but we want to have an officer logged onto your devices, so we get the threat up immediately." Tim looked very concerned.

"I don't know. I need to think about this a bit. You would have access to my texts and emails, I take it?"

"Yes, live access -- to keep you and the kids safe."

"I can't do that. I'm a lawyer. I get confidential emails and texts from clients all day long. I cannot turn over access to those accounts to anyone." She was concerned because Tim should know that.

"Yeah, of course, that's true. We would ignore those emails and messages."

"You can't ignore something until after you've read it. I just can't do it. I could get disbarred for giving access to client communications like that."

"Karen, this is only for your safety, and I -- all of us -- feel strongly that *is* necessary."

"Well, I don't doubt that you are doing everything humanly possible to keep me safe, and I am extremely grateful for that, but the only way you can get access to my emails and texts is if you get a warrant." Karen was firm.

"That's nuts. We're trying to keep you safe, and you're setting up a huge barrier."

"I have no choice."

Karen felt like Tim was not going to give up on this. "Look, I have to leave for another meeting. I'm sorry. I'm super grateful for all you're doing." She stood up and walked him to the door, then went to Chris' desk. She pretended to review some documents Chris had left on the ledge as Tim walked down the hall.

After Tim was far out of view and earshot, Karen asked Chris where Richard's office was, and Chris pointed her to the interior hallway on Karen's floor, to the paralegal offices that were used for summer clerks and some new associates.

Chapter Fifteen

The Recruiting Committee had already put "Richard Adams" on the wall by his partly open door. She knocked anyway.

There was no response, so she peeked around the door as she knocked again.

Richard was sitting at his desk, staring off into space.

"Richard?" He did not respond. She came closer to see if he had ear pods in or something. She didn't see any.

"Richard?" She moved directly in front of him. He looked right through her as though she were not there.

"Richard? Are you okay?"

Karen started to panic. Was he having some kind of seizure? She didn't know what to do. She reached across his desk and gently touched his arm. "Richard, are you okay?"

Richard relaxed, smiled, and said, "Hey, what's up?"

Karen was still a bit startled. "You had me scared there for a second. I thought you might be having a seizure or something."

"Oh, that," Richard said. "Sometimes I just space out a little bit. No seizures. Nothing to worry about."

"Oh, okay." Karen said. But it definitely was not okay. It was very weird. But now he seemed totally fine.

"Did you want to talk to me?" he asked.

She closed the door. "Yeah. I was thinking about the policy," Karen began. "There's just no way we can be together in any capacity at this point. It's not fair to the other summer clerks I work with. What if one of them is incompetent and gets a terrible evaluation and no offer at the end of the summer. That person could file a complaint alleging that you got an offer because you were sleeping with a partner. We just can't be in that position."

"I guess that makes sense. I hadn't thought of that."

"And the same is true if we date and you don't work for me. If we date publicly, partners who depend on me for work may feel pressured to give you good evaluations. And again, someone who does not get an offer might file a claim that he or she did not get an offer because of the same thing."

"Shit, I've really fucked everything up. I'm sorry. So much for my career here. It's all my fault."

Poor guy. She reassured him that his career wasn't destroyed and added that they could reconsider their relationship after his summer clerkship was over.

Why had she added that last part? It was over. Why suggest it might not be? Was it his kindness over the cranberry juice? His willingness to blame himself? Or was it just that he looked so incredibly hot in a suit and tie?

"We need to take you off Wilkommen. I cannot supervise you in anything client-related. But I don't see why I couldn't work with you on a research project or writing an article for publication. I'll have to run it by Denise, but I don't see what would be wrong with something like that. I can teach you litigation skills in the process, but I won't evaluate your work or have any input into whether you get an offer. Something more like a personal project."

"What are you going to give as the explanation for taking me off the Wilkommen team?" He still looked very concerned.

"An abbreviated version of the truth. I was thinking I would write a simple memo that's one sentence long which says that, 'Pursuant to the Firm's policy on sexual harassment, I have concluded that I should not be in a supervisory position with regard to Richard Adams.' If anyone asks, I don't give details, other than to say there was 'something in the past.'"

"Okay, I guess," he said, but a little grudgingly.

"So, think about a topic. Make an appointment with Chris for us to toss around ideas later in the week, okay?"

"Okay."

Karen was still sitting there like there was more to discuss.

"And, there's something else," she said.

Chapter Sixteen

"What did you mean when you said that Director Reilly was a bad cop?"

Richard looked upset, maybe shaken even.

"I -- I can't."

Karen was direct. "You made an extremely serious allegation about the Director of the State Police. He was a witness in number of my cases when I was in the U.S. Attorney's Office when he was a trooper and then a detective. I put people in jail based on his testimony. I never had any reason to question his conduct. Someone doesn't get to be the Director of the State Police if he's a bad cop. I need to know if there is something that I don't know about. He's my ex-husband's best friend, he coaches my son's sports teams, his daughter and my daughter are on the same lacrosse team. If there is something -- anything -- I really need to know it."

"I can't talk about it. I don't have any evidence of anything. I'm sorry I said it." Richard's distress was clear.

"Please, anything, a suspicion even, please tell me."

"No. No evidence. Nothing."

"Then why did you say that? It's a very serious allegation. Surely there's something behind it, or you wouldn't have said it."

Richard sighed. "It was just a suspicion, from a long, long time ago. I don't know anything for a fact. It was just a suspicion. It's getting really hot in here, and I'm feeling a bit light-headed. I'm going to go outside for a few minutes and get some fresh air."

As Richard stood up, Karen noticed sweat stains on his shirt under the arm pits. Richard's forehead was also sweaty. She'd only known him for 72 hours. Maybe she had no right to pry.

"Okay, but can I ask you something else?"

"Sure." Richard was standing by the door.

"If a police officer asked you if they could put a device on your phone and your computer to monitor your incoming emails and texts for threats, what would you say?" She asked the question in a careful manner, making sure not to suggest the answer.

"Get a warrant. That's easy. Otherwise, it would create a huge problem for your clients who send you privileged attorney-client protected communications by email and text. Why are you asking?" he asked, looking perplexed.

"Because Director Reilly just asked me to do exactly that."

"With all his experience, he has to know that." Richard scrunched his face. "That's just bizarre."

"I know," Karen said. "That's why I was asking you about what you said before."

"I thought we were done with that. I said I have zero evidence." He grabbed a napkin from his desk and mopped his sweaty forehead. "Is it okay if I go now?"

"Yeah, sure."

He was out the door before she finished the sentence.

And then it hit her: Richard was a drug addict. The profuse sweating, claiming it was hot in the office when it wasn't, and needing to run outside in the middle of a meeting. That would explain why he thought Tim was a bad cop. Definitely drug addict behavior.

But then, he'd had barely been out of her sight for a forty-hour period where all he had was his bathing suit. He couldn't have raided her medicine cabinets because there was nothing in them to steal. He had a lot of wine -- that was all. Probably not a drug addict. But what then? She was going to look up these symptoms when she got home. Maybe it was diabetes. Maybe the flu. Maybe it was just first-day-at-a-new-job jitters. Whatever it was, it made her suspicious of him and their relationship. Good that the sex part was over. She would make sure it didn't resume. She felt relieved about that.

Chapter Seventeen

Back at her office, Chris updated her. "I spoke to Senator Williams' Office. They can meet with you after the conference with Judge Stewart tomorrow. I told them we wouldn't know exactly when you would be free from the conference, but they said that's fine. You should just go on up when you're done.

"I also spoke to the Marshal's Office. Joe Maldonato -- he was here earlier -- is running your security detail. He said it's fine if you want to go to Senator Williams' office after the hearing, since the courts, the Senator's office, and the Marshal's office are all in the federal building, which is secure. They can escort you to the Senator's office, if you want, and when you're done, you should call downstairs and they can pick you up and bring you back to the office. I assume that the acne team will not be joining you in the meeting with Senator Williams?"

"Yes, that's right."

"Do you really think you need to go in person?"

"You think it's a bad idea?"

"It concerns me. Why take a risk when you don't have to?"

"I know, but it's the principle of the thing. If I flip out every time I get a death threat, they win, you know?"

"Okay, but if you change your mind, let me know and we'll fix the arrangements."

"Thanks."

Karen usually worked in her office with her door open, to appear welcoming for anyone who needed to talk to her, but she closed the door behind her and looked up Ken's number on her cell. He'd been in her contacts since she worked at the U.S. Attorney's office.

"Hi Karen," he answered. His phone obviously recognized her personal cell number. "What's up?"

"Hey, I have some meetings in the federal building tomorrow, and I was wondering if you would be around so I could talk to you about something."

"Sure. What time?"

"I have a court hearing in the Wilkommen case at noon, which should last less than an hour, and then a meeting upstairs with Senator Williams which should also last less than an hour. I'm not really sure about the timing. Are you around generally? Can I call you when I'm done? Or should we schedule something for another day?" Karen was hoping that Ken would not ask what this was about. She hadn't formulated how she was going to bring up the topic yet.

"Sure, that would be great. I'm a little behind with my reports this week, so I'm just planning to be writing reports tomorrow afternoon -- unless some emergency comes up. Just call this number when you get through security, and I'll bring you up."

"Great. Thanks, I appreciate it."

"No worries. See you tomorrow."

Chapter Eighteen

The rest of Monday was as hectic as the morning. Karen ended up grabbing a sandwich in the cafeteria, eating at her desk, and entirely missed the team lunch meeting in the cafeteria. She met with the firm Chairman, Jonathan Kennedy -- who decided to cancel a lunch with a client, a sacrifice of great proportions, to attend with the rest of the executive committee -- to tell them about everything she knew regarding the investigation. She emphasized how important it was to keep the facts confidential. The Committee decided that Karen should tell everyone on the Wilkommen teams that the threats were being investigated; that she had received threats before and they never amounted to anything; but, to be very clear, the Executive Committee had unanimously decided that no one had to continue on the cases if they felt unsafe or uncomfortable. All as she had expected, and pretty much what she had already told the teams. They also offered her armed protection on her daily commute. She told them she would think about it, but she would start by just parking in a different garage each day. Jonathan offered her his spot in the building -- there were limited spots reserved for executives of the largest tenants, which were reached through a secure and largely unknown entry in the back of the lobby.

"That would be really great, if you wouldn't mind, at least until this dies down a bit."

"Of course," Jonathan said.

Karen realized with more than a little bit of fear that her car was currently parked in the garage two blocks away, where she had parked every day for years. She wasn't sure how she was going to get her car at the end of the day. She called Tim, who sent over a junior trooper to collect her car and bring it to the service area of the office building. Chris then arranged with building security for Karen to leave at the end of the day through the service elevator to the basement and out the back in the secured alley behind the building. She'd start parking in Jonathan's spot tomorrow.

She wrote the memo about Richard being off her team pursuant to the sexual harassment policy and gave it to Denise.

Denise read the memo as Karen stood there. "Holy shit. Richard was the naked man?"

"I can't talk about it. I'm sorry. I just can't." Denise was definitely bummed not to get all the prurient details.

Karen left early, at four, because she wanted to be home when the kids got off their respective camp vans.

Chapter Nineteen

Cyndi came home first, distraught, after texting Joey all day.

"Mom, Joey was bullied really bad at camp today. He started crying, and then they got really cruel. Stuff like, 'Imagine how much you'd be crying if your sister died because she took medicine for a pimple.' 'Your mom is a murderer.' He's been crying all day at camp."

"Ugh. That's horribly upsetting. Why didn't I get a call from the camp?"

"Joey said that his camp counselor basically agreed with the kids, and kind of chimed in with the taunting."

Cyndi had always been Joey's protector since the day he was born. They were extremely close. They never fought, and their biggest arguments were over what Karen should make for dinner.

"If you don't call and get that dick-brain fired, I will," she added.

Karen heard the van pull up. She went to the front door and watched Joey as he walked down the path. He looked awful. His face was puffy and swollen like he had been crying. She gave him a big hug.

"Come on into the kitchen. Let's talk." Karen got Joey a glass of water, and pulled out a giant chocolate bar. His favorite. As she sat down, Joey climbed onto Karen's lap and began sobbing as he ate.

"Cyndi told me what happened. I'm incredibly proud of how you handled it. Contacting your sister for support and not getting into a fight. That was terrific."

"Thanks Mom, I just didn't want to bother you at work."

"You will never 'bother' me at work. You and Cyndi are far more important to me than anything I do at work, honey. You can call or text me whenever you need me. Certainly, if something's wrong, you should let me know. I'm sorry my job caused this, but what those kids did was despicable -- taking it out on you when you have nothing to do with it is outrageous.

"So here's the deal. Wilkommen is a long-term client of mine that I have represented for many years. The company has hundreds of drugs that are used all over the world every day, many of which save lives. I don't know -- no one knows for sure -- whether the acne medication or the medication women during took pregnancy caused any deaths or illnesses. The truth is that 99.9 percent of the kids who took the acne drug did not get kidney failure. Tens of thousands of kids thought it was a miracle cure for severe acne that otherwise would have left them with severe facial scarring. When the possibility of a problem was reported, Wilkommen promptly took the drug off the market -- both drugs, actually -- while the experts tried to figure it out. But regardless, Wilkommen has the right to be represented in court."

Cyndi chimed in. "The problem is, they can hire any lawyer they want, why does it have to be you?"

Karen sighed. "It doesn't, I suppose, in a perfect world. But we don't live there. I have a job. Bills to pay. College tuition to save for. My clients aren't perfect, or they wouldn't be sued. But I'm a litigator, and that's what I do."

"What about the death threats?" Joey asked. "Is someone going to kill you?"

Joey was now sobbing again. Clearly, this part was worse than the bullying at camp. She tried to reassure him.

"Why would anyone want to be a lawyer?" Cyndi asked.

"For me, it was because I wanted to change the world, do good things, protect children from human trafficking. Plus, I love to argue -- just like you, Cyndi. But this job pays better."

"Mom," Joey said. "I don't want to go to camp tomorrow."

She agreed that Joey could skip camp and hang out in her office. She left Chris a message to remind her to call the camp about bullying. And the counselor. She was going to bully the shit out of him. And, with surprising unanimity, they all agreed to Thai takeout for dinner.

Chapter Twenty

Karen installed Joey in her office with his phone, hand-held game system -- and e-reader which she knew he wouldn't touch.

The Marshals picked her up at 11:15 in the alley behind the building, where security had set up a fabric screen so no one could see her get into the car. They drove the five blocks to the federal building with another marshal car in front and one behind. It felt like she was in a movie. The assembled press out front was left to figure out how they'd missed her.

All of the benches, and the seats in the jury box, were filled with reporters and a couple of sketch artists, since cameras are not allowed in federal court. Karen politely declined their requests for comments.

Judge Carrol entered the courtroom from the back and sat down at the bench. "Ms. Harding, I have been told by the United States Marshals Office that there have been threats made on your life, threats that appear to be related to this case. Is that accurate?"

Karen stood to address the judge. "Your Honor, I actually have not read them because I was afraid they would be too upsetting, but my understanding from the police is that threats were sent to my email and to some of the lawyers working on this case at my firm."

"I see." She turned toward Marshal Joe Maldonato, who was sitting behind and to the left of Karen. "Marshal, have you read any of the emails that have been described as threatening?"

Joe stood up to address the judge. "Yes, Your Honor. I have read four different emails in total. All were sent to Ms. Harding and lawyers at her office. And all of them, without going into detail, threaten Ms. Harding's life. The indication is that the threats could be related to this case because they came from an email address titled "Justice for Kayley.""

"Thank you, Marshal. I thought it would be appropriate to address the threats in public, here in the courtroom, with the press present. Do any of the parties have any objection to my doing that? Ms. Harding, any objection on your or your client's behalf?" No one objected.

"The threats that have been made in this case, or any other case, will not be tolerated. There are federal laws and state laws here in Illinois that allow for lengthy prison sentences for anyone who makes such a threat, or anyone who takes any action in furtherance of a conspiracy relating to such a threat. If I learn of any threats, I will refer the matter for criminal investigation by the U.S. Attorney's Office, as I have done here. Furthermore, if any threat is made in my presence in this courtroom, I will find that person in contempt of this court and will send the offender directly to prison, without a trial.

"Am I making myself clear?"

"Yes, Your Honor," the lawyers all said in unison.

Judge Stewart continued: "In the United States, our system of justice has depended, for more than 200 years, on the simple but essential principal that all parties in any dispute brought in court have the right to be represented by a lawyer. In criminal law, where the potential punishment includes jail, the right is so important that the state or the federal government provides a lawyer to every defendant who cannot afford one. In civil cases, such as this, corporations are required by law to be represented by counsel. As a matter of law, a corporation cannot defend itself in court without a lawyer.

"Throughout our history, lawyers have been threatened, and sometimes harmed and killed, simply because they were doing their job in representing their clients. This is nothing new. Even Shakespeare, in *Henry VI*, stated that, "The first thing we do, let's kill all the lawyers." But it is not a joke. It is not funny. It is an extremely serious matter and this court will treat it as such.

"Often, lawyers are threatened or assaulted because they are representing an unpopular client or taking an controversial position. In the Great Depression, lawyers who represented banks were threatened and sometimes assaulted. In the McCarthy era, lawyers were threatened and sometimes assaulted because they had the courage to represent people who were accused, often falsely, of being communists. In the Civil Rights era, lawyers who fought for the rights of African Americans to vote and to have equal access to public spaces and public education were threatened and brutalized. Prosecutors who are only doing their job to enforce the law are frequently threatened. Every time a lawyer takes on an unpopular or highly disputed representation, lawyers put their lives on the line for the pursuit of justice. Think of the risks that that the lawyers for some of the most important legal decisions in our history have taken, including the lawyers in *Brown v. Board of Education* (the case that desegregated our schools), *Loving v. Virginia* (the case that held that a state could not make it a crime for a black woman to marry a white man), *Lawrence v. Texas* (the case that guaranteed the right of lesbian and gay citizens to have consensual sexual relations), and, of course *Roe v. Wade*. And if that list tells you anything, it must tell you that the threats don't work. The threats will not stop the course of justice and they will not stop the law.

"This is not to say that I will treat this case differently because of the threats. I will not. I will continue to decide this case based on the facts presented in court and the law and nothing else.

"So, to be clear. This must stop. This is not a joke and will not be treated like one. It is a serious crime. It is a problem not just here in Chicago, but across the country. Our legal system will not survive if our lawyers are not protected. Our legal system will not survive if lawyers are made to feel intimidated or unsafe. I will not tolerate it.

"Any questions or anything else to add, counsel?"

"No, Your Honor," all the lawyers stated in unison as they addressed the judge.

"Thank you, Your Honor," Karen added.

"This Court is adjourned." Judge Stewart stood up. The clerk called, "All rise!" Judge Stewart left, and it was over.

Karen headed upstairs to Senator Shondra Williams' office.

Chapter Twenty-One

"This has to be very confidential," the Senator began.

"Of course, sure." Karen was getting uncomfortable.

"Have you heard the awful news about Steven Palmer?"

Steven Palmer was the current U.S. Attorney for the district. Karen knew him slightly when he had worked in the office as a young Assistant U.S. Attorney, or "AUSA" as they were commonly called. He wasn't viewed as particularly competent when she knew him, but he was politically connected, so it was no surprise that the senior senator from Illinois -- Senator Richardson -- had pushed to have him get the job. Shondra, the junior senator, had never liked Palmer or the senior senator much.

"Again, very confidential here. He has an inoperable malignant brain tumor. The doctors told him that he has four, maybe six months to live."

"Oh my God, that's horrible," Karen replied, truly upset and horrified. "Doesn't he have three young kids?"

"Yes, it's so sad."

"What can I do to help?"

"I want you to be the new U.S. Attorney," Shondra looked intently at Karen. "Can you do it?"

Karen was stunned. First, such awful news; and then, something so totally unexpected (in a good way, maybe).

"I don't know, I mean, this is such a surprise. Something like that, it's never crossed my mind. But why?"

"He learned about the diagnosis on Friday and won't be back in the office. As you are well aware, his First Assistant isn't competent to run the office, so the staff is very upset that there won't be any real oversight, especially since there are lots of very high-profile cases where they need strong leadership now. As you know, the Senate has to confirm the appointment, and the staff has urged me to get the situation resolved as quickly as possible. They feel they can't afford to wait until the Senate comes back after the summer recess."

"Is that even possible? My security clearance will need to be updated. There's not enough time."

"I've spoken to my colleagues in the Senate on both sides of the aisle, it won't be a problem. The clearance can be rushed through because you had a recent check a few years ago for the case you handled for Homeland Security. Everyone understands that the Chicago area cannot be without a U.S. Attorney for months with a dithering First Assistant in charge, and they're very impressed with your credentials. It's just a question of whether you want it."

"I'm incredibly honored by this. I'd love to take it, but I need to think about it. When do you need to know?"

"Wednesday at 5:00? Is that doable? Or sooner, if possible."

"Yeah, sure. I need to talk to my kids. Also, I need to see if I can work out the money part."

"I understand that it will be a huge pay cut."

"Yeah, well, money isn't everything."

Giving up her large law firm salary would be difficult. On the other hand, it wouldn't necessarily be a permanent pay cut. U.S. Attorney's serve at the pleasure of the President. There was a Democrat in office now, and she was being considered because she too was a Democrat. After the next election in eighteen months, if a Republican won the presidency, she would be out of a job. But former U.S. Attorneys are coveted in the big law firms. She could almost for sure return to her current firm, or maybe even start a bidding war between firms. Or maybe teach at a law school and be a legal commentator on a cable news show. The pay cut would be temporary.

They left it there. Karen was so flustered when she left that she forgot to go to the Marshals' office, and she took a cab back to her office. And then she realized that she had completely forgotten about her meeting with Ken Shapiro at the FBI. She asked the driver to take her back to the federal building.

90

Chapter Twenty-Two

"So, do you have good news for us?" Ken asked as he took her into his tiny office.

"What are you talking about?"

"Did you hear about Steven?"

"Yeah, horrible. Really horrible."

"It's really affected all of us. So terribly sad. Makes you think about your own kids, you know?"

"Yeah."

"There are rumors going around the office that you're the pick to take over. People here, they were interviewed by both Senators' staff, and they were pushing hard for you." Ken looked at Karen like he was hoping for a definitive response.

"Can you keep this totally confidential?"

"Sure. You have my word."

"Shondra asked me just now. But I'm not sure. I'm supposed to let her know on Wednesday."

"What's the issue? Money?"

The way Ken said "money" made it sound so vile. "I'm not sure, I just need to think about it."

"Well, if there's anything I can do to convince you to take it, please talk to me!"

"Actually, I came here to talk to you about something else."

"What can I help with?"

"A couple of things. First, something a little weird happened, and I wanted to ask you about it."

"Okay." Ken leaned forward.

"Can this be totally confidential, between you and me and no one else?"

"Absolutely, unless you're about to confess to a felony or something." Ken smiled.

"No, no. It's nothing like that," she laughed.

Karen hesitated before proceeding carefully. "What do you think of Tim? Someone told me recently that he's a quote 'bad cop.' It's someone I don't know well, and the person refused to give me any details. I never had any bad experiences or any concerns with Tim. What do you think? Have you ever had reason to be concerned with him?

"Never," Ken sat back in his chair. "I've known him since we were in the academy together years ago, long before I joined the FBI. I didn't see anything then, and I haven't seen anything at all in the 20 years since. Why? What's up?"

"After you and Joe left the meeting at my office yesterday, Tim came back into my office. He asked me for my phone, and then he told me he was going to put an app on my phone and a program on my computer that would track my texts and emails in real time."

"What?!" Ken interrupted.

"He also said you agreed it was necessary."

"Is he out of his fucking mind?"

"It seemed strange to me, but I thought, maybe I've been out of the investigation business for a long time, you know," she answered, trying to diffuse things a bit.

Ken looked directly into her eyes. "Karen, you know me, I would *never* even suggest anything like that. That's an incredible invasion of your privacy, and it's even worse because you are a lawyer. It would involve getting all kinds of privileged communications with your clients! As you know, when we seize a lawyer's phone records or files, everything has to go to a court-appointed master or to a filter team to make sure that all confidential attorney-client communications are removed before we even get to see a single email or text."

"I know, that's why it upset me."

"Shit. Why would he do that?"

"He said it was so they could get any threatening emails or texts in real time, so as to not have a delayed response if I was off the grid or didn't check my messages for hours. I mean, I'm sure he had good intentions. I was off the grid that entire weekend. And Tim and I go way back -- he's David's best friend since high school."

"I don't know, Karen. Tim's explanation sounds kind of far-fetched." Ken put his hand to his face. "On the other hand, I can certainly see Tim being worried about you -- since you guys have known each other since forever -- and wanting to go that extra mile to make sure you're safe."

Ken looked out the window for a moment. "There's something else, maybe I should tell you. Also confidential, totally confidential, between you and me, okay?"

"Of course."

"You know the four guys in jail for threatening Judge Smith? I had a lot of questions about that case. The kids all confessed, but until they confessed, I really thought we had the wrong guys. I kind of think you should know that, in light of the similarities between the two cases. I've been thinking nonstop since yesterday that maybe we've got the wrong guys in jail. They're just kids. The more I think about it, the less sense it makes." Ken looked very concerned.

"What can you tell me?" she asked.

"I can tell you what's public information. First, their names." Ken grabbed a pad and a pen and wrote down: Jamal Johnson, Kenny James, David Brown, and Thomas Jones. He handed the note to Karen. "All kids of color. All from Chicago. They all had really troubled childhoods. I don't remember the details -- you should check the record from the sentencing -- but they met in juvie or somewhere like that. I think one was a particularly tough kid who was in on a murder charge from when he was ten-years-old, actually.

"Karen, I had some reservations. The thing that got to me at the time was that these kids were not tech savvy. One of them was so poor that he didn't even have a cell phone. Three of them did not own a computer. Jamal Johnson was twenty-one years old, working full-time supporting his mom and little brother and sister while going to community college. The others were eighteen, they had just aged out of the juvenile system.

"Tim said that they were all gang-bangers, and maybe that's true, but our sources in the Crips, the Bloods, MS-13 -- they all said that they had never heard of them, except Jamal. When it came to Jamal, two of our sources in the gangs said he was a good kid who was supporting his mom and siblings and had never been involved in the gangs, and that they left him alone."

"I don't get it. Did you find a motive? Did Judge Smith sentence any of them?"

"The motive was clear. Jamal's mom had a tenant living in the house who was convicted of dealing drugs in their home. Judge Smith ordered the home seized in furtherance of the drug conspiracy, pursuant to federal law. They lost their home. Jamal had been helping to pay the mortgage, and the house was nearly paid off. His mom worked full-time as a nurse. Jamal, his mom, and his little brother and sister ended up homeless. Then Judge Smith started getting the threats."

"I see. Makes sense. So, who confessed?"

"Jamal was the first to confess, then the others followed immediately thereafter."

"So, then you clearly did get the right guys, don't you think? The motive seems clear. Were their confessions supported by the evidence?"

"That's another troubling piece. First, we never found any evidence on any device that corroborated that they had sent the messages."

"Well, they could have erased them. You know, if something gets erased and then overwritten, it won't be there when you do the forensics."

"I know, but it just didn't make sense. The tenant claimed he was framed. Why would these boys threaten the judge who simply applied the law, rather than the cops who arrested the tenant for the drugs, or the prosecutor who asked for the seizure? It just seemed really random to me at the time.

"And another thing, I didn't understand why the other three would have gone along. They had no axe to grind with Judge Smith."

"But they were all friends, right? Did they say why they went along?" Karen asked.

"They were friends, that's true. Tim did all the interviews, and he never asked them why they went along."

"Okay, so like a lot of investigations, not every piece fits exactly into place, but do you have any reason to think that their confessions were false?"

"No, and that's why in the end I went along. But I just had an uncomfortable feeling. Still do. Something just doesn't sit right with me.

I felt they were maybe covering for someone. I figured that they played a role, and that they were guilty, but maybe they were covering for the king pin who was in charge. Maybe it was bigger than the seizure of Jamal Johnson's home. I just don't know.

"I wanted to keep investigating -- get wire taps, etc. But then a second set of threats was sent out. The second threat had disturbing details -- about the Judge going on vacation with his family to a lodge in Michigan, in the UP. They even had the address of the place where he was going to be staying. Only his family and his staff knew that. It was very concerning. That's when we assessed the risk and decided we had to move. There's nothing sketchy about the confessions. All on video. Every interview was clean -- on video -- and by the books. Tim did a good job."

"It really sounds like you did get the right guys, Ken. But why did Tim do the interviews? Wasn't he the Assistant Director then?"

"At first, Judge Smith reported that he thought it was in retaliation for something he had done as a state court judge, so the state police were involved from the beginning. You know Tim, he always wants to help out, and he offered to do the interviews since the case involved a prominent state court judge who had only recently been elevated to the federal bench. It made sense from our perspective to let the State Police take the lead on some things. I *think* we got the right guys in the end, I do. But you know me, I don't like unanswered questions in an investigation. Like I said, there are things that don't make sense -- and now we have a copycat set of threats to you when these four guys have no access to the internet."

"You know, the wardens always claim that the inmates don't have access to the internet, but cell phones get snuck in every day," Karen pointed out. "That's probably what happened. You can get anything in prison for a price. Or maybe they talked about it in jail and someone is just copying."

"I agree. That's all possible. But they would have arranged for others to send the threats from those locations. And why you. Why now. You had nothing to do with these kids."

"Maybe one of them used the acne drug. Maybe they have a relative who died and they saw me on the news on Friday. Maybe I prosecuted one of them or a family member years ago? Those things seem more likely than the odds of the four of them giving simultaneous false confessions, don't you think? Wouldn't they have been held in different facilities since they were co-defendants? The most obvious explanation is that they each just decided to tell the truth."

"Yeah, I have to agree." Ken sighed. "Most of the time, the most obvious conclusion is the right one."

But Karen wasn't sure if she believed what she was saying to Ken, or if she just wanted to convince herself.

Chapter Twenty-Three

Karen went to the marshals' office downstairs. If Joe was aware that she had fled the building and returned, he was at least kind enough not to mention it.

As the marshals drove her back to her office, she tried to thank them for all that they were doing to keep her safe. She got a polite nod in return. They were way too busy watching everyone and everything to take time out for conversation.

"How'd it all go?" Chris asked as she followed Karen into her office.

"Good. Nothing too exciting. Judge Stewart gave a nice speech about how she won't tolerate anyone threatening lawyers."

"And Senator Williams?"

"I'll have to talk to you about that tomorrow. It's a long story." Karen wanted to tell Chris, but she felt she should keep it quiet until she had made her decision. It would not be appropriate, and Senator Williams would be upset, if she let out that she had been offered the job if she was just going to turn it down. She drove home with Joey.

Cyndi was waiting for them in the kitchen. It wasn't often that Karen got home in time to take the boards out after work, and the weather was perfect. The water was still unseasonably warm, Caribbean blue, and there were no waves or whitecaps.

They all went out, paddling close to shore and jumping in for a swim when they got tired. After a while, Karen saw a man standing at the shoreline. It looked like he was holding a rifle. And it was pointed directly at her. "Jump off your boards, now!" Karen screamed.

They all jumped into the water.

"Keep your heads down!" she yelled.

"Mom," Joey asked, "Are you thinking that man with the black whiffle bat, playing ball with the toddler, is trying to kill you?"

"Huh?" Karen looked closer. "I don't have my glasses on. Is it really a whiffle bat?"

The kids started laughing hysterically. "You've got to me kidding me mom," Cyndi said, "You thought we were going to be murdered by a whiffle bat?"

"I guess I should get some glasses I can use on the lake," she said sheepishly.

"Or contacts," Cyndi said, "so you don't look like a lawyer even when you're out paddling."

"You know, mom" Joey said, "you always warned us that whiffle bats aren't safe as you think!"

"That was when you were playing in the house."

"Yeah, definitely a deadly weapon!" Cyndi added.

As U.S. Attorney, where she wouldn't have to bill clients for 2500 hours of her time each year, she'd have more time to do stuff like this with the kids. That would be priceless.

When they sat down to dinner -- Chinese takeout again! -- she broached the topic. After first getting Cyndi and Joey's commitment that they fully understood that they could tell absolutely no one about it until it was announced to the public, Karen told them about the conversation with Senator Williams and her offer to be the next U.S. Attorney.

"Would you be home more?" asked Joey.

"Wouldn't you get more threats as the U.S. Attorney than you do now?" asked Cindy.

They talked about all of the pros and especially the cons. Less money. Eating out less, and less take out, which, since Karen never had time to cook, would mean a lot more pasta-sauce-in-the-jar dinners on weeknights. Fewer vacation trips. No fancy summer camps. Not as many Amazon deliveries. A reduction in many things they'd come to see as entitlements.

"Mom," concluded Cyndi, "I think you should go for it. I think you would feel better about what you're doing every day -- working to protect children and marginalized women from being trafficked, stopping the flow of fentanyl into the community and things like that. I would be really proud to have a mom who did that work. Even if it meant that the threats were worse or more frightening."

"I agree," said Joey. "Money isn't everything, you know, Mom?"

"Okay. So, it's a go then." Karen thought she should accept the offer quickly, just in case, God forbid, Shondra had changed her mind and was thinking of withdrawing it. She texted Shondra's cell with her decision.

"I spoke to the kids, and I gratefully accept your offer to be the next U.S. Attorney for the Northern District of Illinois. I will let my partners know first thing in the morning. You can feel free to issue a press release any time after 10:30 a.m. -- if that schedule works for you. Thank you, again! I am very excited about the opportunity to serve our District."

Those three dots you see when someone is typing popped up on Karen's phone. Karen had a moment of terror that maybe Shondra had changed her mind.

"Terrific news! We'll issue the release at 10:30. Staff will make sure you get the security clearance forms first thing tomorrow so we can get that process started."

She texted Jonathan, the firm's chairman, to let him know.

Chapter Twenty-Four

First thing next morning, Karen met with Jonathan to discuss reassigning her cases. Jonathan Kennedy was a "lifer" at the Firm, who started as a summer clerk in law school and rose in the ranks until he was elected Chairman five years ago. He was a brilliant lawyer with a national reputation as one of the best litigators in the country, and he was an equally skilled Chairman, who could negotiate the daily high-level stress of law firm politics -- an atmosphere where people who were highly paid to argue for a living seemed to never be able to stop arguing about anything, no matter how minor, including the color of the carpets in the hallways, or more particularly, how much they should each be paid come December when the firm's profits were divvied up. Karen had always liked Jonathan since she worked at the Firm as a summer clerk before she went to the U.S. Attorney's Office. Jonathan was a fifth-year associate when Karen was a summer clerk, and he had always been kind and supportive of her career at the Firm.

Hardly to her surprise, the Executive Committee, all white men with a lone white woman who was elected by the Executive Committee only because they knew she would do what she was told, had already divvied up Karen's cases amongst themselves and their friends -- rather than to the more qualified lawyers who'd worked on the cases with Karen for years. It was everything she hated about the firm. The stupid, short-sighted decisions that were invariably based on greed or self-interest. In the end, she was able to save a couple of cases for the people who deserved to run them, but, for the most part, the cases were now in the hands of people who were not particularly smart and lacked prior experience with such matters. Jonathan said he felt a bit bad about it, but there was nothing he could do.

The one thing that made Karen really sad was losing Chris -- it would be a huge pay cut for Chris to go to the U.S. Attorney's Office. Chris would be fine -- she had an amazing reputation at the firm, and the partners would be jockeying for her. When Karen told Chris, the two of them cried and hugged.

Now that she had transferred oversight to all of her cases to other partners, Karen had time on her hands to think about the research project with Richard. She reviewed his very impressive resume. University of Michigan's Honor's Program with a double major in psychology and Spanish, a perfect GPA, Summa Cum Laude, Phi Beta Kappa, and various other awards. Perfect grades in law school (he had one A-), and recently elected editor-in-chief of the Law Review. In the bargain, he worked his first summer at an inner-city civil rights organization for youth involved in gangs; and during his second year, in addition to Law Review, he did independent research which resulted in two published articles, while he also somehow managed to volunteer at the mental health residential hospital for children downtown.

To say that she had never seen a student's resume like that would be an understatement. Near-perfect grades from top schools and law review were the norm for summer clerks at the firm, but working with kids in gangs, volunteering at a juvenile mental health facility, and publishing articles in leading law journals were each, in their own way, extraordinary.

His articles evidenced a strong interest in protecting children: "A Fifty State Survey of the Evidentiary Rules Regarding Child Witness Testimony Outside the Courtroom," and "Does the Americans with Disabilities Act Authorize Courts to Grant Testimonial Accommodations to Children with Disabilities?"

Just reading the titles of Richard's articles hit home for Karen. She had spent three years at the U.S. Attorney's Office prosecuting child sex-trafficking cases, and she had had countless cases where she had no choice but to offer monstrous defendants ridiculous plea agreements because she knew the child would never be able to testify. The most upsetting part of the process was that the worst offenders -- those who had caused the most damage to the children, thereby rendering them too terrified to testify -- often never spent a day in jail, and, instead, were free to traffic more children. When she finished reading the articles, she picked up the phone and asked Richard if he could stop by her office. A few moments later, he was sitting in the chair facing her desk.

"I read your articles. Pretty impressive," she told him.

He looked almost uncomfortable with the compliment. "Yeah, studies have shown that children with disabilities are criminally victimized -- sexually, physically and by neglect -- at rates that far exceed their non-disabled peers, but the cases are rarely prosecuted when the kids can't testify in court, which leaves the perpetrators free to hurt more children."

"Absolutely, I know from experience how challenging it can be to prosecute a case if the victim can't speak, or has intellectual disability, or is too traumatized to take the stand."

"Exactly. But there are ways to accommodate their disabilities to enable them to testify."

"How so?"

"Well, the U.S. Supreme Court has held that child victims of sexual abuse can be allowed to testify outside the courtroom, right?"

"Yes, of course."

"Why doesn't that apply to other cases? Like a domestic violence case? In some states, children who are victims of domestic violence are allowed to testify outside the courtroom, but in many states, they have to testify in front of the abuser. It seems to me that if a sexual abuse victim is allowed to testify outside the courtroom, the same principles apply to a child of domestic violence."

His voice was rising with passion. "Did you know that in juvenile proceedings, when the Department of Children and Family Services wants to remove a child from the home because of violence against that child, many states require the child to testify in court in front of the abuser? That's insane. The end result is that children cannot testify, and they returned home and suffer more abuse.

"And the same goes for children who witness abuse. Why shouldn't a little sister, who saw her father beat her brother or mother, be allowed to testify outside the courtroom? These rules are harming children."

"I agree," she responded. "But what about the right to confrontation?"

"Well, look at the original draft of the Magna Carta in 1215, when King John of England agreed to protections against illegal imprisonment and fair trials."

King John? Magna Carta? No wonder he was Phi Beta Kappa, and he wasn't even a history major.

"The final version," he went on, "which became the law in England in 1297, provided for the right to a trial by jury. But the right to confront witnesses didn't exist until much later. Here, the Bill of Rights included the Sixth Amendment, which provides a criminal defendant the right 'to be confronted with the witnesses against him.'"

Having dealt with the issue in some of her old cases. Karen was familiar with the history. "The right of confrontation in the Sixth Amendment was carried over from English common law, where it was a response to anger over abuses, most notably the trial of Sir Walter Raleigh, who was tried for treason in 1603 and convicted on the written confession of his former friend, Henry Brook, 11th Baron Cobham. Raleigh repeatedly requested that he be allowed to question Cobham: '[Let] my accuser come face to face, and be deposed!' But the court denied Raleigh's requests, a jury convicted him, and Sir Walter spent 13 years in the Tower of London, where tourists today can still see his cell."

"Of course," Richard replied. Right, she thought, of course he knew. "And did you know that Sir Walter finally was released from the Tower in 1616," he went on, "only to get in further trouble, so he wound up beheaded two years later? His last words were to the Executioner: 'Strike, man, strike!' Sir Walter's head was embalmed and given to his widow, who kept it in a velvet bag until her death 29 years later, at which point Sir Walter's head was returned to the remainder of his corpse in the tomb at St. Margaret's Church, where you can visit both the head and the corpse together today."

She laughed. "Okay, so you one-upped me there. I knew about the history of the Confrontation Clause, but I missed out on the head-in-a-bag part of the story."

"The point," he continued, "is that the right to confront witnesses obviously can be fulfilled with technology that didn't exist 500 years ago. Today, a witness can testify outside the courtroom by live video and the defendant can see and question the witness in the same manner without the witness feeling physically threatened by the defendant. All states need to allow that, to protect children, and also to protect adults with disabilities, like PTSD. If you have an adult with PTSD, like a domestic violence victim, that person might not be able to speak to testify in front of the defendant, but might be able to do so outside the courtroom. That needs to be accommodated."

"Yeah, but what's the legal basis for your argument? You need a law or a case or something to support that theory."

"Two things. First, when the U.S. Supreme Court decided in *Maryland v. Craig,* in 1990, that the Confrontation Clause permitted a child to testify outside the courtroom by means of one-way television so the defendant and the jury could see the child testifying, but the child could not see the defendant, the Court held that, while our system of justice maintains a 'preference' for face-to-face confrontation, 'a State's interest in the physical and psychological wellbeing of child abuse victims may be sufficiently important to outweigh, at least in some cases, a defendant's right to face his or her accusers in court.'"

"You have that quote committed to memory?"

"Yeah, I guess that's a little embarrassing."

"No, it's a skill that will make you a top litigator. But tell me more. What else have you got?"

"I've got the Supreme Court's 2004 decision in *Tennessee v. Lane*, where they held that the Americans with Disabilities Act applied to State Courts."

"How does that case support your position?"

"In that case, the state of Tennessee made George Lane, the named plaintiff who was a paraplegic, crawl to the second floor of the courthouse to face some minor criminal charge. He crawled to the second floor. Then, on a second occasion, he refused to crawl up again to the second floor for his court hearing, and the state charged him criminally for failing to appear in court. He sued, and the State of Tennessee argued that the state had the right to treat people with disabilities that way -- and they continued to argue that all the way to the U.S. Supreme Court.

"The Supreme Court found that the conduct of the officials was covered under the Americans with Disabilities Act, and that the plaintiffs had the right to sue state officials for failing to provide them reasonable accommodations to access the state courts."

"So, you think that the Americans with Disabilities Act requires state and federal courts to provide testimonial accommodations to children and adults with disabilities in order to give them full access to the court system?"

"Exactly."

"Brilliant."

"Do you know how the justices voted in *Tennessee v. Lane*?"

"No, but I could guess."

"Justices Scalia, Thomas, Kennedy and Rehnquist wrote dissenting opinions."

"No surprise there."

"Yeah, I guess they had no issue with allowing a state to humiliate a paraplegic and make him crawl to the second-floor courtroom -- or the fifth floor, for that matter -- and he would have no recourse to stop it and no defense to the criminal charge for not showing up. Really sick stuff."

"Agreed." Karen often thought about how so many people focus on typical "conservative" and "Christian" issues like abortion when they vote for the president who will pick the next Supreme Court justice, but they don't realize the damage the Supreme Court can do to everyone else in the country who is not trying to have an abortion. Including the voters who likely put the president in office. Where were the "Christian values" when it came to people with disabilities like George Lane?

"So, my thinking is that, while George Lane needed an elevator, others might need to testify without seeing the defendant; they might need to testify in writing or by texting or typing their answers, they might need the same kind of accommodations they get in school. There ought to be a process by which the rights of witnesses with disabilities for accommodations during testimony should be arranged by the court.

"And how often are criminal cases with victims with disabilities never even charged, or settled with ridiculous plea agreements, because the prosecutor knows that the victim won't be able to testify in the courtroom? And what happens to those defendants who are free to abuse more children and more people with disabilities?"

Karen was blown away. Richard's arguments were so simple, so brilliant, and so right.

"This is really ground-breaking. No wonder your work is published in two of the top journals. Very impressive!"

"Thanks."

"Do you want to work on a similar research project with me? What do you have in mind?"

"I do have an idea, but it isn't legal research."

"Tell me what you're thinking."

"Um," Richard hesitated, but then he began. "You know how all these prestigious boys prep schools have had scandals recently, kind of like the Catholic church, and the boy scouts -- about teachers and staff sexually abusing the students from years ago? I was thinking how we hear all about the prep schools because the kids who went to those schools are educated and affluent and have the money to hire lawyers and know how to go public. But what about the schools that house the most vulnerable kids? Like the residential programs for delinquents and unmanageable kids -- places like that. I think no one is looking out for those kids, and the old victims who are now adults could shed light that will help protect current students at those facilities if someone helped get their stories out."

"Powerful idea." Again, she was really impressed. "But how do you even begin to do that?"

"A few weeks ago, I set up a Facebook page. It's called 'Victims of Stern Harrison and Southern.' I don't know if you know about the old facility at Southern -- the state used that facility to house kids who required something slightly less than a total lock-down facility due to delinquency or, for whatever reason, couldn't be placed in foster care. It closed twelve years ago, and now the state sends those kids to the facility at Stern Harrison. I had some initial contacts from the Facebook post, but I'm trying to keep the Facebook group incredibly closed and private because I don't want the wrong people to find out. People send me requests and I have to approve them. But, as of last night, the Facebook group has 27 members. Men are telling their stories. The stories are awful. As I kind of suspected they would be. I want to interview everyone, interview them under oath even, find out their stories, write a report. It's kind of gotten out of hand much quicker than I expected. Stern Harrison is still operating. There are over 150 boys there today. I feel like I need to move super-fast, but I don't know how to interview people, or get started, or anything."

"Wow. Incredible. But don't you think this is something that should be passed on to law enforcement?"

"That's an issue with this population. These kids, and now they're adults, had bad experiences with law enforcement and the state. They got arrested for serious crimes and that's how they ended up there. They don't trust the cops. Or they were removed from their families and placed there because of emotional or behavioral issues, or neglect. They don't trust the State of Illinois. But I think -- I'm hoping -- they might trust me."

"Do you think this is something that could turn into a contingency fee case for the firm? The Catholic church, as you know, has paid millions and millions of dollars."

"I don't know. Maybe. I don't really know how that works. I would expect that a lot of the cases, if there was abuse, it was probably so long ago that the statute of limitations has expired. My goal is really to make the issues public so the current kids can be kept safe."

"Do you know when the statute of limitations expires?" she asked while she turned to her computer and looked it up.

"I don't know," Richard said. "That's a good point."

"Okay. . . here it is," Karen said as she pointed to her computer screen. "It's ten years after the victim turns 18 -- so 28 -- except that it is five years after the victim realizes that the abuse occurred and that their injuries were caused by it. That's the PTSD exception. So, if someone gets diagnosed with PTSD at 40 years-old from child sexual abuse, they have five years to file a lawsuit. But we also need to check when that law went into place for anyone who was abused prior to the new law. Let's see. This gets pretty complicated." Karen was still checking on her computer.

"The new law went into effect in 2003. So, what I just read applies to those who were abused after 2003. For others, we would have to go back and find out what the law was at that time. Very complicated. I see there's also an exception if the perpetrator threatens the victim -- that also extends the deadline for filing a lawsuit. And there's usually a threat of some kind. A threat not to tell.

"Of course, some states are amending their laws to make it possible for people to sue over old child sexual abuse claims," he pointed out. "We'll need to check with the legislature to see if that's in the works for Illinois.

"I think the firm would definitely be interested in looking into this, although I'm not sure how it would play out. You know, every case has to get approved by the Contingency Fee Committee or the Pro Bono Committee, and whenever you try to protect people who can't afford to hire lawyers, some partners will complain -- especially if the case will be high-profile and has the potential to create political issues for the Firm's conservative clients.'"

"Yeah, I get that, and I wasn't really thinking about it in those terms. I really don't know if the cases will have any dollar value. Most of the kids who were sent there were juvenile delinquents. They've committed crimes. For all I know, they might all have adult criminal records. I'm not sure if these are people juries would sympathize with, you know? Juries might not even believe them. And we're talking about old cases, with no physical evidence and no eyewitnesses. Why would any juror believe them?"

"True, but that's what makes kids like that all the more vulnerable. I think this project is a really important idea, and we should look into it. Whether the firm wants to take it, whether there's financial value in it -- those are considerations for another day when we know more. Although, I can tell you from experience, you'd be surprised at how fast the 'political issues' can go away for a law firm if there's a potential to make big money on the case. Anyway, first we'll have to run conflict checks to make sure the firm doesn't represent the organizations that control the facilities, or anyone involved in management. And we'll also have to run conflict checks on the people who are contacting you on Facebook. It would be a disaster, for example, if we represent a spouse in a divorce and you're getting confidential information from the other spouse on Facebook without him knowing that the firm represents his wife."

"Yeah, thank you. Hadn't thought about the conflicts issue."

"That's always a very important issue for law firms. We need to clear conflicts first before we get any confidential information from any of these people."

"Got it. I printed out copies of everything for you." Richard reached for the files he had brought, placed them on the table, and pushed them toward Karen.

Karen started to look at the documents. She noticed that it was already 12:30. She was hungry but wanted to talk about this more. It was really interesting. The kind of case that had made her want to go to law school in the first place. The kind of case she had not done in a really long time.

"Hey, it's 12:30, and I'm hungry. Do you want to have lunch?"

"I'd love to, but is that okay? I mean with the harassment policy and everything?"

Besides his great credentials, she couldn't help but notice his brown eyes, the out-of-place wisp of hair on his forehead, his perfect teeth, his chin. She had been so mesmerized with the interesting discussion -- the kind of discussion that only lawyer nerds could enjoy -- that she had momentarily stopped paying attention to those little details. She wasn't a religious person, but she found herself thinking that some kind of divine intervention was at work when it came to Richard. The sudden windstorm that broke his mast line, his ending up in her yard, the power going out, the fallen trees keeping them captive in the house, Twisted Sister giving Joey the condoms. And now Karen was being handed the U.S. Attorney position, where she would be free to pursue her relationship with Richard if she wanted to. But did she? There would never be a future with Richard. Yet, as her mother used to say, "God works in mysterious ways." And she couldn't help but think that divine intervention was interfering in her good judgment right at this very moment.

"Yeah," Karen said. "About that, there's something you should know. It looks like I'll be leaving the firm soon. I've been offered the U.S. Attorney position, and I've accepted. I have to get through the security clearance process, and my appointment has to be approved by the Senate, but it should all go through."

"Wow! That's awesome! Although I'm sorry you won't be here anymore."

She just nodded. "Meet in five minutes in the lobby?"

Chapter Twenty-Five

"Hey, do me a favor, and make sure that I keep the receipt," she said as she walked up to where he was waiting. "I have to give it to Chris, and I always forget."

As they walked toward the glass revolving doors, Karen was seized with panic. She hadn't taken the regular elevators or left the building outside the front entrance all week. She had forgotten about the threats. What if someone was waiting for her? It was prime lunch time. They would be looking for her now. And then she stopped herself. "I can't live this way," she told herself. "If I live in fear, they win." But just the same, that didn't mean ignoring it altogether.

"Before we go outside the building, I just kind of like to look around and make sure no one suspicious is waiting outside. Do you mind if we just give it a look through the windows before we step out?"

All clear, to the extent that all the people on the street didn't look any scarier than normal. They headed to the Thai restaurant in the alley, a place so dirty and dingy that Karen had long assumed they had a connection with the Health Department or paid cash for their passing certificate. It was Chicago, after all. The place had a few booths that looked like they had been there since the 1940s, with high backs and sticky cracked vinyl upholstery, holes covered with dirty used-to-be-gray duct tape. The floor was made of linoleum squares so old that you couldn't tell whether the cracked tiles were filthy or just permanently the color of dirt and grease, with black swirls consistent with the asbestos tiles of the 1960s, Karen knew, having handled some asbestos tile litigation. But she figured the asbestos was not getting in the food or the air. She had used the bathroom, once years ago, and decided that she'd rather wait until she got back to the office in the future. She hoped that none of the cockroaches had climbed on for the ride. None of this mattered because the food was delicious. Maybe the asbestos, roaches and the decades of grease made it taste better. She didn't care.

"Hey, thanks for taking me to such a fancy place."

"The food's to die for."

"Not literally, I hope," he smiled. "I'm game."

They took a booth in the back, out of view from the door and the one small window in the front that was partially boarded up to hold a window air conditioner at the top. As they sat down, Richard's leg touched her leg. Inadvertently? As they repositioned themselves, Richard kept his right inside calf pressed against the outside of Karen's left calf, and she didn't move her leg away. Although every rational thought had convinced her over the last few days that this relationship was impossible, over, and not happening, being with him and looking into his eyes made her question every decision she had ever made in life. She had always been the "good girl" who made "sound" decisions, and look where that had gotten her in her relationships.

And then there was this issue of Richard's eyes. His pupils were dilated in that sexual way. He had that puppy dog look that was so endearing. He was looking at her intently, like he was in love with her. And, given how she was feeling in the moment, she figured that her eyes were probably giving him the same look back. She felt his leg against hers. The sensation of that simple touch was welcome and also a bit overwhelming. She had not expected to feel this way. They were doing so well in her office talking about his research. It had been so professional. As she reached for her napkin, she felt her hard nipples brush against her shirt through her bra. She was wearing a thin, light-colored crepe blouse. Richard glanced briefly at her chest. She was sure that he had noticed.

After a while, Richard said, "I have a question." He hesitated. "About the sexual harassment policy."

Their legs had been pressed against each other the entire time, and it didn't much seem like harassment.

"Does it still matter, if you leave the firm? I mean, I guess there's the remote possibility that you won't leave, but, um, what do you think?"

Richard was looking down at his food, clearly uncomfortable.

"Regardless of how I feel in this moment, I don't see any way that this can work. I'm old enough to be your mother. We're at different stages in life. I don't see ever hanging out with you and your law school friends, and I can't see you fitting into my life either."

"Then why are you looking at me like this?"

Richard pulled his foot out of his shoe, and started to rub Karen's ankle with his socked toes. Karen felt his gentleness, recalled his kindness, and it moved her. She looked around and confirmed that no one could see them. She reached for his hand. Their fingers met and intertwined.

"Um, do you have a busy afternoon?" he asked.

"Not really, I have to work on transferring my cases and closing files. Nothing urgent. Why?"

"My apartment is two blocks from here, my roommate is away, and I would really like to be alone with you. I've never done anything like that, you know, leave work in the middle of the day, but we don't have to do anything or, you know. I just really want to hold you and kiss you and I can't do that here."

Karen's heart started to pound.

"Not now, not while I'm still at the firm."

She spent all afternoon regretting it.

Chapter Twenty-Six

Back in the office, Karen was finding it impossible to focus. She thought about arguing with Jonathan and the Executive Committee about their choices of the partners who would take over her cases, but complaining would accomplish nothing and piss off a lot of the people who would be in a position to decide whether to welcome her back as a partner once her term as U.S. Attorney was over. Her mind kept wandering to Richard. His touch, his kindness, his eyes, his body. The sex. She wished she was at his apartment right now, but she knew she had done the right thing.

Most of the clerks were in the firm's suite that night to watch the Cubs get bludgeoned by the Dodgers. Except Richard, and his absence was noted. Jonathan came up to Karen.

"Hey, I heard from Denise that you and Richard Adams were friends or something before, and I'm wondering, do you know why he's not here? He didn't attend the clerk event last night either."

Karen was sure Jonathan had seen the memo she had written. She wasn't sure if he was being polite by saying that she and Richard were "friends or something before," or if he just found it unfathomable that Karen could ever have sex. "I have no idea. Maybe Denise knows."

"He's the best recruit we've had in as long as I can remember. The Dean at Northwestern told me he's the best student they've had there in a decade. He's only been here a few days and people are already raving about his work. We ought to be giving him the full court press. If there is some reason why he's not attending the events, we ought to figure that out and fix it."

"I really don't know him that well," Karen said awkwardly. Thankfully, Denise walked up to them.

"Denise, do you know?" Jonathan asked.

"Know what?"

"Do you know why Richard Adams isn't here or why he didn't go to last night's event?"

"Jonathan, I told you about this when we gave him an offer. He was the clerk who let us know he would not be able to attend events on

Tuesday evenings, Wednesday evenings or Sundays. Remember? You said that was okay." Denise often found Jonathan aggravating, but she was trying not to show it.

"Oh yeah, yeah. I forgot completely. That's fine. We should let people know that, so they don't think he's disinterested in the firm or anti-social. But do you know why he's not available?"

"I have no idea. He didn't say, and I didn't think it was my place to ask."

Karen wondered. Richard was uncomfortably secretive about being unavailable Sunday and missing the Cubs game, and now Karen had just found out that he also had something going on every Tuesday night. She would question Richard about it. Not that it was her business, since they were not going to be involved anymore. But nonetheless.

"Jonathan," Karen said, "Richard wants me to work with him on a really interesting project. He's exploring the possible sexual abuse of kids who were housed in Illinois state homes -- like the mental health hospital for children in Chicago, and the residential facility in the southern part of the state. He's set up a Facebook page for survivors of abuse from the residential center down south, and he has already gotten a pretty strong response. He wants to interview potential victims of abuse and publish a study. I think it's pretty compelling work, and it could end up with a strong contingency fee case for the firm if we take the project on and the evidence supports his theory. What do you think?"

Karen knew that the idea of collecting millions in fees for sexual abuse cases would be very attractive to Jonathan. The firm had stupidly turned down the initial cases against the Catholic church because two of the partners were closely connected to the Cardinal and those partners had convinced Jonathan that the cases would never be worth any money. Big mistake. They never got any business from the Cardinal and lost millions in fees that went to a smaller firm that had the good sense to realize the potential.

Jonathan gave Karen a look that was both unexpected and made her uncomfortable. Could he possibly be imagining her naked with Richard? Maybe she was just being paranoid. She'd known Jonathan forever. They had always had a very friendly but completely professional relationship. He'd always been someone she could go to when she needed help with anything at the Firm.

Furthermore, Jonathan Kennedy was not the fool-around type, and he never flirted with women. He was happily married to a psychologist for 20-something years, with four kids. He was ruggedly good looking -- so much so that people who didn't know him assumed that he was one of "those" Kennedys, with wavy dark brown hair and crystal green eyes that women generally found irresistible. In terms of sexual harassment, multiple female lawyers, paralegals and secretaries had been spoken to about their brazen flirting with him; how it made him uncomfortable; and how they needed to stop and keep it professional, or they would be asked to leave the firm. Jonathan was also regularly propositioned by some of the female lawyers and executives who worked at the major corporations that sent him business. He had mastered the skill of politely putting them off while accepting whatever work they sent his way.

"Whatever Richard wants, we should let him do it," he concluded.

Was it because Richard was such an exceptional recruit, Karen wondered? Or was Jonathan giving Richard special treatment -- and if so, why?

Karen texted Richard to let him know that Jonathan had approved the project, and that they could work on it pretty much full-time until she left. The message was "delivered," but Richard did not respond, and still hadn't responded by the time she left for work Thursday morning.

Chapter Twenty-Seven

The more she thought about it, the more upset she got.

Other than his wonderful academic record, she knew absolutely nothing about Richard. She didn't know him at all. He had never shared a single personal fact, even something as basic as whether he had siblings, who his parents were, where they lived, where he grew up. Nothing. He had not even mentioned that he went to the University of Michigan. Every fact Karen knew about Richard was on his resume. She did not even know if he had grown up in the United States. For all she knew, he could be a Russian agent. Okay, so that was a stretch, but still. Maybe he was in some kind of trouble. Maybe he had gotten in with the wrong group of people and couldn't get out. He had done that work with the kids in gangs last summer. Maybe he was in some kind of trouble with a gang. Maybe he was into drugs. Maybe he was a drug dealer. Her anxiety escalated, more irrational with each minute that he failed to respond to her text. She tried to tell herself that his life was none of her fucking business, but that didn't help.

A half-hour later, he stopped by. His hair was wet like he'd just got out of the shower. He looked hot as ever in his suit. He purposefully closed the door and took a seat in one of the two chairs facing her desk.

"I'm sorry, I just read your text. Of course, I'm thrilled and that's great news. But I wanted to talk to you about something else. I was up all night, worried about this. I know that David lied to you all the time and kept secrets. I'm not that person. I'm really upset with myself that I can't tell you about my schedule, but I'm working really hard to be able to."

Richard looked like he was about to cry, and it seemed like maybe he was trembling. She started to feel guilty.

He continued. "I know that no real relationship can have secrets, and I don't want to ever have any secrets from you. Whether we have a friendship, or a professional relationship, or maybe something more, I need to be honest with you. But there are things that I cannot talk about, ever. Please understand, it's not that I'm *unwilling* to talk about it, it's that I'm *unable* to talk about it. I'm working really hard on a plan. I'm hoping that it might work, but I can't really promise anything right now. But I'm thinking that, if you could come over for dinner on Thursday, I might be able to tell you more."

Since he had so far told her nothing, telling her "more" was a start.

"Next Thursday?"

"Yes, and it would just be dinner. Nothing physical. I just can't tell you these things in a restaurant. I need a quiet, private space, and my roommate will be out of town."

Whatever resolve Karen had had was long gone. "Sure, I can make sure that the kids are at David's or have them stay with friends. It should be fine."

"Great. Again, I can't promise, but I'm going to try. And, is it okay if you don't ask me about it? Don't ask me anything at all until Thursday?"

Richard was definitely trembling. And sweating. Profusely.

"Sure, whatever you need."

But her mind was racing with so many questions. How could he be "unable" to talk about something? Was he involved in the mob? Gangs and drugs seemed more plausible. But maybe it wasn't something illegal. Was he working as a secret agent? Maybe with the CIA? Maybe he was wearing a wire for a federal investigation? Maybe he was investigating someone at the firm or a firm client? Maybe it wasn't so far-fetched to think that he was a Russian agent -- after all, many people thought the President was.

Working as an informant for the FBI made the most sense. But for what? Could it be linked to the project they were working on? Karen felt her heart beating rapidly. Could *she* be a target? Was it a coincidence that Richard appeared at her door on the day that Senator Williams had first tried to reach her to ask her to be the U.S. Attorney? Was he sleeping with her because he was a spy? And what about that whole thing with Tim Reilly? Was Richard afraid of Tim because he was with law enforcement? Did Tim know something about Richard that Karen ought to know? Should she talk to Tim about Richard? Could Richard be behind the threats?

"I need to get some air," he suddenly said.

And just like that, he was gone.

Chapter Twenty-Eight

"Mom, Joey and I think that something's up and you're not telling us."

"What are you talking about?"

It was Friday night, and Karen was looking forward to spending the weekend with the kids, and to spending time alone with Richard next Thursday night. She realized that she hadn't been this excited about a boy since junior high. Surely, she was losing her mind due to early menopause or something. *Very* early menopause. She looked up the menopause symptoms. Having the hots for a much younger guy wasn't included. So nope, not menopause. Maybe she should not have agreed to meet at his apartment, but she was confident that she would not give in to her impulses this time. She would not drink wine or anything other than water. She would be okay. They'd eat dinner, have a discussion, and she'd leave. There was no relationship. It was over. But why was she feeling this way?

"You're not your normal self, Mom. You don't seem upset about anything. You haven't complained about Dad or Twisted Sister for days. You haven't yelled at us. We want to know what's up. You're just different."

"Other than making us jump off the boards because we were about to be shot by a whiffle bat, I agree," said Joey.

"Well, um, you guys surprise me. I guess I'm excited about going to the U.S. Attorney's Office."

"Really? Is that all? We thought maybe you had a boyfriend."

Shit, was it that obvious that she'd actually had sex for the first time in three years?

"No, no boyfriend. I did have a date with a nice guy, but it's not going anywhere because he's too young for me."

"What? You have your first date in three years, and you think the guy is too young for you? How old is he? Is he at least old enough to legally consent?"

"Cyndi, this is not an appropriate conversation."

"He's under 17? Are you kidding me?"

"No, I meant that mothers don't talk to daughters about people they are dating. He's over 17, but not enough over 17 to make it viable."

"19?" Joey chimed in.

"No, not 19. And I'm not discussing this further."

"Yeah, but Mom," Joey jumped in, "you have a terrible track record of picking jerks. You *need* input from us."

"Don't call your father a jerk Joey, that's not really fair."

"Okay, an immature asshole, then."

It was hard not to laugh, and she wasn't going to argue. True, she didn't want to encourage them to think or say bad things about David, but she also didn't want them to grow up to be like him.

"Tell us about this mystery man," Cyndi demanded.

"There's really nothing to tell. He's nice. We had a couple of dates." Karen never lied to her children, ever. Was a "couple of dates" a lie when it was a weekend tryst? "But it didn't work out. End of story."

"If it didn't work out, why do you seem so happy?" Joey wasn't buying it.

"So exactly why didn't it work out?" Cyndi wasn't either.

Karen felt like she was being cross examined. Well, she knew where they got that from. "He's way too young for me."

"Well, as long as he's legal, who cares." The kids obviously were not going to let her be unless she gave them details.

"He's 24."

"That *is* kind of creepy," Cindy said. "He's the same age as Twisted Sister. Can't you and Dad find people your own age?"

"Everyone their own age is probably dead already, she needs to be flexible," Joey joked.

Cyndi stopped with the negative comments. "If he's really nice, I guess the age shouldn't matter."

"Age does matter. I cannot see myself hanging out with his law school friends or having him hang out with mine."

"Another lawyer? Where does he go to school?" The kids wanted details.

"Northwestern."

"So, he's super smart." Cyndi caught herself accidentally complimenting her mother, and quickly fixed that. "I hear it's a lot harder to get in there now than when you applied."

"Yes, he's one of the smartest people I've ever met."

"Well that would be a nice change from Dad." Joey did not think much of his father.

"This conversation is a waste of time. I've already told him that I can't see him anymore."

"Well that was stupid. Text him and take it back." Why did Cyndi always act like a parent?

"I think we should meet him," Joey said.

"No."

"But Mom. . ."

"No. And I don't want to talk about this anymore."

"At least tell us his name so we can track him on the internet and find out if he's a sociopath or serial killer on the sly," Cyndi said.

"He's not a sociopath or serial killer."

"And you'd know that how?"

"Have you seen any of those Netflix shows?" Joey added. "A lot of them lead normal lives."

"Richard Adams. He's a nice guy. Not a sociopath."

"We'll check him out and get back to you."

Later that evening, she overheard Joey say to Cyndi, "Hey, do you think that Mom is finally getting sex?"

"Nah. Not possible." They were laughing.

Later, after the kids were in bed, Karen thought she ought to do some checking herself. "Richard Adams" is a common name, and while she found plenty of people with that name on all the social media sites, she didn't find Richard. He didn't even have a professional resume page -- odd for a law student.

After giving up on stalking his social media, she checked out the Facebook page Richard had created for the investigation. She logged in using the password he had given her and read the posts from the men. It didn't take long to realize that Richard was onto something big. Some of the men had posted about how "everyone" knew that children were being abused and no one did anything about it. Several men posted about their own abuse. A few named names. Others responded to those names with more information of what they knew or had been told by others.

She immediately suspected that there were more victims who had not yet come forward. She knew that countless studies had shown that children delay disclosing sexual abuse, and that many children never disclose it at all -- ever. And as bad as the disclosure rates are for girls, the disclosure rates are much lower still for boys, and these facilities were for boys only. In addition to all of the reasons that girls have to withhold disclosure -- fear, shame, believing it was their fault, being threatened by the abuser if they tell (the list of reasons for nondisclosure goes on and on), boys have additional reasons not to disclose, especially if their abuser is a male. The whole gay element can be overwhelming for boys who are not gay. And then there's the fear of the false stigma that boys who are sexually abused as children all grow up to be sexual predators.

In light of all these factors, the fact that so many men had indicated that they were victims of sexually abuse at the facility, and that forty-plus men had now joined the group -- 13 more since Richard had told her 27 had joined -- because they believed sexual abuse was "rampant" at the facility, made Karen suspect that some of the men in the larger group had been victimized but had never disclosed the abuse. And hundreds (thousands?) of kids had been placed at the two facilities over the years. The Facebook page probably had not reached 99% of the former residents.

She picked up her phone to text Richard about the interviews, and she saw that she had a text from Jonathan Kennedy.

"Want to do lunch one day this week?"

When the Chairman asks to do lunch, the answer has to be yes. So, she promptly texted him back. "Sure, that'd be great. What day works for you?"

They agreed on Monday, even though Karen was swamped with witness interviews for the project.

Then she texted Richard about her thoughts about the interviews. To her surprise, he responded immediately. They texted back until 1 a.m. with ideas for the interviews and how to manage the investigation. When they finished and texted good night, he sent her a heart emoji.

As she tried to get to sleep, she could not stop thinking about it. Was it a normal thing for someone that age to send a friend a heart emoji? She didn't even know what emojis were until Cyndi told her about them. Was his emoji suggesting something more? Why did she care so much about this? She was driving herself crazy, when all she really wanted was to be asleep. And why did Jonathan want to do lunch?

Chapter Twenty-Nine

On Saturday afternoon, Karen and Cyndi went to watch Joey's summer basketball league game. To her shock, Karen saw Richard sitting in the bleachers on the other team's side, with a beautiful woman who looked like she was around his age. She was tall, thin, with sandy-blond hair, and a classic style that bordered on being overdressed for a little kids' basketball game. The woman also was sitting next to a man who was obviously her father. He had the same sandy-blond hair but with specks of grey, the same facial features, and he, too, was a bit overdressed for the game -- wearing a blazer and a white button-down shirt. Next to him was a little girl, who looked exactly like the woman and her father. Next to the girl was an older woman, who Karen figured must be their mother. So, Richard was sitting with this woman and her family, and they were *definitely together*. They were sitting too close not to be. And he too was overdressed -- also wearing a nice shirt and a blazer.

That lying asshole. Karen was livid. She had thought Richard was different from David, and that he was honest. Yet again, she had shown terrible judgment.

She did not want to be caught staring, but she looked at them out of the corner of her eye at every opportunity. Richard didn't look well. Maybe he had seen Karen? It was hard to tell from the distance, but he looked nervous and kind of out of it. Karen didn't acknowledge him either. She certainly was not going to show him any courtesy. The woman held Richard's forearm and, at one point, put her head on his shoulder as they talked. Karen wanted to throw something at them she was so angry. Richard's relationship with this woman was obviously not new – after all, here he was spending time not just with her, but with her entire family. What a liar!

When the game ended, Karen and Cyndi walked down to the floor to congratulate Joey, who had made a key jump shot and two free throws in the game's final minutes. Richard, the pretty young woman, and the rest of her family walked right by them as they went to greet a boy from the other team. Richard looked right through Karen as though she wasn't there, he didn't even acknowledge her. His beautiful date was holding onto Richard's arm, pulling him in another direction.

Karen tried to tell herself it was just as well. That she didn't want anything to do with Richard anyway. Or maybe any other man. That it would have never worked out. But still, she felt betrayed and the same sense of loss of self-worth that had descended on her when David cheated and lied. Obviously, no man who was nice and honest -- if such a creature even existed -- would ever want her. She only attracted the dirt bags. Maybe she should go to a therapist and find out what was wrong with her. She obviously was lacking whatever it was that *good* men wanted.

She was now dreading seeing Richard. Dreading seeing him on Monday morning. Dreading having dinner at his apartment even more. She didn't want to hear how it was all her fault. She knew it was. She never should have gone to bed with him in the first place.

At 9:00 a.m. on Monday morning, Karen walked into the conference room where Richard and the rest of the interview team were waiting. It was going to be a long day. It was going to be an even longer few weeks before she was out of here and at the U.S. Attorney's Office.

Karen started the meeting by outlining the things that needed to get done -- legal research on the statute of limitations to see whether the claims of child sexual abuse were time-barred, and critical research on the people they were going to be interviewing. The team needed to do the work that defense lawyers later would replicate: find out how each witness's past might affect their credibility as witnesses and get the facts to explain away anything worrisome in their history. Trouble with drugs and crimes are common for people who are sexually abused as children, and sometimes a troubled history makes the sexual abuse claim even more credible.

Richard followed her back to her office. She told him she was busy, but he came in anyway and shut the door. "What's wrong?" he asked as he sat on the couch.

"I saw you Sunday at the basketball game. With a woman. Your girlfriend?"

"That's all? No, not my girlfriend."

"Who then?"

132

"We need to talk about this on Thursday. I can't discuss it now."

"Tell me who she is. You looked awfully cozy there on the bleachers."

"You agreed that you wouldn't ask any questions until Thursday."

"I wasn't expecting to find you with a girlfriend."

"I can't talk about it, because the discussion will get complicated very quickly. But she is not a girlfriend. Never was. Never will be."

"This is bullshit Richard. Stop lying to me. There is no reason why you can't tell me who that woman is. Who were those people you were sitting with?"

Tears started streaming down his face. "There is a reason. On Thursday, I promise."

She grabbed a box of tissues off her desk and handed it to him.

"It's hot in here. I need to go out and get some air."

Richard stood up. There was a knock on the door. Jonathan, ready for lunch.

"I was just on my way out," he said as he turned to face Jonathan and went out the door without saying anything more.

Back in his office, Richard's cell buzzed. The screen said "Unknown Number" but he answered anyway. The voice was mechanically distorted but thoroughly understandable: "We always know where you are, and we know who you're with. If you don't stop this Facebook bullshit you're up to, we'll just have to make you stop." The call cut off. Richard stared into space for a while, then pulled himself together enough to write down verbatim what the caller had said, pack up his briefcase, and head home to his apartment.

*   *   *

"Do you want to go to that dumpy Thai place in the alley I took you to when you were a summer clerk?" Jonathan Kennedy said.

"Love to."

At lunch, Karen again couldn't help but have the uncomfortable feeling that Jonathan was trying to imagine what she looked like without her clothes on. One of the great things about approaching middle age

133

was that men didn't give her that look anymore -- a look she had always found unwelcome and sometimes threatening. Jonathan had never looked at her that way before. Obviously, the thought of Karen and Richard had made him look at her differently.

They took a booth in the back -- the same booth she had been in with Richard. As they sat down, Jonathan asked, "Are you still a big fan of their Gai Ka Prow?"

"That's my favorite."

"I remember."

"You can remember what I ordered for lunch all those years ago?" She was a bit taken aback.

"I have a good memory," was all he said.

But after they ordered and the waiter walked away, Jonathan went on, "Or maybe because I've had a crush on you since that lunch. I can even remember what you were wearing. A navy pin stripe suit with a straight skirt, matching navy heels, a white silk blouse. You bought the suit at Brooks Brothers. I saw it on the racks there the next time I went in. The blouse too."

Oh no, she thought, he really is hitting on me, like he must think I'm readily available. "You're making me uncomfortable," she curtly told him. "You were married then, you're married now, and I'm not interested." She tried hard to smile, to show she wasn't angry with him.

"I'm sorry. Totally inappropriate. I'm really sorry." He seemed genuinely upset. "But the thing is, I'm not going to be married much longer. Mindy and I are getting a divorce."

Karen was stunned. Jonathan and Mindy had the happiest marriage of anyone she knew. Their youngest was in Cyndi's grade. Kyle and Cyndi traveled in the same peer group -- the five or six kids out of the thousand or so in their grade at New Trier who were vying to be valedictorian two years on at graduation. Kyle had a realistic chance; Cyndi not so much. Jonathan's three older kids were in college or grad school. All great kids. Great family. Great parents.

"I'm sorry. I had no idea."

"I haven't told anyone at the firm, and please don't tell Cyndi or Joey yet. Mindy fell in love with another psychologist at her office and moved in with *her* six months ago. We decided, for the kids' sake, we

134

would wait six months and see if Mindy was happy before we made any final decisions. It's been six months. This is what she wants, and, while it is really devastating to me, I want her to be happy. Nothing is going to be contested. We're splitting our time in the house now, so Kyle doesn't have to move between parents. I've been living half of the week at the Winnetka Suites for the last six months. I don't know how long we're going to keep doing that -- whatever is best for Kyle. I guess if it goes on for a while, I'll get an apartment somewhere.

"As I'm sure you understand, it's been a big shock for him to find out that his mom is gay, and his parents are getting divorced. Changes are hard for him, and this is a big one. He's our focus. We're trying to make sure that we do this in a way that limits the damage to him and the girls."

"That's so impressive. I wish I had that kind of relationship with David."

"From everything you've said, David was a total shit. I pride myself on being a decent human being. It's not like Mindy wanted this. She grew up in a really religious family, and it took a long time for her to accept who she really is. It's been a really rough road for her, for me, for all of us. But it is obviously not her fault."

"You've always been such a kind person Jonathan. Ever since I was a summer clerk. Remember how you helped me with that first legal memo when I had no idea what I was doing?"

"Yeah, I was so glad to do it. So, anyway, I apologize for hitting on you. I had always assumed that, after David, some wonderful guy would come along and sweep you off your feet. But when I read the memo about Richard Adams, I realized that maybe that wasn't the case. Life is about timing, you know? I didn't want you to leave the firm without letting you know how I feel and that I'm not going to be married anymore. I figured this is my last chance before you leave."

"You're nuts. I'm damaged goods, and don't men your age marry trophy wives in their 20s? Something is really wrong with you," she laughed, "if you're attracted to me."

"As I said, I'm not David. I prefer a woman with substance. Someone who is brilliant, successful, kind, a loving parent. And, it helps that you're gorgeous, but that's an afterthought really. But are you seeing anyone? Is Richard really in the past? He seemed pretty upset in your office a little while ago."

"Richard and I had a fling. That's all it was. I've never done anything like that in my entire life, and I'm struggling with it. It happened before he started at the firm. I didn't know that he was going to be working here, or it never would have happened. The truth is, I was never with anyone after David left. Richard just, you know, happened."

"He's a great kid though. I could see why you would be attracted to him. He's a genius. He's the smartest summer clerk I've worked with since back in the day when you were a summer clerk."

"You exaggerate my skills, but thanks. He's eight years older than Cyndi, and can you see me hanging out with his law school friends? Going to Bar Review on Thursday nights?"

It was a tradition at Northwestern law school for the students to meet every Thursday night at a designated bar downtown. It was jokingly called "Bar Review" -- a play on words about the class they would all ultimately take when they were studying for the bar exam.

Jonathan laughed.

"Look, if you swear not to tell a living soul, can I tell you how it happened? You won't believe the story. But you have to promise not to hold it against Richard."

Jonathan was still laughing. "Of course."

After she told him the general outline, Jonathan concluded: "So, bottom line: there was a naked man in your house for 40 hours, you were both single, and there's nothing for you to be ashamed of."

Still laughing, Jonathan said, "I mean, he is old enough to legally consent. And he's a nice guy, don't you think?"

"I'm not sure. I don't know him that well, and I have some concerns, but we're having dinner on Thursday so he can explain some things to me that seem pretty inconsistent. But the issue at this point is whether we can be friends or colleagues going forward. He's way too young for me."

"Have you guys gotten together since that weekend?"

"No. We had lunch -- here, in fact, in this same booth. That's the full extent of the time I've seen him out of the office."

"So, back to my issue about timing. Any interest in having dinner one night this week?"

Karen's head was spinning. She didn't handle surprises well, and everything about this was shocking. Although she didn't always agree with Jonathan's decisions (for example, giving her clients all to old white men), he was a wonderful father, a brilliant lawyer, and a generally decent guy. She had always been fond of him. He would be a huge step up from David.

"Before I say yes, and I will say yes, you need to be public about the divorce. If not, word will get out first that we're seeing each other, and people will wrongly think that I broke up your marriage."

"That's true, but I haven't been telling anyone because of Kyle. Half the partners have kids at New Trier, you know. As soon as I tell one person here, the nasty kids will be hounding Kyle in the hall, and since he's on the autism spectrum, as you know, he's already a target for bullying from time to time from a few kids. Not from Cyndi of course."

Cyndi, actually, had a huge crush on Kyle, who was every bit as good looking as his father, and a really nice kid -- in addition to being a genius. Karen certainly could not share that fact with Jonathan, or her daughter would disown her. "Makes sense. Cyndi always says great things about Kyle, by the way."

"Nice to hear. So, anyway, I don't know about going public. I'll have to talk to Kyle about it and take his lead. But I'll definitely talk to him about it."

"Why don't we figure out some place pretty private, and go slowly, at a speed that works for Kyle," Karen suggested.

The waiter brought the bill and Jonathan handed him a credit card. He turned to Karen, "That why I've had a crush on you. Your judgment. Your kindness. Plus, how beautiful you are without any makeup. How's Friday night after work? Maybe we could do something downtown. Do you have the kids?"

"They're at David's this weekend. Kyle?"

"With Mindy. You pick the restaurant. I'm good with anything."

As they left the Thai place, Karen could not believe it -- first her weekend with Richard, and now she'd be going on a date with Jonathan Kennedy.

Chapter Thirty

Karen was surprised and concerned when Richard texted her that something unexpected had come up, so he was going home and would be a little late, but in time for the first interview. They were still on for later at his apartment, however, and he said he had something new and extremely important to discuss. It seemed so out of character.

Richard and another clerk, Jackson Bennett -- the only non-white summer clerk -- had prepared separate interview outlines for each witness and collected anything relevant from social media and criminal records searches. The clerks then would sit in as Karen interviewed the witnesses.

Jackson was, Karen learned, a friend of Richard's from Northwestern. They were both on Law Review. Jackson always dressed conservatively in high-priced, perfectly tailored pin-striped suits, pressed white shirts, stylish ties, and office shoes that were perfectly polished. He topped off his look with a hip set of short dreadlocks, which made him look like he was walking the runway for a Burberry show rather than working at the staid law firm of Christian & Johnson -- but Karen loved the dreadlock look. She'd known his father slightly when they were both summer clerks, many years ago. His father had a great career as a lawyer and was now general counsel for the Merc. Karen wondered what had possessed Jackson to accept the firm's offer after his dad had, justifiably, called it quits after one summer. In its 100-year history, the firm had consistently been on the wrong side of civil rights issues, starting with its founding in 1910 when it provided free representation to Chicago citizens accused -- and no doubt guilty -- of killing Chinese men for sport; through the 1950s when several partners, with firm approval, testified on behalf of Senator McCarthy's anti-communist witch-hunts to help destroy countless lives; in the decades since when it provided pro bono representation to guilty police officers accused of criminal misconduct against minorities; and now representing pay-day loan scammers who preyed on minority communities by offering instant cash at usury interest rates.

Karen herself, of course, was representing Wilkommen, but at least she could rationalize about Wilkommen being a legitimate company with many drugs that probably saved more lives than they ended. Well, she liked to hope so, anyway.

The firm was now a huge operation, with over a thousand lawyers in its two offices, many of whom were wonderful people who did a lot of good things. But a huge number of the partners were still, in Karen's view, blatantly racist. Sure, they were educated enough not to use the "n" word, but they had substitutes they used with equal derision, like "southside."

It was a miracle that an academic star like Jackson had accepted the offer. Like Richard, Jackson could have gone anywhere. But here at the firm, there were only a handful of non-white partners to mentor him, and none of them came up through the ranks. They were all lateral hires, who tended to stay a few years before they went on to better opportunities where they didn't have to hit their heads against a wall trying to change the "culture" at the firm. On the other hand, associates who stayed a few years could go just about anywhere with Christian & Johnson on their resume. If she had a chance, she'd talk to Jackson about going to the U.S. Attorney's Office, where his brains and talent would be genuinely appreciated, in case he didn't want to stay at the firm.

Karen's objective was not only to do the interviews, but to give the clerks a road map for dealing with the witnesses they themselves would later take on. She started all of the interviews by trying to make the witnesses comfortable and by easing any concerns they might have. As she did when she was prosecuting sex trafficking cases at the U.S. Attorney's Office, she began by saying that she understood that some things might be hard to talk about, so the witnesses should feel free to write or text their answers. She'd bought a prepaid phone for this purpose. A few chose that option for the traumatic parts of their story. By the third or fourth interview, all of the witnesses started to blend together in Karen's mind. When she interviewed a lot of witnesses in a short period of time, with no time to process in-between, she found that the facts remained, but who said what was impossible to remember. She was surprised the number of no-shows was so low. No one wants to talk about traumatic events. The fact that so many witnesses had actually showed up was pretty shocking.

By the end of Thursday, the witnesses had provided compelling testimony. Fifteen ultimately disclosed personal sexual abuse at Stern Harrison or Southern. Moreover, they were able to specifically identify five abusers; and most had been sexually abused by more than one of the five. By piecing together different accounts, Karen and the clerks were able to figure out first and last names of four of the abusers. The fifth was more difficult. The men only knew him by his nickname, "Stoner."

The men described similar acts of abuse. The details were so consistent: the rooms where it took place, the time of day when no one was around, the way the boys were "groomed" by the perpetrators, even the words specific perpetrators had said. There was no way they could have all gotten together and made this story up. It was just too consistent, across too many witnesses, across too many years. It was real, and it was compelling

Karen had also asked everyone in the interviews about whether there was any corroborating information that might be available. Had they ever told anyone of the abuse, or had any boy, perhaps a best friend, ever told them that he was being abused? Had anyone seen or heard something, anything? Only one or two of the victims had told someone else contemporaneously. A few told a girlfriend or wife years later. Most had never told anyone -- but Karen was encouraged by how many others remembered seeing or hearing something that corroborated one or more of the facts in the victims' stories. She knew these kinds of corroborating details could be crucial evidence of credibility in court-- for example, that "Stoner" took boys alone to the gym at night; or another abuser always had candy in his pocket and offered it as a reward for his "favorite" boys; and a third was seen bringing his "favorite" boys (one at a time) out to his car for trips to town.

Together, the witnesses told a cohesive story of sexual and physical abuse by the same perpetrators over the course of fifteen years. Karen had no idea whether any of these monsters might still be employed in youth services, so she asked a summer clerk to find out.

The clerk checked websites and social media and came up with nothing, so Karen told her to call Stern Harrison and ask to speak to the individual men, but to hang up before she got connected. Bingo. Four of the five perpetrators were still there. Boys were almost surely still being abused. Karen emailed everyone: they needed an emergency meeting. Did they have to stop what they were doing and turn the case over to law enforcement? She also called Jonathan Kennedy to give him -- as the head of the firm -- a heads-up on what was developing.

She looked up the Illinois mandated reporter law while they were on the phone. In some states, anyone who has reason to believe that a child *might* be in danger of abuse is legally required to report the concern within 24 hours or face potential criminal charges for failing to do so. In other states, the mandate to report only applies to select groups -- people who work in schools, social workers, and the like. In Illinois, there is a long list of professions where people are mandated reporters, but lawyers are not on that list. Of course, nothing *prevented* them from reporting -- but should they, and if so, when? They decided to hold off on a decision until the team discussed it tomorrow morning, and Jonathan decided to get a junior lawyer to research the issue immediately. In addition, since at this point, they lacked permission from the witnesses to get law enforcement involved, they needed to ascertain whether they needed to get clearance from the victims.

Karen was exhausted and in desperate need of a break. The last thing she wanted was to go to Richard's apartment for dinner and a discussion of whatever his excuses were that she did not want to hear. She'd make it quick, hear what he had to say, and head home.

Chapter Thirty-One

Karen had expected to find Richard living in typical law-student housing: a third-floor walkup in a 1920s brick building with chipped lead paint and windows that shuddered with every el train that went by, unsafe wiring, drafty windows, and heat that barely approached the legal minimum of 68 degrees in the winter. She was surprised when he texted her the address and particularly shocked when her taxi pulled up in front of the building.

He lived in the newest and hottest residential building in the city. Designed by a famous architect, the building had been marketed to the ultra-wealthy and celebrities for the security and amenities it offered. The doorman at Richard's building and the people at the security desk were expecting her and welcomed her by name. They escorted her into the secure elevator lobby and pushed the button on the elevator for her, using their key.

Richard greeted her at his open door down the hall from the elevator.

Karen had never been in an apartment like this. The outside walls were floor-to-ceiling glass, with spectacular views of the lake and downtown. The furniture was all modern, all white leather. She felt like she was in a photograph from an architectural magazine.

"Wow. Nice place."

"Yeah, I'll explain that later."

Richard had ordered her favorite food delivered from the dumpy Thai place in the alley. The food containers were on the glossy-white dining table. Richard had put plates out, and water glasses. No wine glasses this time.

"Let's eat first, since the food is hot. Then I'll . . . explain."

"Okay," she said, sliding onto one of the all-white leather dining chairs. "But what was the new thing that you wanted to talk about?"

"Later," he said. "But I have a question. It's kind of awkward. You don't have to answer. Are you seeing Jonathan Kennedy?"

"Kind of, maybe. I'm having dinner with him tomorrow."

"He's a really good guy. Or at least, he's been really good to me. I don't know him that well."

"I think he's generally a good person. I've known him for years, but so far, we've had lunch twice in all the years I've known him."

"Yeah, I guess he didn't get around much when he and his wife were together."

Karen was surprised by Richard's comment. "What do you mean?"

"Well, obviously, you wouldn't be seeing him if he and his wife, you know. I assume he told you, or you wouldn't be having dinner. I know the divorce is a secret for his son and all."

"How do you know all this?"

"He told me at lunch today. He told me not to tell anyone. I assumed you knew if he was telling me."

"I did know about the divorce. I didn't know the Chairman took summer clerks out to lunch."

"I guess he does. Next week, Jackson is joining us."

"That sounds good. Jonathan must like your work."

Now it made sense. Jackson was on the Wilkommen team and, she was told, doing great work (although Karen could not tell Richard how another clerk was doing), but it was clear that Jonathan was taking an interest in *particular* clerks. Richard, the superstar, and Jackson, the academic star who was also the sole non-white law student in the summer clerk program who would help -- if Jackson could stomach it -- to add diversity to the firm.

"Yeah, so far, Jonathan has been pleased with my work. He keeps giving me new assignments, so I guess it's going well."

"That's great to hear. Having Jonathan on your side bodes well for an offer at the end of the summer."

"I figured. So, I'm working really hard on his assignments. On everything, really."

After dinner, they cleared the table together, and Richard loaded the dishwasher.

"Before we sit down," he motioned toward the enormous L-shaped white leather couch in the living room, "I want to show you something in my room."

He took her down the hallway, past a bedroom, obviously a woman's, with a flowery quilt on the bed, to his bedroom next door. Karen was surprised that his roommate was female, but at least she had a separate bedroom.

He walked Karen over to the dresser in his room. And he pointed to two framed photographs that were displayed on top.

"No questions, yet, ok? But I want to show you pictures of my family."

The first picture was of two little children with their parents, playing in the sand on the beach in Evanston. A little dark-haired boy around five years-old, a blond girl a few years older. The children looked exactly like their parents: the mother was dark-haired like the boy, and the father was sandy-blond and looked just like the girl.

"That's me, my sister Dennie, my Mom, my Dad."

Then he pointed at the second picture. Richard was wearing his cap and gown. It was a graduation picture from the University of Michigan.

Karen immediately recognized the gorgeous blond woman from the basketball game. "This is my sister Dennie, all grown up, who, by the way, lives in the bedroom we just passed. She's the woman you saw at the basketball game. This is my Dad."

She recognized his father from the basketball game as well.

"This is my step-mom, Susan; my little half-brother Robbie -- he was playing in the basketball game -- and my little sister, Katy. You probably saw them too on Saturday."

Karen felt embarrassed and also angry. Yes, she'd made a mistake, but if he hadn't been so secretive, she would have known about his family.

"I'm sorry, but I don't see why you couldn't have told me that right off the bat."

Richard said nothing. They walked back to the living room. Karen sat down in the middle of the smaller side of the "L"; Richard took a seat on the other side.

"Karen, what I'm going to say is really hard for me to talk about. I'm going to try to tell you things that I've never told anyone, but I don't know if I can.

"But first, I want you to know. I don't want to have any secrets from you." He slid a small piece of paper on the coffee table toward her. "Here's my phone password, my cloud password, and my email password so you can track me, anywhere any time. You can read anything and everything on my phone -- ever -- no need to ask."

"Richard," Karen began, "you really don't need to do this."

"I know I don't *need* to do it, but I want you to know that you can trust me to always be completely honest and to not have any secrets."

Richard looked down at the floor.

"On Wednesday nights, at 7 pm, I have a telephone appointment with my therapist in Ann Arbor who got me through college, and law school and still is an essential part of who I am. If I'm having a bad day, it helps me to know that I will be talking to him Wednesday evening, and I can hold it together.

"Richard, really." She paused as he grabbed a tissue from the box on the end table, and dabbed at his eyes. "You don't need to do this."

"Yes, I do. Trust me, I do.

"On Tuesday nights, I have dinner at my Dad and stepmom's house, with Robbie, who is ten, and Katy, who is twelve. Dennie comes over as well when she can, but she has a busy schedule because she's a resident at the University of Chicago Medical Center. My stepmom, Susan, is a nurse at Northwestern Memorial. My dad, Kent, is a cardiothoracic surgeon at Northwestern Memorial. I also spend every Sunday with them. My family is my whole world. They keep me grounded. If I'm having a bad day, I know I can get through it because I'll be seeing them on Tuesday and on Sunday, and I live here with Dennie so she can support me. The truth is, I would not be alive today without them."

"Richard. Really. Enough. You don't need to tell me anymore."

"I need to tell you because you won't understand me unless you know everything. I've never been able to have a close relationship with anyone outside of my family and Dr. Kendrick because I can't tell these things to anyone. I feel like you and I have potential for something special. I'm scared to death that if I tell you, you will run as fast as you can. But I can't keep secrets from you anymore. I have to take that chance."

"Richard, really, it's okay. Either way."

"There are things I need you to know. You deserve the full truth, even if it does make you run away." By now his eyes were filled with tears.

"So, I've been practicing speaking about it since I met you. Practicing with Dr. Kendrick, practicing in the shower. Practicing talking and speaking out loud about what happened. But I realized, I just can't do it, and that gives me this overwhelming sense of failure. But then, in the interviews, when you offered those men the opportunity to text, I thought I might be able to do that. Can we try?"

"Of course." Karen was wishing that she was sitting next to him on the couch rather than across from him.

He slumped down across the couch and texted Karen the following: "Please google my mom, Rachel Adams and 'Officer Michael Connolly.' Please read a few of the news stories and let me know when you're done."

Karen did as he asked. The headlines popped up immediately:

"LAWYER DIES AFTER BEING SHOT BY POLICE OFFICER"

"RACHEL ADAMS' FIVE-YEAR-OLD SON IN CAR WHEN SHE DIED"

"Oh my God, Richard. Is this you?"

"Yes," he texted. "Please read the news articles and let me know when you're done."

Karen read with horror. There were a lot of news stories in the *Tribune*, the *Sun Times* and every local television website. Rachel Adams was a young lawyer who worked as a juvenile public defender. She represented kids who were charged with crimes. One day, nearly twenty years ago, she went to meet a teenage client at one of the worst housing projects in the city. Her colleagues reported that she went there to give the client the small camera that belonged to the office, for the

147

boy to take photographs of his living conditions -- the syringes on the pavement, the broken heat pipes, peeling paint, the shot-out lights in the hallway. She had also asked him to take photographs of the refrigerator and kitchen cabinets in the apartment, because he had told her that there was no food in the house because they had no money ever since his mother had lost her job after she was convicted of possessing a small amount of marijuana.

The boy, Darnell, was facing a felony criminal charge for stealing food from the big grocery store down the block -- food he stole because he and his younger siblings were hungry. DCFS had investigated previous complaints about the kids being neglected; found on two prior occasions that there was insufficient food in the home -- once after Darnell was arrested for stealing a coffee cake from the same store; and determined that the kids were all undernourished, and that Darnell, the oldest, was missing school to take care of his younger siblings while his mom was looking for work. Nonetheless, DCFS did *nothing*. The DA didn't care and charged Darnell with shoplifting, according to Rachel Adams' colleagues who were quoted in the paper. Because Darnell had previously been convicted of shoplifting, the new charge was a felony. What had he stolen this time? A loaf of Wonder Bread, a package of sliced turkey, and a package of American cheese slices. An employee noticed the Wonder Bread because it didn't really fit inside his jacket. The store manager called the police, not because he wanted the boy arrested for stealing food, but because he wanted DCFS to do *something* for the neighborhood children who were so hungry that they came in every day to steal food.

According to Rachel Adams' colleagues, after Darnell took the photos that Rachel had requested, he ran to Rachel's car to give her the camera. His running toward the car caught the attention of Officer Michael Connolly, who called dispatch to report a robbery/carjacking in process. As Darnell reached inside the car to give Rachel Adams her camera back, Officer Connolly shot at Darnell. But, at the moment he fired three shots into the car, Rachel Adams turned toward Darnell to get the camera.

Everyone agreed about how she died: she was shot three times in the chest. The medical examination showed that one shot was through the heart, and she would have died in a matter of minutes or seconds.

Karen looked over at Richard. Tears were streaming down his face. His nose was running, and he was blotting it with a tissue. And he was now curled up in a fetal position on the couch.

"Richard, I'm so sorry. Can I hold you?"

"Not yet," he texted. "There's more. Google 'Michael Connolly acquitted.'"

She did as he asked.

"MICHAEL CONNOLLY ACQUITTED AFTER RACHEL ADAMS' SON REFUSES TO SPEAK IN COURT"

"OFFICER CONNOLLY ACQUITTED AFTER JUDGE REFUSES TO ALLOW VICTIM'S FIVE-YEAR-OLD SON TO TESTIFY OUTSIDE COURTROOM"

Karen read the stories. Officer Connolly had testified that Darnell was holding a gun, not a camera, and was about to shoot Rachel Adams. That Connolly fired three quick shots at Darnell, but that "the decedent" turned just at the moment and "apparently" got hit.

Karen realized that the forensics of the bullet fragments taken from the autopsy must have proved that the bullets came from Connolly's service revolver -- not some unknown, missing gun -- or he wouldn't even have admitted that his bullets were the ones that killed her.

Connolly further testified that Darnell ran away as Officer Connolly fired the shots, and Connolly could see the gun in Darnell's hand as he ran away. Then, after Connolly tended to "the decedent" and realized that nothing could be done, he searched the car and there was no camera. A gun was never found either, but, of course, Darnell had lots of time to get rid of the gun before they found him. And besides, why would he run if he was just handing her back her camera?

The papers noted that Darnell was black, and neighbors complained that the police had shot at yet another unarmed black child.

Darnell testified at the trial. He had used Mrs. Adams' camera to take photos of his living conditions, as she had instructed him to do, and he was reaching his hand into the car to hand the camera back to Mrs. Adams when the shots were fired; he did not have a gun and did not own a gun; he dropped Mrs. Adams' camera into the car when the shots fired; and he ran because he was scared that he was going to get shot. There were often shootings in the neighborhood, so he freaked and ran as fast as he could.

Other police officers testified that they also searched the car and never found a camera. Rachel Adams' camera never turned up.

It seemed obvious to Karen that Connolly was lying. Darnell's story was far more credible. Why would he run to his lawyer's car and threaten his own lawyer with a gun? The camera story was the only logical explanation for what had happened. And the new digital cameras back then were metallic and about the size of a handgun. It made sense that Connolly might have *thought* it was a gun, but Karen also knew from prosecuting Connolly five years after this for selling seized guns to teenage gangbangers, that he was a very dirty cop and a liar. Certainly, he was the kind of scumbag who would never admit that he made a mistake about anything.

But at the trial involving Richard's mother's death, it was Officer Connolly's word against the word of a black teenager who now had a felony conviction for stealing food. The jury was told that Darnell had a felony conviction, but the court ruled that the jury would not be told what the felony was. So the jury never heard that Darnell's only crime was stealing food to feed his little brother and sister. A jury -- without those facts -- would assume the worst.

The news stories reported that Rachel Adams' son, who had just turned five a few days before his mother's death, had been interviewed by the police and DCFS the day after the shooting. He told them that Darnell did not have a gun, and that Darnell reached inside the car to hand Rachel Adams her camera. He also told the police that Darnell dropped the camera on the passenger seat when the shooting started, and that, after the shooting stopped, Officer Connolly picked up the camera, and then saw the boy sitting in his car seat in the back, and said to the boy, "You'd better keep your [expletive deleted] mouth shut about what

150

you just saw unless you want the same thing to happen to you." The boy said that Officer Connolly then put the camera in his squad car, and when another police car arrived, the boy heard Officer Connolly say, "I'm so fucking sick of these n*****s" as he walked up to the policeman's car. Mrs. Adams' son had since been diagnosed with PTSD as a result of witnessing his mother's death, so the prosecution filed a motion asking to allow the boy to testify outside the courtroom, because the boy's therapist believed that he would not be able to testify in front of the officer who had killed his mother and threatened him. The judge denied the request. The boy was called to the stand, but did not respond to a single question, including when he was asked to state his name.

As a result, none of what Richard had told the police was ever revealed to the jury.

Members of the jury who spoke to the media afterward reported that, without the boy's testimony, there was reasonable doubt. "It was a 'he-said, he-said' case," said one juror. "On the one side, you have a respected cop with no prior disciplinary history; on the other, you have a teenage punk with a felony criminal record. We just couldn't convict on that evidence."

Karen put her phone down and stopped reading. "Richard, I'm so sorry. But I'm so proud of you for the work you've done -- and are doing -- to correct this injustice, and to change the laws nationwide, going forward. You are a hero to so many kids, everywhere."

"There's more," Richard texted. "After the acquittal, I tried to kill myself. I spent a few days in the state juvenile mental hospital, and then I tried again, and I spent a week there."

"You do know that that's pretty normal for any kid who went through what you went through."

"Yeah, I know," Richard texted. "I finally turned the corner after the second time. My Dad told me that he needed me. Something about feeling needed -- it really turned it around for me. Sure, I still had periods when I really missed my mom, and I still get the freeze response sometimes -- I kind of zone out -- you probably noticed. But I was doing really, really well for years.

Richard continued to text. "When I was ten, I watched your trial of Connolly. You prosecuted him for selling seized guns to kids in that same housing project. My dad told me about the trial, and I asked him if he could take me to see it. You were amazing. You destroyed that piece of shit on cross. Your closing argument was incredible. Dad and I watched the whole trial together. The day the jury convicted was the happiest day of my life. We went to the sentencing, and I was so happy that he was going to jail. I felt safe, really safe, for the first time since the thing happened. And I knew that I was going to be a lawyer. I wanted to be like you. To protect kids, like my mom worked to protect kids, and like you."

Richard continued to text. "After your trial, life was good. Really good. I was doing great in school; things were great at home. And then on Friday afternoon after Connolly's sentencing, Trooper Tim Reilly showed up at my school and took me away. He lied to me and said my dad told the court that I was unmanageable. He lied to my dad and said the school had called the police on me. To this day, I have no idea why I was put away. Dad hired the best lawyers, and they couldn't understand it either. There was no evidence, it was all made up. The lawyer said that the fact that the original order was insufficient didn't matter, because the people at Southern testified at every hearing that I posed a risk of harm to myself and others. So, the juvenile judge kept me there for years based on nothing other than their lies."

"Oh my God. That's horrible. How did you get out?"

Richard texted: "Google 'Director Stephen James' and 'sex assault.'"

Karen did as he asked. There were dozens of headlines.

"DIRECTOR OF SOUTHERN CENTER FOR CHILDREN CONVICTED OF SEXUAL ASSAULT OF TWELVE-YEAR OLD BOY AT THE FACILITY"

"STEPHEN JAMES' VICTIM REQUIRED EMERGENCY SURGERY TO REPAIR SEXUAL INJURY"

"STEPHEN JAMES' VICTIM'S LIFE WAS SAVED BY NEW NURSE AT SOUTHERN CENTER WHO DEFIED ORDERS

AND SNUCK VICTIM OUT IN THE MIDDLE OF THE NIGHT TO TAKE HIM TO THE HOSPITAL"

"LOCAL HOSPITAL IMMEDIATELY CALLED FOR MEDICAL TRANSPORT BY HELICOPTER AND SAVED BOY'S LIFE"

"SOUTHERN CENTER FOR CHILDREN PERMANENTLY CLOSED AFTER REPORT OF SEXUAL ASSAULT BY DIRECTOR"

"CHILD VICTIM IN SOUTHERN CENTER SEXUAL ASSAULT GETS $5 MILLION SETTLEMENT FROM CENTER AND STATE OF ILLINOIS"

"Richard, is this you?"
"Yes," Richard texted.
"Can I hold you now?"
"Yes."
Richard texted, "I've never been able to tell anyone these things before. I'm still not able to speak about it."

Karen laid down on the couch behind Richard and wrapped her arms around him while he cried. "I'm here for you, and I will support you, 100 percent. You're a good person. I hope you know that none of this was your fault. You didn't deserve this."

Richard texted. "I always felt like it was my fault. When Mom was shot, she called out to me. I tried to undo my seatbelt to help her, but with my useless hands, I couldn't do it. She called out to me before she died, and I couldn't do anything to help her. Every time I struggle with a seatbelt, I have a flashback of being in the car with my mom calling me."

"When I was prosecuting Connolly, I read the file on your case. There was nothing you could have done to save your mother. I remember the report -- she was shot through the heart like the news articles said. She would have died within seconds. There was nothing you could have done to save her."

"But I still can't help feeling responsible." Richard texted.

"I understand how trauma victims feel that way. But there truly was nothing you could do." And then she asked, "Did you ever figure out why you were taken away?"

"No," Richard texted. "That's what I really want you to help me to figure out. Why did Tim Reilly pick me up from school that day? Why me? And why did they keep me there for two years?"

"Absolutely, I'll do whatever I can. But how can I help?"

Richard texted. "My step-mom was a nurse at the Southern Center. She wasn't my stepmom then -- Dad married her later. Anyway, she carried me out in the middle of the night and took me to the hospital. The hospital called for a helicopter, and she flew with me to Northwestern Memorial. She called my Dad and he met us there. They operated right away. When I woke up, she and Dad were there. Two of the people from Southern got there, and they demanded that they were going to take me back to Southern. They said they had a court order. Dad -- who you know now, works at the hospital -- called hospital security and they actually put the guys in handcuffs. Dad told me that the police were coming to interview me, and that he would not be allowed to be in the room with me, but that I would only have this one chance to tell the police what had happened. He told me he knew it would be really hard, but he told me to think about what it felt like when he was holding my hand -- and he grabbed my hand and rubbed my hair on my forehead -- and to imagine he was holding my hand from outside the room, and that he would be outside the room and I could yell if I needed him and he would rush in. He told me that the only way I would be safe and not go back to the Southern would be if I told the police what happened.

"The police came in with a child social worker from DCFS and I told them everything. About the Director who hurt me -- that only happened one time, and only by him. But I also told the police about two other men who regularly performed oral sex on me. One of them was one of the two guys from the school being held in handcuffs by hospital security outside my door. I told the police everything, and they arrested him right there. I heard it all from my hospital room, I could tell there was a struggle.

154

"His name was John Stone. We all called him Stoner." Richard texted and looked at Karen for her reaction.

"The same Stoner we've been hearing about?"

Richard nodded yes. "The director agreed to plead guilty because the police had his DNA from my injury. The case was solid, whether or not I testified. Plus, they had him on other charges for directing people not to take me to the hospital. Adults could testify to that. But with John Stone, it would have been my word against his. There was no physical evidence. And I had a history of not being able to testify at trial, so they dropped the charges against him. And they never even pursued the other guy at all.

"This spring, I googled the men who abused me, did Facebook searches and finally tracked them down. After Southern was shut down, they moved to Stern Harrison. Stoner and the other man are still there. That's why I started this project, because they must still be abusing boys, and maybe -- just maybe -- I could find someone who *could* talk, to stop it this time, even if I'm unable to speak about what happened to me."

"You're amazing."

Richard sat up and spoke for the first time. "I think it's all connected somehow to the sexual abuse. I thought you could help me stop all this and figure out why Tim Reilly picked me up from school that day, and whether there are others. Except. . . ."

"Oh my God," Karen said. "Tim is Joey's coach. Except what?"

"Except we have to stop."

"Stop? How could we?"

He took a deep breath. "I got this call this afternoon." He took out his notes and described the call. "So, it's not safe to go on. I'd be willing to take the risk for myself, I've thought it over all afternoon, that's why I rushed home to think about it. But I can't drag you and anyone else along. It's just not right. Especially since you're already getting death threats."

"No," she said, raising her voice. "I've been threatened before, and I vowed I wouldn't let it stop me from doing the right thing. And that's the end of it. Period."

He smiled, weakly. "I thought you'd say that. But I think that the death threats you got are somehow related to me. I don't know how, or why, since they started that weekend when we got together for the first time. But that can't be a coincidence. I think we have to be careful."

Chapter Thirty-Two

Richard continued. "Also, I want to be very clear about Director Reilly. He never abused me. I have no evidence of him abusing anyone. But I do feel like he picked me to be abused by others. I don't know why. Yeah, I do have this suspicion about him maybe abusing kids, but it's just a hunch, and none of the witnesses has identified him. So maybe that was wrong. If he was an abuser, someone would have named him in the interviews."

"Yeah, maybe," Karen said, frowning. "On the other hand, he's the guy in charge of the State Police, and people would be absolutely terrified to name him. What was your hunch based on? Can you tell me?"

"I spent a lot of time looking out of my second-floor window. I would watch the people come and go -- the staff, the visitors -- I would stare and wonder why I couldn't leave, and I would pray to God to get me out of there, but then when I stayed for two years I gave up on God. One time, when I was looking out my window, I saw Reilly drop another boy off. And then, about an hour later, I saw him walk up to his patrol car. As he was about to get into the car, he dropped something -- it looked like some white envelopes or maybe folded white papers. He picked them up, and then he looked around to see if anyone was looking -- there was no one there and he didn't look up to my window. Then, I saw him put his hand in his pants and adjust himself. I felt in that moment that it was like -- like I felt after someone, you know, did stuff to me -- I don't know how to explain it. It was just a creepy feeling. Of course, guys adjust themselves all the time, and there's probably nothing to it. But in that moment, I felt there was."

"I'm so grateful for you telling me this. I need to speak to Joey and Cyndi about Tim to make sure they're safe. Joey is friends with Tim's son and is over his house all the time. I don't know exactly what to say to them -- I need to figure it out. Obviously, I'm not going tell anyone anything you've told me tonight."

Richard looked concerned. "You have to be very careful. I have no evidence that Reilly's ever done anything wrong. You can't suggest anything -- we can both get sued for defamation."

"I agree, but there is no way they're going over there again or spending any time alone with Tim. In the meantime, though, have you ever documented what you remember?"

"What do you mean?"

"Well, if he ever sues us, it is always good to have a record of your memory. You should type it up and send an email to yourself, so you'll have a record of what you remember today, just in case."

"Okay, that's weird, but I guess that's good advice. I'll do it later. Anyway, I thought you suspected something with me and Reilly."

"Why? I mean you told me he was a bad cop, but . . . ."

"Well, the first time -- just hearing his name mentioned -- I went into the freeze and then the flight response. Surely you noticed?" Richard looked at Karen.

Karen laughed. This was such a relief. "I thought you might be a drug addict! Trauma didn't occur to me. Running from the police because you were a drug addict made much more sense."

Richard laughed -- it was good to hear him laugh again. "I'm not a drug addict and I don't do drugs -- although a lot of people in my situation do -- but that's pretty funny. Didn't you notice it at Joey's game? I saw Reilly down on the court and completely froze. That's why Dennie was holding on to me to get me out of there."

"Well, I completely misinterpreted that. I'm so sorry."

"And there's one more thing we should talk about," Richard said. "This is really awkward for me, and I don't know if it matters anymore since I guess we're not going to be a couple, but I feel like I should say it anyway.

"I get triggered by certain things. In sex. Maybe you noticed."

She immediately put it all together. Richard did not like to be touched down there. Whenever she touched him, he pulled her hand away. Sometimes he startled. And when she had tried to go down on him, he had suggested something else.

"I hadn't really thought about it, but now that you mention it, I'm guessing there are some things you don't feel comfortable doing, so tell me and I'm fine with that." Karen realized as the words came out of her mouth that her relationship with Richard was apparently not over.

"Okay, the list: I don't like to be touched down there, oral sex on me is completely out of the question, and if you ever want me to engage in anal sex with you, I'm just not that guy. Is this okay?"

"Are you kidding? It sounds like you are a gift from heaven. I'm fine with all of that."

Richard laughed.

Karen snuggled him closer. She wondered if she had already blown this relationship, or whether Richard was still interested. Except, it was over, right?

"So, about this apartment. Dad saved all of the settlement money for me. After college, I really wanted to come home to Chicago and go to NU for law school, like my mom. I wanted to walk the halls that she had walked, sit in the classrooms and maybe the same seats even. Some of her professors were still there, and maybe they would remember her. But I never felt safe in Chicago. In Michigan, I felt safe because they were *Michigan* cops. Here, every time I see someone in uniform, I freak. It's ludicrous, I know, but even guys who work for UPS and FedEx can set me off.

"Dad told me that some architect was building a new building here in Chicago for celebrities and the like, and it was supposed to have the highest level of security. He said he thought it would be a good investment if it didn't work out, because we could always sell it. Dennie offered to live with me, and that helped a lot. So that's why I live here. I know all the security guards. They know how scared I am of the police. They get it. They keep me safe. And sane."

Richard looked pensive. "And also, do you understand now why I can't ever have kids? I couldn't function. I would be worried sick about their safety. It would make me completely crazy. I worry to death about my little brother and sister, but I can handle it because my Dad and stepmom are on top of it. It's not my responsibility, you know? I will never have kids, because I would be traumatized every single day that I looked at them -- traumatized with worry that someone would pick them up from school, traumatized with worry that someone would hurt them like people hurt me. I just absolutely can't handle it. And I also couldn't handle the fear of losing you with the risks of childbirth and everything. I've lost my mother; I can't handle even thinking about losing another woman who I -- I'm close to."

"I understand that now."

"I also have to keep this all a secret because of how people react. They don't see you like a robbery victim but like you're unclean, or something's wrong with you, or you had bad parents who were drug addicts and didn't protect you. People make all these horrible assumptions that aren't true. Like they don't think you're safe around their children. And then there's the gay sex thing."

"Pedophilia is not gay sex Richard. Being assaulted as a child doesn't make you gay or a pedophile."

"I know that, and believe me, I don't think there's anything wrong with being gay, but when I'm feeling low, I have these intrusive thoughts. I mean, I've always been attracted to women, not men -- but it makes me question everything, you know?

"Richard," Karen took a stern tone, "you were a little boy. You didn't send off any signals. You were not responsible in any way for what happened to you. You're thinking of this like all child-sex assault victims do -- but the truth is that you did not deserve this, it wasn't your fault, and it makes you no less of a man today and it certainly doesn't make you gay any more than it would make you heterosexual if you were assaulted by a woman. You are what you are; being assaulted doesn't change that. And it certainly doesn't make you a sex offender."

"Thanks. I know that on an intellectual level, but when I'm down, I struggle with it emotionally. But let's stop talking about it now. I'm exhausted. Can we watch a show or something to help me stop thinking about this? I mean, unless you need to talk about it more."

Karen reached over Richard to grab the remote on the coffee table, but she couldn't reach it and had to position herself on top of him a bit as she stretched. Their eyes met. She put her lips on his and started kissing him instead. He reached his hand inside her shirt. It didn't take long before they were in his bedroom.

Afterward, she rested her head on his shoulder while he wrapped his arm around her neck and began to talk. "There's one thing I forgot to mention, I was taken into state custody on Friday, February 13th, of

President's Weekend. It was in the middle of the school Valentine's Day party. Valentine's Day is always a painful memory for me, and I know it is for you -- I think we should plan a blow-out Valentine's Day to replace all our bad memories."

"I totally love that idea," she said. "Maybe go to some amazing beach somewhere."

"Awesome. What do you think about taking your kids? I want to include them in our lives."

"What a wonderful suggestion."

"Do you have the kids this weekend?"

"No, they're at David's."

"Doing anything Saturday night? Dinner maybe?"

"Saturday would be great."

Before long, he fell asleep, but for her, remorse was setting in. Why was she doing this? Why couldn't she just say no? The sex was amazing, and he was brilliant, kind, and had lived through a nightmare. But it all came down to one thing: there was zero chance this would ever work out. Showing up with him somewhere -- anywhere -- would be embarrassing. Everyone would assume he was her son. And why did she stupidly suggest going to a beach? She shouldn't be leading him on like this. She convinced herself she would put a stop to it once and for all, and finally dozed off.

In the morning, Karen remembered she had left her phone in the other room when they moved to the bedroom. As soon as she retrieved it, she saw a string of text notifications.

She had eight messages and a ton of missed calls from David.

Chapter Thirty-Three

Karen got her glasses, and quickly read the most recent message from David: "Look, I left a message for my lawyer and unless you agree, I'm filing an emergency motion for full custody."

"What the fuck?" Karen quickly scrolled up to the first message and began to read the messages, as Richard sat up in bed next to her.

> Karen, I need to talk to you about the kids. It's urgent.
>
> Karen, please pick up your phone.
>
> I've been trying to reach you for hours. I need to talk to you about the kids.
>
> Okay, so you're not picking up and not responding to texts. I hear you have a new boyfriend, and I don't think he should be anywhere near the kids. He's dangerous. If you don't agree I don't care. This is non-negotiable.
>
> Tim told me that he spent YEARS in a mental health facility!!! Did you know that? YEARS!!!
>
> And Tim said he was raped and repeatedly sexually assaulted as a kid. HE IS NOT SAFE AROUND OUR CHILDREN!!!
>
> He is to be nowhere near them! This is non-negotiable! If you don't agree, I don't care -- my lawyer says I have good grounds for custody, regardless of what the kids want -- because of the risk of harm!!

"What's the matter?"
She showed him the messages.
"And your ex knows we're spending time together?"

"My kids cross-examined me, and I gave in under pressure and told them I'd had a few dates with you, and they asked for your name, so I told them."

"Why were they cross-examining you?"

"They said that I seemed unusually happy."

"Well that's interesting. Maybe something you should think about?" he said in a distracted way, as he read through the messages. "But I don't think it's really about your kids. I think it's all connected to that call I got. Whoever is behind this is showing me they can go after you. And anyone else. And clearly, Reilly is playing some role."

"I'm really pissed and I'm going to text David to fuck off."

"Let's think about this. We need to figure out what's going on and respond in a way that's to your advantage.

"Obviously Tim Reilly is involved in this, somehow. But remember, it's all based on my juvenile records, which are confidential by law. If Reilly told David about anything in my records, he broke the law. It's a crime, Karen. If we can really trap David into giving us the details of what Reilly told him, that will help you prove in court that the information was obtained illegally, and that David -- who is a lawyer -- conspired in criminal conduct to get it. A judge isn't likely to take any action to remove the kids based on information that was obtained in violation of the law. Instead, Reilly and David will be the ones at risk."

"Damn, you're good!"

"This is obviously very upsetting to me, also. I would be 100% safe around your kids – I'm certainly not attracted to children and could never hurt a child after what happened to me -- and David and Reilly are defaming me. I would never hurt anyone."

"I have no worries about you, Richard."

"Yeah, but this is like my worst nightmare. What if I hadn't told you first? And to treat me like a pedophile just because I was victimized as a child. It just brings the shame back all over again. And why is Tim Reilly doing this to me? What did I ever do to him? Why does he still want to destroy my life? Wasn't taking me to Southern enough? And I don't even understand why that happened. I told you he was bad.

"So, let's get even, let's set the trap. Why don't you text David something like, 'I don't know what you are talking about. What exactly did Tim tell you?'" Richard looked pensive, like he was trying to come up with the best words.

"I'm not sure about that," Karen replied, "because it's not exactly true. I do know what he's talking about, and I don't want to put in writing something that suggests that you have not been forthcoming with me, when you have been. We've known each other for less than two weeks, and you told me very personal things last night."

"True. How about just texting, 'What exactly did Tim tell you? I don't understand the issue.'"

"That's good." Karen texted that to David, and then spoke to Richard. "And by the way, I really don't understand the issue. Your history from when you were five-to-twelve years-old does not create a risk of harm twelve years later."

"I know, but the stigma is real. People make assumptions."

"This really sucks. I'm furious at David for putting you through this. If he goes forward, we're going to have to figure out if you are able to testify."

"Yeah," he said, his voice rising, "but if we can nail him and scumbag Tim Reilly, it's worth it. I can handle that. I won't have to go into the trauma details if we can establish that Reilly gave those details to David. Furthermore, what I've accomplished since I was released at twelve is better evidence of who I am as a person, and I can certainly talk about that." She'd never seen him angry before, but still, he was like steel. Under control. Confident. A real warrior. He clearly would excel in legal battles.

Karen's phone buzzed. "Look, he took the bait!" she said triumphantly, showing him David's response.

"Hook, line and sinker!" he said as he read it:

> Tim told me that Richard Adam's mother was murdered when he was five and that he had a complete nervous breakdown, tried to kill himself multiple times, was hospitalized multiple times for extended periods of time, that his father refused to help him and he became so unstable that the court finally ordered him into state custody when he was ten. That he spent two years in a

165

mental health ward. That he was raped so violently that he needed emergency surgery and almost died. That he was sexually assaulted on a regular basis by two other guys who were never prosecuted. Tim told me that guys like him go on to sexually abuse children and that he is not safe around Joey or Cyndi, and especially Joey. Tim knows what he's talking about. THIS GUY IS NOT SAFE AROUND MY CHILDREN.

That was close, but not perfect. David could claim it was some other Tim. So, she texted, "Who told you this? Tim Reilly?"
David replied:

Yes, Tim Reilly, the Director of the State Police. He has access to this guy's records. And he knows this stuff. He knows the risk. You have to agree to keep Richard Adams 100% away from the kids or I am going to court.

Still not perfect. David needed to admit that the records were juvenile records, so she texted, "What records are you talking about?"
David again gave them what they wanted:

Tim said he was familiar with Richard's juvenile records -- that he read the records of Richard's early hospitalizations when Tim took Richard into custody when Richard was ten, and that he followed Richard's juvenile case until he was released from custody when he was twelve.

"What a total idiot your ex is," Richard laughed. "He has no clue what he's done."
"I told you he was an idiot," said Karen, laughing along.
Richard, however, began to look pensive. "Let's look at this in detail. First, it is interesting that Reilly admits that my mom was murdered, since the official position of the State Police was that it was an accidental shooting. That's helpful.

166

"My hospitalizations after my mom was murdered, that's true, and it is 100% protected confidential juvenile information. It was a crime for Reilly to tell David that.

"The part about my dad not helping -- that's just a lie. Dad has always been there for me from day one. He would drive Dennie down to see me every single weekend when I was at Southern -- they never missed a weekend. It was a four-hour drive each way, and they stayed over Saturday night so they could visit me on Saturday afternoons and Sunday morning until it was time for them to drive home. If it was a three-day weekend, they stayed the whole time, and during school breaks, the whole week. They didn't have a life for two years. Dad and Dennie gave up everything: sports, a social life, everything -- to support me.

"The part about the court order is true, except that I was not unstable. That order is a confidential juvenile record, as is the fact that I spent two years in state custody -- it's a crime that Reilly told David that.

"The stuff about me being a victim -- I don't think that's a crime for Reilly to disclose that. My name is probably in the court record somewhere in the criminal case. I'm not sure, but there might be a mention in the official court record of my interview where I also named the other men. Plus, I was released from State custody as soon as I disclosed the abuse and my juvenile records ended."

Karen interrupted. "That might not be a crime, but it violates a lot of rules about the rights of victims. You probably also have a civil case about all of this -- invasion of privacy, wrongful and malicious release of confidential personal and juvenile information, maybe other causes of actions. There's also a clear intentional interference in our relationship, and intentional infliction of emotional distress."

They agreed that Karen would talk to Jonathan about the firm potentially representing Richard in a civil lawsuit against David and Tim, but they would wait to file a complaint until after the custody hearing. If David knew that his testimony would get Tim in trouble, he'd surely lie.

But they had so many questions. If Tim had really cared about the kids' safety, he would have picked up the phone and talked to Karen about it. Getting David to go to court to accuse Richard of being a pedophile who was a risk to the kids? Forcing Richard to try to convince a judge that he wasn't a pedophile (how can you ever prove such a thing?) when Richard was a young lawyer, just at the start of his career? It seemed like Tim Reilly was out to destroy Richard, but why? It just didn't make sense that, after complying with a legitimate court order to take a ten-year-old boy into state custody, he was still going after that little boy 14 years later.

Chapter Thirty-Four

All of the witnesses had signed release forms for the team to get their juvenile records, and the firm had requested the records on an emergency basis from the juvenile courts and DCFS. Richard had also confidentially provided his records to Karen in case they might help her for the custody hearing with David.

They now had the complete records for four of the victims. The four commitment orders were signed by four different judges. One order was signed by Judge Harold Smith, who also signed Richard's commitment order. Later, when he was a federal judge, he was the one who had been the subject of death threats similar to Karen's.

As a federal court judge, Judge Smith was generally viewed as stupid and lazy, but at least he had a reputation of being a decent person who tried to make fair and equitable decisions. He had always been very politically active, rising to head the Chicago Democratic Party until he became a judge.

Karen looked at the DCFS records of the victim who had been committed by Judge Smith. Nothing looked out of the ordinary. The parents had testified that the boy was unmanageable; the family had been working with DCFS, which had put supports in place a year earlier, but the boy's behavior was just getting worse. The straw that broke the camel's back was when the dad sent the boy to his room for a time out, and he snuck out his window, got a can of gasoline from the garage, and set the house on fire. Everyone was okay because the amount of gasoline available wasn't much more than fumes, but the house had been damaged enough to need repairs before it would be habitable again. The boy's parents were staying with friends and they had no means -- and no desire -- to keep the boy with them. And DCFS couldn't place a juvenile arsonist in foster care. Judge Smith's commitment order was fully supported by the DCFS records.

That emphasized to Karen how odd Richard's own situation had been. In his file, there was absolutely no support for the commitment order. Zero. No record of anyone asking him to be committed -- an obvious first step, since judges don't just issue commitment orders out of the blue -- and no record that DCFS was even working with the family at that time or had put prior supports in place. Juvenile residential placement is always a last resort. Even if a parent isn't capable of parenting, DCFS must by law first look for family members who might take the kid in, and then if those efforts fail, foster care is the next option. In a case where a kid has committed no crime -- and there was certainly nothing to suggest that Richard had done so -- you can't lock kids up unless they pose a huge risk to themselves or others, and then they go to the mental health facility -- not Southern.

Moreover, although there should have been a record at the time showing why he was placed in custody, oddly, it wasn't in the file. There were only records of DCFS' very limited involvement during Richard's brief hospitalizations when he was five years old. Those records showed that a social worker met with Richard at the hospital each time and spoke to Richard's father and the treatment providers. DCFS determined Richard's father was taking appropriate measures and closed the file each time shortly after DCFS had finished its interviews.

The next document in Richard's file was the commitment order -- five years later, when he was ten years old. After that, there was a transcript of an emergency hearing that was held on the Tuesday following his commitment on Friday, February 14th.

Three different people from Southern testified that Richard was suicidal. They said he spent much of the three-day weekend curled up in a fetal position, and that he neither spoke nor responded to anyone. "He *refused* to speak, and he tried to smuggle a knife from the cafeteria into his room after dinner, we think to cut himself or worse," one testified. Another witness said Richard had told him "he wanted to kill himself." Richard's father had retained a top-notch lawyer, who pointed out how that testimony was inconsistent with the testimony that Richard refused to speak at all. Each of the three witnesses testified, based on their training and experience, that Richard posed an immediate risk of harm to himself and needed to be in a secure facility where he could be watched carefully and receive constant care.

Richard's lawyer tried to call Richard's father and witnesses from Richard's school to testify that there was no basis to commit Richard to custody based on their observations. But Judge Smith ruled that the circumstances prior to Friday's commitment were irrelevant in light of the testimony that Richard's suicidal condition now required residential placement.

Richard's lawyer argued that any child with Richard's trauma history could be expected to be in a fetal position and unable to speak after being suddenly removed from school by the police and taken to a residential facility for reasons that the boy -- and his family -- did not understand. The lawyer also said that the witnesses from Southern were lying, that Richard had not attempted to take a knife to his room, and that Richard had not said that he wanted to hurt himself, let alone kill himself.

Then, Judge Smith interrogated Richard in open court, in front of not just the lawyers and the court staff, but also the people from Southern who had transported Richard to the hearing. Richard remained mute, failing to respond to a single one of the Judge's questions. Judge Smith determined that he had no choice but to find that the witnesses from the facility were telling the truth, because Richard failed to deny it himself, and his lawyer's statement was just argument -- not evidence. Moreover, Judge Smith found that Richard's refusal to respond to questions evidenced a "refusal to cooperate in the proceeding, which suggests a severe mental disturbance" and "further warrants residential placement at the facility where supports are in place to keep him safe from self-harm." Judge Smith concluded that Richard was a continuing risk of harm to himself and extended the commitment order.

Karen finished reading the hearing transcript with horror. She had never thought about how, once a child is placed at a facility, the people at the facility have total control over whether the child stays there. No judge would ever release a child after three experienced professionals had testified that the child posed an imminent risk of grievous self-harm, even if the child (unlike Richard) could speak and deny it. The repercussions if the child were released and committed suicide would be a political nightmare. The judge surely would not win reelection -- a thought that would be on the mind of any judge in a state like Illinois, where judges are elected.

Indeed, no one would believe the kid anyway -- since all kids want to be released and go home, no matter what their homelife is like.

The people at the facility could simply lie and keep the child institutionalized until his 18th birthday -- based on nothing but fabrications.

But why did they lie? Three different people? It would make sense for a ten-year-old boy with Richard's history to be suicidal under those circumstances. And it would also make sense that he might now misremember that traumatic time in his life. But Richard was quite adamant that they made it all up.

After the first hearing, Richard's file was replete with records of hearings held every few months at which continued placement at the facility was recommended by the treatment providers at Southern, and supported by DCFS. Richard's father had world-renowned experts assess Richard, and they opined that he was not at risk of harm to himself, and, even if he were, he would be better off at home with his supportive family. But Judge Smith found those experts less credible than the people at Southern who were "just doing their jobs to keep kids safe."

Richard's father testified at every hearing that, while Richard had had a problem with self-harm and suicide attempts immediately after his mother had died, Richard was no longer at risk. Dr. Adams also testified that he visited Richard every weekend, spending all day every Saturday and Sunday with him; spoke to Richard every day by phone; and that Richard was not at risk of self-harm. At every hearing, Richard's lawyers claimed that the people at the facility were lying, but Richard was never able to testify to prove it. Again and again, Judge Smith ordered Richard to be held in custody for Richard's safety, because, he said, the people at the facility were in the best position to assess the state of Richard's mental health.

As she finished the last pages of Richard's file, Karen confirmed that there was not a single record to explain why Richard was ever committed to the Southern facility in the first place. Something was clearly missing. Maybe Richard didn't have all the files. Maybe he didn't give her all the files. Certainly, the total absence of any records that would support the commitment order was strange -- to say the least.

Meanwhile, they decided to go forward with the interviews that had been scheduled for Friday, and the interviews were much the same as the prior days. Karen let the summer clerks conduct the interviews, and they generally did a good job, with occasional prodding and redirecting from Karen by way of notes she would hand to the clerk conducting the interview.

Richard, however, was exceptional. One witness, whose brother had committed suicide a year after he turned 18, was describing how his brother had told the witness and their mother during a visit that he was being sexually abused, at which point the witness quickly muttered something about "the police knew and did nothing about it."

Richard immediately followed up, and bringing out the fact that the witness and his mother had gone to the State Police barracks in person, in Chicago, to make a formal report that her son was being sexually abused. The next day, the state trooper they had spoken to came to their house and told them that the report of sexual abuse was unfounded, that there was no evidence of sexual abuse, and that the boy had denied any abuse when questioned. The witness and his mom went to visit the boy a few months later -- Richard brought out the fact that they could not afford to visit him very often because the mother worked two jobs to pay their bills and couldn't afford the gas or the time off. At the visit, the boy told them that no one had ever spoken to him about it. "The cops lied," the witness said. "They never did any investigation. They just hushed it up." Richard asked if the witness remembered the name of the trooper, but he did not. Richard asked the witness to describe the trooper and he answered: "white, about six feet tall, clean shaven, really fit, with a shaved head, in uniform, maybe in his thirties." That description fit about seventy percent of state troopers nationwide. Richard asked if the witness could identify the trooper in a lineup, and the witness laughed: "Yeah, that'll be the day!"

Around 11 a.m., Karen got a text from David: "My lawyer wants to know if you will accept service of our emergency motion, or do you need to be served by a sheriff."

"Happy to accept service. Have him email it," she texted back. Karen couldn't believe that David was really going through with this; but, then again, he had always used this sleazy and cheap lawyer whom Karen suspected made whatever little money he could muster by filing frivolous actions and harassing people.

As Karen contemplated whether she should say anything to the kids about the motion David was filing, she got a text from Cyndi.

"We're at the house now. We are so livid at Dad that we left his place first thing this morning. We knew you wouldn't mind, under the circumstances. Joey and I decided that we are NEVER going back there. We hate what he is doing, and we want to talk to the judge!!! This is Dad's biggest asshole action EVER. We are so done with him. We don't want to live with him. What kind of asshole doesn't get that? Is he brain damaged? How could you have ever married such a fucking idiot. We haven't even met this guy and Dad is turning our lives upside down just to get MORE MONEY from you."

Karen responded, "I'll call your lawyer so you two can talk to her and let her know your position on your father's motion. Unfortunately, we shouldn't talk about it until the judge decides the motion because I don't want to be accused of trying to influence you guys. I will support whatever position you two take."

"Thanks," Cyndi texted back. "It's nice to know that we at least have one grown up for a parent."

During lunch break, the kids called.

"Dad's a fucking asshole." Karen didn't bother telling Joey to watch his mouth.

"We'll live on the street before we live with him and Twisted Sister," Cyndi added.

"We told the lawyer that we'll never spend another night at Dad's because of this, and that he just wants your money," Joey said.

Karen tried to present herself as neutral. "As I said, you have nothing to worry about. For as long as you want to live with me, I'll do whatever the court requires for that to be approved. Don't stress about it."

"We're not stressed, we're figuring out how to get even." Classic Cyndi.

"Dad doesn't give a shit about our safety. Remember when Cyndi was in the hospital, and he didn't even bother to visit?" Joey said.

"He was out of town." Karen couldn't believe that she was defending him.

"Yeah, at one of his loser casino vacations."

And then the kids announced that they were both sleeping at friends' homes, so no need for her to rush home. At least she could still have dinner with Jonathan.

Karen realized that Cyndi and Joey would meet Richard for the first time in court. Not exactly what she had planned. Meanwhile, she started to fantasize -- maybe when she drove home after dinner downtown with Jonathan, she'd happen to come upon David and Twisted Sister in a crosswalk in front of her. Accidents happen, right? Everyone sometimes mistakes the accelerator pedal for the brake?

Richard interrupted her homicidal thoughts by peaking his head in the door.

"Great job on the interviews today." She genuinely meant it -- he had done a terrific job.

"By the way," she added, "about Saturday. . . ."

"You need to cancel? That's okay."

"I'm sorry, but . . . ." She told him about how the kids had texted her about being angry with David, and how they were going to be at the house instead of David's all weekend."

"But they're not going to be there tonight, when you're having dinner with Jonathan?" He smiled -- like he was jerking her chain?

"No. They're staying with friends. I'm not making this up. Do you want to see the texts?" She held up her phone.

"No, the one thing I do know is that you won't lie to me."

After Richard left, Karen thought how, after going three years with no one, she suddenly was juggling two different, and very attractive, nice guys. Considering her track record, she was sure she'd manage to blow it with both of them.

Chapter Thirty-Five

Jonathan looked a bit rumpled after a long day at the office, but his blue eyes didn't look as tired as his suit, and his broad smile made her want to throw her arms around him.

The lobby was empty except for the security guards at the desk. They'd managed to escape prying eyes.

"Do you like burgers? Ever been to Hanrahan's?

"Not in years! Sounds perfect!"

Hanrahan's was a pricy and upscale Gold Coast eatery, around since forever and known for its enormous burgers that provided your cholesterol for the week, crisp white tablecloths, quiet atmosphere, and lots of privacy. Years ago, before smoking was outlawed in restaurants, there was a cloud of cigar smoke from noon until closing, but now you could breathe and talk without choking. Many corporate takeovers had been plotted in the booths in the back of the narrow space that had the feel of a railroad dining car -- except the booth seats had very high backs so no one could see anyone sitting in the next booth or hear their conversation. It was a place to go when you didn't want to be seen, and you wanted to be able to talk privately.

They took a booth in the back, and, after they both ordered bacon cheddar burgers (something they found out they had in common) and a bottle of wine, Jonathan started right in on the topic she desperately wanted to avoid.

"How was your night with Richard?"

Karen was taken aback. Did Jonathan know that she spent the night with Richard? Or had he just used that term "night" loosely?

"Okay."

"Did you work out the concerns that you had?"

"I worked out my concern about his honesty, but I still don't think the relationship is going anywhere long term."

"Richard's an honest guy. Did you have a good time?"

"It was pretty emotional, actually."

"Oh. Did he tell you about his mom?"

"You know about his mom?"

"I was friends with Rachel in law school. We hung out in the same crowd. Everyone admired her. Brilliant, like Richard. And committed to social justice. She'd worked for several years before law school at a local woman's shelter. Richard didn't fall far from the tree. I was with her the night she met Kent, Richard's dad, at a law student-med student mixer."

"Wow. So that's why you're paying special attention to Richard."

"That's part of it. I had lost touch with Rachel and Kent long before she died -- we were all married young professionals with no time -- but I read all about it in the papers and everyone in our class was talking about it. I saw Kent at the funeral, of course. He's a really good guy. Richard is a great mix of his parents. He's a dead ringer for Rachel. It's hard for me to talk to him without thinking of her."

"So how did you reconnect?"

"Did you hear about my Dad having emergency heart surgery last fall?"

"Yeah, of course. But he's fine now, right?"

"Yeah, he's fine, thanks to Kent. Kent was his surgeon. That's how we reconnected. He told me that his son was a second year and that, while he was certain that Richard would end up like his mom working as a public defender for children or something, he thought it would be good experience for him to work in a law firm for a summer to make connections, see another part of the law practice, get the kind of training a big firm can offer."

"Makes sense."

"So, I met with Richard in my office before official recruiting began, and he met some other people on the recruiting committee, and we gave him an offer on the spot. With his credentials, it wasn't like I needed to twist anyone's arm.

"Then Kent asked me to look out for him. He thought Richard might require some support. I knew about Rachel's death, of course, and Kent told me about some other stuff -- did Richard tell you about that?"

"Yes."

"And Kent told me about Richard's fear of the police. Which, of course, makes a lot of sense, given what he's been through. As you know, there was a time when I was an associate, and I needed support, so I told Kent about that and that I'd make sure Richard was protected. You know how it is at the firm -- keep him away from the assholes, make sure he works with nice people. Like you.

"Of course, I didn't know that you two had already managed to work that out." He paused, a bit dramatically, and smiled. "In a way I hadn't exactly anticipated."

Well, if Karen was going to tell him about having sex with Richard last night, maybe now was the time, but Jonathan fortunately changed the subject.

"By the way, I told Kyle I was having dinner with you tonight. He seemed fine with it. Said how much he liked Cyndi."

"That's good. He's such a great kid."

"Yes, he certainly is. He's overcome a lot, as I'm sure you remember. He barely needs any support now, but this stuff with Mindy has been really hard for him."

"As it would for any kid, I'm sure."

"Maybe you and I have dinner once or twice a week? Ease him into this for a few weeks, then maybe you can join us for a dinner at home? And then, maybe we can all get together, with Cyndi and Joey?"

She was thrilled that Jonathan wanted to keep things going, and once or twice a week sounded ideal in light of their childcare responsibilities -- and whatever might be ongoing with Richard. It was like having a great rookie starting pitcher, with an experienced veteran in the bullpen if he ran out of gas. The Cubs should be so lucky.

"Sounds like a plan," was all she thought she needed to say.

"So, tell me about this investigation you guys are doing," he asked.

Three hours later, they realized that the restaurant was closing, and the wait-staff was anxious for them to leave. They had talked nonstop. About the investigation. Their kids. New Trier politics. Winnetka politics. National politics. Karen's becoming U.S. Attorney. Jonathan's cases. Wilkommen. Talking to Jonathan was so easy. They were grown-ups sharing the same interests and they had the same background, grounded in law, litigation and their kids. She couldn't help but contrast it with Richard. What did they have in common besides legal work -- and in bed?

She realized that she hadn't brought up the subject of the firm potentially representing Richard in a civil suit over Tim's release of Richard's juvenile records. She broached the subject as they walked to her car.

"Do you know Tim Reilly?"

"Never heard of him."

"Head of the State Police?"

"Still never heard of him."

Good to know that Jonathan wasn't Tim's source for the info that she had seen Richard last night.

She told Jonathan about the texts with David, the threat of custody, the illegal disclosure of Richard's juvenile records, and the custody hearing that was happening on Monday.

Jonathan was off-the-charts furious. "Of course, we'll handle that. That's outrageous. Disgusting. He's a young lawyer just getting started and this guy -- what did you say his name was?"

"Reilly."

"And this guy Reilly does that to him? Can you file the complaint in federal court? Or does it need to stay in state court? You can't be involved, obviously. Talk to the whoever is handling litigation assignments lately and get a partner assigned. I'll talk to Richard about it. Let's get this filed after you've got it all on the record in the custody hearing, and you have a transcript of exactly what was said in court. Have you done a conflict check yet? If we have a conflict, let's get another big firm to handle it. Pro bono. Tell Richard it won't cost him a cent. We'll cover the costs."

Great, she thought, he was really stepping up to the plate.

As they walked toward Karen's car in Jonathan's normal parking spot in the garage, they moved closer to each other, with their arms momentarily brushing. As they got to the car, Karen fumbled in her purse for the car key, then unlocked the doors. Jonathan stepped closer, put his hand gently on her waist inside her blazer, and kissed her.

Chapter Thirty-Six

"All rise," the court security officer called out to the small, mostly-empty courtroom as the family court judge presiding over the custody motion took her seat at the bench. The parties were arranged at three tables: one for David and his lawyer; one for Karen and her lawyer; and one for the kids who were sitting with their lawyer, who would help them present their views to the judge. Karen and David split the cost of the kids' lawyer, and Karen was pleased to consider how much this escapade was costing David. Richard, whom David's lawyer had served with a subpoena to be a witness, was waiting outside in the hallway until it was his time to testify.

"Please be seated," Judge Catherine Carroll announced.

The judge, a gray-haired veteran of decades in family court, first spoke directly to the children. "Thank you for coming here today. I want you to know that you have an absolute right to be here under the law, but your attendance is voluntary. Sometimes, kids find it helpful to hear the evidence in cases like this; but it also might be too upsetting to hear. You may, at any time, step out of the courtroom and wait in one of the conference rooms outside. If you need us to take a break for any reason, just tell your attorney. If you want to leave for the entire proceeding, that is also okay, but you can't leave the building, and your attorney needs to know where you are. At the end, I will want to talk to you both about what you want to do, going forward."

Cyndi and Joey stood up to address the judge and said, "Thank you, Your Honor," in unison. Karen was wondering where they learned such good courtroom behavior -- maybe all those law shows they'd watched over the years.

The judge continued. "We are here today on the emergency motion brought by father, who claims that mother's current boyfriend was a victim of child sexual abuse and was hospitalized in mental hospitals and placed in the State's residential facility for children, and that, because of what happened to the boyfriend when the boyfriend was between five and twelve years-old, father believes that the boyfriend poses an unreasonable risk of harm to the children. Did I state the issues correctly?"

The lawyers agreed. David's lawyer called David as his first witness. He took a seat on the witness stand, which directly faced the children. He was trying very hard not to look at them.

David testified about the current custody arrangement, which he described as "flexible and informal." He got the kids every other weekend during the school year, and more in the summer. He got them for one week of vacation a year, if he wanted to take them on vacation, but he usually didn't because his schedule was too busy. The custody schedule was very flexible because his wife sometimes had extremely long hours, which could be unpredictable depending on her cases, so he was always available to take the kids at the last minute, and he often did so, including last week, when Karen had been very busy conducting interviews.

He then testified that he had never met Richard Adams. Instead, his friend, Tim Reilly, the Director of the State Police, had called, very upset, that Karen was in a relationship with him. Director Reilly very strongly stated that Richard Adams was not safe around the kids and urged David to go to court to protect the children. David asked Director Reilly why, and Director Reilly explained that Richard Adams was mentally unstable; had tried to commit suicide many times when he was a child; had been institutionalized for a period of YEARS; and had been sexually abused by multiple men. David then offered his opinion that men who are abused as children become child sexual predators, and that there is no way that Richard should be with Joey for one second.

Cyndi made a loud, teenage snort of disrespect.

"Miss Harding," Judge Carroll interrupted. "This is a formal court proceeding, and outbursts like that are not acceptable. Please refrain from that in the future." Cyndi apologized.

The judge continued. "Although hearsay testimony can be considered in a family court proceeding, do you have anything else to offer concerning the risk Richard Adams allegedly poses to your children besides what Mr. Reilly told you, Mr. Harding?" the judge asked, looking none too pleased.

"As I said, he's mentally unstable. He's been sexually abused by multiple men, and everyone knows that men who are sexually abused generally go on to abuse children. Just look at the priests, you know? Many of them said that they were abused when they were altar boys."

"Objection, Your Honor." Karen's lawyer, Melanie Carlson, stood up to argue to the judge. "I move to strike that statement from the record."

The judge cut off Karen's lawyer before she could make further argument and ruled promptly: "Mr. Harding has presented no evidence, and I am aware of no evidence whatsoever, that shows that boys who are sexually abused grow up to be sexual predators, and Mr. Harding's unsupported statement about supposed anecdotal evidence is not relevant to this proceeding. I will strike that statement from the record." She turned to David's attorney. "Proceed Mr. Hamilton."

David's lawyer asked him: "Why do you believe that full custody should be awarded to you?"

David responded as he looked directly at the judge: "Because I love my kids, it makes me crazy to think of them being abused, and I want them to be 100% safe. I know they will be safe with me."

David's lawyer spoke to the court: "That's all the witnesses we have, Your Honor."

"Thank you, Mr. Hamilton," Judge Carroll said. "Just to be clear, you do not have any expert testimony, any studies, any evidence whatsoever, that links child sexual abuse to child predation later in life, is that correct?"

"Yes, Your Honor, that is correct." David's lawyer sat down.

"Ms. Carlson, do you wish to cross examine?"

"Yes, Your Honor," she said as she rose.

Melanie Carlson, now well up in her 60's, was among the best family law lawyers in Chicago. First in her class at Howard, she came home to Chicago for law school, excelling at the University of Chicago, just blocks from the dilapidated tenement where she grew up. She'd aimed to be a litigator at a big firm, but all the Chicago firms she interviewed with discouraged her ("It's so rough and tumble for a woman, and the hours! -- you'll need to be getting home to make dinner"), so she settled for a small family law firm where she knew that at least she could get into court. Capable of being a lioness in the courtroom, but with the empathy needed in many family law situations, she had built a renowned and lucrative practice and was respected by everyone.

Tall and rail-thin, she stared David Harding down and then began her cross examination.

"Mr. Harding, first, do you know whether Richard Adams has ever met your children?"

"I assume he has."

"So you don't know?"

"I assume he has because Tim Reilly said that Karen was seeing him."

"I see. So, if I were to tell you that Richard Adams has never met your children, you have no evidence to refute that, do you sir?"

"No."

"And how exactly do you know that Ms. Harding is seeing Mr. Adams?"

"Tim Reilly told me that."

"And do you know how Director Reilly knew that?"

"I do not. But I know that Tim doesn't lie."

"Mr. Harding, you say that you want custody to keep your kids safe. Is that the only reason?"

"Yes, and of course, I love them and want to be with them."

"Is it your testimony that the financial benefit you would get if the Court granted you custody has nothing to do with why we are here today?"

"Nothing at all, I'm just concerned about their safety."

"Isn't it true, Mr. Harding, that you pay child support because Ms. Harding has custody the overwhelming amount of time, but you get a reduction in your child support payments for every night the kids spend with you beyond every other weekend?"

"Yes, but that has nothing to do with this."

"Really?" She gave the judge, whom she had practiced before for years, and with whom she shared a mutual respect, a side-ways look. "Well I have some questions about your financial situation, Mr.

Harding. You and your girlfriend live in a two-bedroom apartment in the Hancock building, is that right?"

"Yes."

"Do you rent or own?"

"We rent."

"You'd describe that as a very upscale building, would you not?"

"Sure. I'm proud to live there."

"Where does Joey sleep when the kids are there?"

"Sometimes on the couch, sometimes, if my girlfriend and I are up late in the living room, he sleeps on the floor in the other bedroom with Cyndi."

"Did you ever think that you could live someplace less posh and have a bedroom for Joey?"

"I like living downtown."

"So, that's a no."

"Correct."

"And your girlfriend is a paralegal, is that right?"

"Well, she was. She lost her job last month."

"Oh, I see. So, the two of you have had a sudden loss of income within the last thirty days or so?"

"Yes."

"Are you struggling to pay the bills, Mr. Harding?"

He hesitated.

"Mr. Harding?" the judge interjected.

"Yes. I suppose."

Melanie Carlson smiled. "Now, Ms. Harding, she makes much more money than you do, is that correct?"

"Yes."

"And, if the Court were to grant you full custody, you would no longer have to pay child support, and instead, you would receive substantial child support from Ms. Harding, is that correct?"

"Yes. But that isn't the reason why I'm here. It's because I want the kids to be safe."

"Please just answer the question asked," the judge said impatiently.

Karen's attorney continued. "In fact, Ms. Harding's child support payments, which are mandated by law, would exceed your current family income, is that correct?"

"I don't know how much she makes, but probably, yeah."

"Now, I'm going to ask you some questions about the children. Does Joey play sports?"

"Yes. He's on a basketball team."

"Have you gone to a single basketball game of his in three years?"

"No, my girlfriend doesn't like basketball."

"And Cyndi, does she play sports?"

"Yes, she plays lacrosse."

"And when was the last time you attended one her of lacrosse games?"

"I don't remember."

"More than three years ago?"

"Yes."

"Does your girlfriend also not like lacrosse?"

"I don't know."

"What's the name of the children's pediatrician?"

"I don't know. Karen always handles it when they get sick."

"Have you ever taken the kids on vacation with you since the divorce?"

"No."

"Isn't it true that you have taken vacations with your girlfriend, to the Bahamas, to Door County in Wisconsin, to Los Angeles, to Atlantic City, and two trips to Las Vegas?"

"Yes."

"And you never brought the children on any of those vacations?"

"No, they were in school. But I did take them to Detroit recently for a weekend."

"Is there some reason why you could not schedule vacations for when they were not in school?"

"I was busy at work."

"I see. What's the name of Cyndi's best friend?"

"I don't know."

"What's the name of Joey's best friend?"

"I don't know."

"Have you ever allowed either of the children to have a friend over to your apartment?"

"No, our place is too small."

"I see. And if the judge grants you custody, would you continue to not allow the children to have friends over?"

"No, with the additional child support we could get a bigger place."

"Finally! And that is what this is all about, isn't it Mr. Harding, you wanting more money?"

"No, absolutely not. It is about the kids' safety."

"Right. And how are you planning to get them to school in Winnetka every day?"

"We'll need to find a school downtown."

"Oh. I see. So, your plan for custody also includes the children changing schools?"

"I haven't really thought about it."

"Do you know what grade Cyndi will be entering into in the fall?"

"Junior year." David seemed relieved that he actually knew *something* about the kids.

"And you're not concerned about moving your daughter junior year?"

"No. She's a great student. She'll do fine."

"I see. Now, as a part of your divorce settlement, Ms. Harding paid you $200,000, is that correct?"

"Yes."

"And that was just three years ago, isn't that correct?"

"Yes."

"Did you spend that money on gambling and prostitution, Mr. Harding?"

"Prostitution, no, definitely not."

"So, you spent it on gambling?"

"I spent some of it at the casinos, yes. I like to play a little blackjack when I'm on vacation. It's not like I blew a lot of money or anything."

"I see." She stared hard at him again. "But you claim that no money went to prostitution?"

"That's correct." Now, he was started to sweat and squirm.

"Okay, let's go back in time, Mr. Harding. When you were married to Ms. Harding, you frequented so-called 'spas' that were later busted as places of prostitution, human trafficking, and child sex trafficking. Is that correct?"

She grabbed a stack of papers on the desk and held them up.

"Objection, Your Honor," said David's lawyer, standing. "This is not relevant and should not be allowed. And, furthermore, these records were not provided to us prior to the hearing."

"Your Honor, it is highly relevant, and Mr. Harding has had these records since the divorce negotiations three years ago, where it was a significant issue, so it's hardly a surprise. Furthermore, Your Honor, Mr. Harding has claimed that Mr. Adams is not safe around children because Mr. Adams was a victim of child sexual abuse. But the evidence, these credit card statements, will show," she added, waving the papers, "that Mr. Harding regularly frequented so-called spas, which were later busted by the federal authorities for human trafficking and the sexual trafficking of minors. That's extremely relevant given the Court's choice of placing the children with their mother, where they will have little or no contact with a man who, in any event, has no record of child sexual abuse; or their father, whose record of sexual perversion is disturbing, to say the least."

Hardened as she was by years on the bench, even Judge Carroll seemed taken aback. "Overruled. You may proceed."

"Mr. Harding, do you need to see the credit card bills over fifteen years to answer that question?"

"No, I do not need to see the bills. Yes, I went to spas for massages. Some of the spas were later busted. I never knowingly received a massage from anyone whom I had reason to believe was underage or being trafficked."

"I see. Now, isn't it true, that every time a spa that you frequented was busted by the police, you found a new spa for those same, um, shall we say, 'services'?"

"For massages, yes."

"I see. Can you explain whether those massages include, shall we say, 'massages' of your penis?"

David was really squirming now in his chair. "Sometimes, yes."

"Isn't it true that every time you went to these spas, you obtained -- what do they call it Mr. Harding, a 'happy ending' -- with a 'massage' of your penis?"

David looked like he wanted to crawl under a table. "Yeah, I mean probably."

"To be clear, did you ejaculate during these massages?"

"Yeah, I mean, that's what they do. Everybody goes there from time to time. It's a common thing."

"I see. And what, if anything, did you do to confirm before you received such services, that the person providing those services was not underage?"

"I just assumed that they were all adults, that's all. They looked like adults to me."

"And you assumed that, even after multiple spas you had attended had been busted for the sexual trafficking of children?"

"Yes. They did not look underage to me." David was now sweating profusely and looking just about anywhere other than at the children.

Karen was worried about the kids and was watching them out of the corner of her eye the whole time. She had worked out a plan with her lawyer that, if she saw any signs of stress in Joey, the lawyer would stop this line of questioning. But she thought the kids were both old enough and ought to know their dad's history, and it looked like Joey and Cyndi were both handling it fine. They didn't seem surprised at all and at times looked rather amused as their father squirmed on the witness stand. Joey glared at his father in disgust.

"One last set of questions, Mr. Harding, about your conversation with Director Reilly regarding Mr. Adams. Was it one conversation, or more than one conversation?"

"We had one conversation, where he told me the stuff I testified to, and a second conversation yesterday where he encouraged me further to go forward with this hearing for the well-being of my kids."

"Okay. When you spoke to Director Reilly in the first conversation, and he gave you the information about Mr. Adams, did you have any understanding of how Director Reilly knew that information?"

"Yes, Director Reilly told me that he had reviewed Mr. Adams' juvenile records, and that the information was from Mr. Adams' juvenile records."

"And tell us about the second conversation with Director Reilly, the one that occurred yesterday. Can you please tell us about that conversation, who was present, what was discussed, etc.?"

"Yes, Director Reilly called me yesterday. We spoke for just a couple of minutes. He wanted to make sure that I was going forward with the custody matter."

"Can you please tell me his exact words?"

"Yeah, more or less. To the best of my recollection he said, 'I'm calling to make sure that you are doing whatever is necessary to protect the kids. Richard Adams is very dangerous.' And I told him that I was going forward, and I told him we had a hearing today. That's all."

"Thank you. Mr. Harding, I believe you are a lawyer, correct?"

"Yes, I testified to that earlier."

"Are you aware of the Illinois law that makes it a crime to reveal confidential information from juvenile records?"

"Yes, generally speaking, I know that is a crime."

"So, you were aware that it was a crime for Director Reilly to reveal information from Mr. Adams' juvenile records?"

"I hadn't really thought about that at the time. Actually, I don't really know the law. I don't know if I've ever read it. I just kind of know maybe a little general stuff about it. So, I need to change my earlier answer." David gave a very worried glance at the judge, who looked back sternly.

"Mr. Harding, the fact is, you conspired with Tim Reilly to get unlawful access to information from Mr. Adams' juvenile files in order to change custody, which, you've already admitted, would give you a financial benefit, isn't that the case?"

"I don't know how to answer that question. Maybe I shouldn't talk anymore at all." David looked at his lawyer.

David's lawyer jumped up, "Your Honor, we have moved into unexpected areas of testimony now, and I need to confer with my client about whether the Fifth Amendment is appropriate."

"Interesting that they think it's unexpected, Your Honor, since Mr. Harding was the one who testified explicitly about the confidential juvenile records," Karen's lawyer said with a smile. "But that's okay, Your Honor, because I have no need for further questions of this witness."

The judge spoke. "Any redirect, Mr. Hamilton?"

"No, Your Honor. We don't have any more witnesses, so we rest."

The judge turned to David. "Mr. Harding, you may step down." He looked like he would be glad to descend through a trap door if the courtroom had one. She then turned to Melanie Carlson. "Please call your first witness."

"Mother calls Richard Adams, Your Honor."

The security guard went out into the hallway and returned with Richard, who walked across the room, took the oath, and sat on the witness stand.

Now adopting a far more-gentle tone, Karen's lawyer started to question him. "Mr. Adams, we heard a little bit about you from another witness. Can you please tell the court a bit about your background?"

"Yes, of course." Richard appeared nervous as he looked directly at the judge. "I grew up in Evanston. My Dad is a cardiothoracic surgeon at Northwestern Memorial, my mom, who is deceased, was a lawyer. My stepmother is a nurse at Northwestern Memorial. I have an older sister who is a doctor and a resident at the University of Chicago Medical Center, and I have a little brother and a little sister that my Dad and step-mom had a few years after my mother passed."

"Can you tell us about your education, Mr. Adams?"

191

"Yes, I graduated first in my class from the University of Michigan, and I am going into my third year as a law student at Northwestern, where I will be the editor-in-chief of the law review."

"Can you tell us about your grades in law school? Northwestern doesn't rank its students, is that right?"

"That's correct. My grades are very good, I have one A minus and everything else has been an A plus."

"And have you published any articles?"

Richard briefly described his published articles in the law journals.

"Mr. Adams, we heard testimony about your childhood. I understand that you have been diagnosed with PTSD, is that correct?"

"Yes."

"When were you diagnosed with PTSD?"

"When I was five years-old."

"Do you still have PTSD?"

"Yes."

"Are you able to speak verbally about traumatic events that happened when you were little?"

"No, I am not." Richard turned to the judge. "Your Honor, I am neurologically unable to speak about these things. But I think I could nod my head if I'm given a yes or no question, or I might be able to write or text my answers."

Judge Carroll spoke: "Is there any real dispute about what happened to Mr. Adams?"

The attorneys agreed there was no dispute.

"Okay, since this is just background information, and we're in family court where the rules are a bit relaxed, I am fine with you leading your witness, and with the witness nodding his head or communicating in any way in which he is comfortable."

"Thank you, Your Honor," Melanie Carlson said.

The judge then spoke to Richard. "Mr. Adams, if at any point, you need a break, let us know, okay?"

"I will, thank you, Your Honor."

The judge then directed the court stenographer to record whether the Richard nodded his head 'yes' or 'no,' and then turned to Karen's lawyer. "You may resume, Ms. Carlson."

Karen's lawyer took Richard through his mother's killing, and the subsequent trial where the officer was acquitted.

"Mr. Adams, is it true that after that, you went through a difficult time, and you were hospitalized, twice?

Richard nodded yes.

"Is it true that you had largely recovered from that before you turned six?"

Richard spoke. "I can't say that I was largely recovered, but I was no longer suicidal. I no longer had suicidal ideations, and there were no more attempts and no hospitalizations. And, even before, I had never acted out at home or at school. I just tried to hurt myself. But I had stopped doing that by the time I was six." Richard looked down as he spoke the last statement.

"Mr. Adams, are you able to speak about what happened when you were ten?

Richard shook his head no.

" Now when you were ten, Tim Reilly, then Trooper Reilly but now the Director of the State Police, came to your school, is that right?"

Richard nodded his head yes.

"He took you away, pursuant to a court order, and brought you to the Southern facility for children, is that right?"

Richard nodded yes.

"Do you have any understanding of why you were placed there?"

His anger permitted him to speak, with his voice rising. "To this day, I have zero understanding of why I was placed at the Southern facility. There was no reason for it. I was behaving perfectly at home and at school. I had perfect grades. I had not threatened or attempted to hurt myself in years. I am now working on an investigation to determine whether other boys, like me, were abused at Southern or removed from their homes and placed there for no reason. And I believe, quite firmly, that Tim Reilly is going after me now because of that investigation."

"A judge ordered you into custody when you were ten, isn't that correct?"

"Yes, but the order does not describe any basis for the decision -- as, I understand now, custody orders always do -- and there was no motion for custody filed by DCFS. The order is highly suspect, in my opinion. Neither I nor my family have any idea why I was taken into custody."

"Mr. Adams, I'm going to show you Ms. Harding's Exhibit which has been marked as Exhibit 1 for identification. Do you recognize this?"

"Yes. That's the order that directed that I be placed in state custody when I was ten years old."

"And did you provide this to me?"

"Yes."

"And because this is your own juvenile record, do you have the legal authority to share it with me and with this court?"

"Yes."

"And are you willing to waive your rights of confidentiality regarding this document such that it may be used in this proceeding?"

"Yes."

"Do you authorize me to provide a copy to Mr. Harding's counsel?"

"Yes."

Karen's lawyer handed a copy to David's lawyer. "Your Honor, I move to admit Mrs. Harding's Exhibit 1, the court order directing that Mr. Adams be placed in state custody when he was ten years old."

"Any objections?" the judge asked.

"Yes, Your Honor, we object," said David's lawyer. "This is not relevant in any way."

"How is it relevant, counsel?" the judge asked.

"Your Honor, unlike any order directing a child to be taken into state custody that I have seen in my forty-odd years of practice, this order provides no basis in support of the decision. Since the father has directly put in issue Mr. Adam's character, including the fact of his being in custody as a child, the extremely odd and questionable nature of the custody order is highly relevant."

194

Karen's lawyer handed the order to the courtroom deputy, who handed it to the judge, who read it, who then peered over her reading glasses as she addressed the parties.

"I have been a family court judge for nearly as long as Ms. Harding's counsel has been practicing, and I must say, I too, have never seen an order like this. I will admit the Exhibit 1 over Mr. Harding's objection for the reasons Ms. Carlson stated."

Karen's lawyer continued. "Okay, Mr. Adams, can you talk about what happened to you at Southern?"

Richard nodded his head no.

"Is it true that you were sexually abused there by three men over the course of two years?

Richard nodded his head yes.

"Is it true that you suffered severe internal injuries in the last sexual assault?"

Richard nodded his head yes.

"And you were twelve years old at that time? You had been there two years?"

Richard nodded yes.

"Is it true that your life was saved because a school nurse defied direct orders and snuck you out to a hospital in the middle of the night?"

"Yes, she later became my step-mother. She saved my life," Richard managed to say.

"And you were helicoptered to Northwestern Memorial and had emergency surgery?"

"Yes," Richard spoke.

"And your father then was able to get a court order releasing you from state custody?"

"Yes," Richard spoke.

Karen looked at the judge. Judge Carroll, hardened as she was from hearing years of testimony of every possible horrible thing that could ever be done to a child, was doing her best to hold back tears -- and she was not succeeding.

"And the director of the Southern facility was convicted of sexually assaulting you and was sentenced to serve 40 years in prison?"

"Yes."

"Now to be clear, Mr. Adams, have you had any contact with Ms. Harding's children?"

"No. I've never met them, although I would like to at some point."

"Can you tell us how, if at all, your PTSD and your childhood experiences could impact your interactions with Ms. Harding's children?"

"Sure," Richard began slowly. "I am very fortunate in that I never get the fight response. You know, there are three neurological responses that people with a trauma history can have. Fight, flight and freeze. You don't get to pick which neurological response you'll get, or how your brain will react in any given situation. But I am very fortunate that I have never reacted to any trigger with the fight response. I have never become verbally or physically aggressive, at any time in my life. When I get triggered, I freeze -- sometimes I dissociate, and kind of look off in the distance for a while -- and sometimes I feel the urge to flee. When that happens, I'll just say that I need to step outside for a minute and get some air. I don't usually go far, and I can control that response usually pretty well -- like I've never left my little brother or sister unsupervised or anything. Mostly, I just get quiet. Unable to speak."

"Mr. Adams, have you ever sexually abused a child?"

"No. Of course not. I never have, and I never will." Richard looked directly at the judge. "Your Honor, I was hurt physically, mentally and neurologically by what those men did to me. It had a powerful impact on me, but the strongest lesson that I learned is to never hurt anyone. I'm constitutionally incapable of hurting anyone, especially a child. I want to be a lawyer, like my mother, who worked to help kids and keep them safe. That's why Ms. Harding and I are working on this investigation of child sexual abuse at state facilities, as I mentioned a moment ago. I plan to dedicate my life to keeping kids safe. I can promise you that I pose zero risk for Cyndi and Joey."

Karen looked over at the kids. They were both reaching for tissues on the table and wiping their eyes.

Karen's lawyer spoke. "I have no other questions for this witness, Your Honor."

"Any cross examination, Mr. Hamilton?" asked the judge.

"No, Your Honor," said David's attorney, who, dumb as he was, knew that further questioning would only do more damage.

Melanie Carlson addressed the judge. "Your Honor, our only other witnesses would be the children, Cyndi and Joey, but I assume that Your Honor wants to conduct that questioning."

The judge ordered a break so Cyndy and Joey could speak to their lawyer privately outside the courtroom about what they wanted the judge to do. After ten minutes, they came back into the courtroom with their lawyer, and Judge Carroll spoke to Cyndi and Joey directly. "Do either of you want to say anything? And, if so, we can arrange for you to speak to me privately, outside the presence of both of your parents, in my chambers."

Cyndi stood and said, "We've spoken with our lawyer, and we want speak here in the courtroom. Joey has asked me to speak for both of us." Joey nodded in agreement.

"Okay," the judge said, and let the record show that Joey Harding has nodded 'yes' to his sister's statement that she will speak for them both. "What do you both want me to know? Specifically, I'd like you to tell me where you'd like to live."

"Your Honor, we want to live with our mother. When we first learned that Dad had filed this motion, we fled his apartment in a rage. We were extremely angry, and we are still. We recognize now that maybe he just made a mistake, and he is our dad so maybe we don't really want to cut him out of our lives completely. But we do not want to live with him, ever. We were okay with spending time with him every other weekend, and when Mom needs us to stay with him, but no more than that. And right now, even that's too much. We're old enough to stay by ourselves until Mom gets home, or with a babysitter if Your Honor thinks that's necessary, although I'm old enough to babysit myself and I've done it.

"And, after hearing the testimony from Richard Adams -- who we've never even met -- we have absolutely no problem being with him, but we do want an order that we are to have no contact with Tim Reilly. The testimony today was very disturbing to us. We did not understand why Mr. Reilly said those things to Dad about Richard, because Richard, frankly, seems like a much better potential dad to us than our own father. It all made no sense to us, but now, we believe that the only plausible explanation for all of this, for us being here today, is that Mr. Reilly is somehow out to get Richard, and maybe always has been, and we want no part of that. Mr. Reilly is Joey's basketball coach, but Joey does not want to be near him. To the extent that we maintain contact with our father, we want to ask you to issue an order that Mr. Reilly will not be present."

Karen had tears in her eyes and was so proud of Cyndi's articulate presentation. She could envision law school in her future

"Thank you, Cyndi." The judge looked at Joey. "Joey, do you agree with everything your sister said?"

"Yes, except one thing I want to add, Your Honor. My Dad does stupid things sometimes. Even despicable things. But what he did today, by stressing us all out, and what he did to Richard Adams, making him come to court where he had to testify about very private things, things that are so upsetting to him that he can't even speak . . . in front of all these people who he's never even met, like us, I think that's unforgiveable. I don't want anything to do with my Dad, Your Honor. I don't want to have to visit him. If my mom has to work late, I would rather stay in her house alone than be with him."

"Thank you, Joey. We are going to recess now, and I expect to issue my order within the hour."

They stepped outside into the hallway after the judge left the bench. David exited the courtroom area with his lawyer as quickly as possible, leaving Karen, Richard, the kids and their lawyers in the hallway.

Cyndi walked up to Richard. "Nice to meet you. I hope we get to see more of you, because you sound much cooler than our father. Sorry about today. It's really embarrassing what he did."

"Yeah," Joey said, "we're nothing like our Dad. You might actually like us."

The four of them went out to lunch together at the food court in the Thompson Center, grabbed some caramel and cheese popcorn for dessert, and the kids took the train home.

When Karen and Richard got back to the office, Judge Carroll had emailed three orders. Karen and Richard read them together.

Chapter Thirty-Seven

First, there was a confidential family court order denying David's motion. In her decision, the judge lauded Richard's remarkable accomplishments, including how he had successfully overcome the traumatic events of his childhood. She found that there had been no evidence presented that would support, let alone suggest, that Richard posed a risk of harm to the children. Instead, all the evidence demonstrated that he was a caring and conscientious adult. The judge also noted in a footnote that she had been the sentencing judge in countless cases where men had sexually abused children, and in all of those cases, the men were asked as a part of their pre-sentence investigation whether they had been sexually abused as children. She noted that it was extremely rare for convicted defendants -- who were presumably honest in the sentencing interview since they would get some credit for childhood trauma -- to report child sexual abuse. She stated that while this was not the basis for her decision, it called out for further study. Finally, she noted that Joey had requested that Tim Reilly not have contact with the children, and given the testimony regarding Mr. Reilly, she supported Joey's request and barred all contact, including at school where, given Richard Adams' testimony, it was especially important that the children feel safe.

Second, in another confidential family court order, the judge noted that the evidence raised a significant question as to whether it was *David* who presented a risk of harm to the children, given his admission of regularly receiving sexual services at multiple establishments that were later convicted of child sex trafficking. Therefore, she ordered that he have no unsupervised in-person contact with the children until after he had submitted to a psychosexual evaluation, after which the court would hold a hearing on the issue of future contact.

Finally, in a third order, the judge made a criminal referral to the FBI for investigation of David and Tim Reilly for what she described as "a potential conspiracy to obstruct justice" by unlawfully revealing Richard's protected juvenile information in order to impede the investigation Richard was working on with Karen. The judge was very careful not to name Richard or provide any information that could be used to identify him. In addition, she referred the matter to the state lawyer licensing authority to investigate whether David had violated the rules of ethics, and whether he was fit to practice law.

"Holy shit," said Richard. "I've never seen a case where a judge made a criminal referral before."

"It's extremely rare, I've only seen it once before in all my years of practice," Karen said.
"It also means that David could lose his law license, and he might also be prosecuted and end up in jail with Reilly -- which would be unfortunate for the kids. Of course, they brought it on themselves. Really brilliant, going to court over custody with no basis and by illegally revealing confidential juvenile information. But David's always been an idiot with no judgment when it comes to pursuing what he wants in the moment, and I think Tim Reilly just used him here as a pawn. You were right, he's a really bad guy. I had no idea. You think you know someone, you know? I assume he'll be placed on leave while the matter is investigated."

Getting back to work, Karen set up an impromptu team meeting to learn about the interviews that had taken place while she was in court. Several more victims had spoken out, and three additional witnesses had provided corroborating evidence to much of the testimony. The new victims had reported abuse by a combination of the five men already identified, so there was nothing new there. And no one seemed to recall Tim Reilly.

The latest interviews only affirmed her view that it was time to stop conducting interviews and turn everything over to law enforcement. Normally, she would have referred this case to the state Attorney General's Office, but because of Reilly -- the Director of the State Police -- trying to obstruct the investigation, only the FBI could handle it.

The interviews were proving that the widespread sexual abuse at the two facilities constituted an ongoing trafficking case that had continued unabated for years and was undoubtedly still going on. Therefore, the civil statute of limitations clock would probably only start ticking with the last case, rather than the first, and perhaps all of the criminal cases could be prosecuted, no matter how old.

What she found particularly puzzling was Tim Reilly's role. What could he possibly be up to? If he had really been worried about Richard having contact with Cyndi and Joey, the obvious move would have been to call Karen directly. But he knew that it was bullshit, and that no judge would ever order a transfer of custody on that record. His only purpose could have been to threaten and intimidate her, to stop her from having contact with Richard. But why?

Richard joined her in her office. "Did you notice, Karen, that David testified that he heard about your relationship from Tim Reilly -- not from the kids? Do you think they told him?"

"I don't think they would have done that. I swore them to secrecy when I gave them your name. But it's possible.

"How else would he know we were spending time together?"

"I don't know."

"It's kind of concerning, don't you think?"

Karen didn't respond, and, with Richard on speaker, she called Ken at the FBI to report all that had just happened, including Richard's history, and the results so far of their sexual abuse investigation. Then they described how Tim Reilly had unlawfully revealed Richard's juvenile record to David, and their sense that Reilly was attempting to obstruct the investigation. Karen told Ken about the court order and the criminal referral, and finally had Richard describe the threatening call he'd received.

Ken listened and took notes throughout the call, frequently asking them to repeat facts so he could get them down accurately. When they got to the piece about Tim, Ken whistled. "Shit," he said, "this is huge. Why would he do that? He's got to know that's completely frivolous bullshit. It's hard to imagine he wasn't trying to intimidate you to stop the investigation, but why?"

Ken asked them to stop all interviews so the FBI could take the case moving forward. Karen agreed, and told Ken that, with the permission of the witnesses, she would hand over all of their records.

"That piece about Tim really troubles me," Ken said, "especially since he asked to install that program on your phone and your computer. Were you investigating this at that time?"

"No," Karen said. "Not at all."

"Actually," Richard said, "I had set up the Facebook group the week before I started at the firm, but I don't know how he would have known about that. He certainly didn't ask to join the group. At least, not unless he used an alias or something."

"Interesting," Ken said.

By the time they finished the call with Ken, it was nearly seven. Richard left her office to head home, but she still had some emails she had to respond to before she left for Winnetka.

Fifteen minutes later, Karen was just about done when her office phone rang.

She recognized the phone number -- it was from the after-hours operator. "Ms. Harding? There's an emergency call for you from the front desk, from Shawn Jeffries. Do you want us to put the call through?"

Karen had no idea why Shawn was calling her. He had never called before. "Yes, please put him through, thank you."

"Ms. Harding? It's Shawn, from the front desk. That young man that you are friends with? That you had lunch with the other day? He was attacked in the elevator. We're not sure if he's breathing. We've called 911 for an ambulance. I didn't know who else to call."

"I'll be right down." She grabbed her bag and laptop and ran to the elevator.

Chapter Thirty-Eight

The elevator took forever to get to 59 and forever again to get to the ground floor. As Karen bolted out into the lobby, she immediately saw a commotion by one of the elevator doors. There was an empty stretcher sitting outside the door. As she got closer, she saw Richard crumpled on the floor against the corner wall of the elevator, being attended to by two EMTs. He appeared to be unconscious. He wasn't moving, and he was sickeningly pale. Karen completely panicked and started to hyperventilate. Tears started streaming down her face. Richard looked dead. They put him into a supine position on the floor of the elevator and began working on him.

The EMTs were taking his vitals and checking his airway. She was relieved to hear that he had blood pressure, and a pulse. She heard them say that his oxygen level was low but getting better. He was breathing on his own now, but that had not been so clear in the beginning. They had undone his tie and ripped his shirt open all the way down and had wired those sticky tags to his chest. Shockingly, his neck was deep red, and there was the clear outline of a handprint -- where someone's fingers had pressed into his neck. The red outlines of someone's fingers were so clear that Karen could see it from outside the elevator.

Shawn came up to her, and she felt him put something in her blazer pocket. He quietly said, "We got it all on video Ms. Harding, with audio." And then he leaned closer and said in a very low voice, "I put it on a thumb drive for you in case the master file disappears when the police get here. That Tim Reilly, he's a really bad man, a very dangerous man. You two need to be careful."

"Tim Reilly did this?" She was incredulous, but, at the same time, somehow not surprised.

Shawn whispered, "That man is a monster. I knew that before, but wait until you see the video. I knew he was up to something. He was waiting on the 59th floor for 30 minutes -- that's on the video too. I got worried, and we started watching closely. When he saw your friend get off alone on 59 and go into the other elevator, bam, Reilly went into that elevator and started the attack. There was just the two of them in the elevator. You could see and hear how Reilly wanted your friend to take a swing, I guess so Reilly could arrest him for assaulting an officer, and Reilly got really angry and strangled him when your friend refused to fight. I thought he was going to kill him. He would have, if the elevator ride had been a minute longer. The video picks up his threats and his voice is really clear. You'll hear it. Your friend did nothing wrong. He did nothing to provoke this. We're not telling the Chicago or State Police about the video, unless they ask. But you have it now. I don't know how to get the FBI involved, but the State Police can't handle this. Please do what you can before they start to destroy the evidence."

Karen saw the blue light of state police patrol cars coming down the block. She pulled out her phone and called Ken Shapiro.

"Ken, thank God I got you. This is an emergency. She told him what had happened, that the EMTs were working on Richard in the elevator, and she had a video of the assault.

Ken told Karen to tell the State Police and Chicago cops that this is an FBI case, so they should secure the scene and do nothing else until the FBI arrives, which should be momentarily. He also said that, obviously, the EMTs should do whatever they need to do to care for Richard and get him to a hospital. He asked Karen to take photos of Richard in the elevator now, and to photograph his injuries, making sure to photograph the front and back of his hands as well.

"Have the police call me at this number. I was just heading home. I'm in my car. I'll be there in less than five minutes."

Much to her relief, Richard was now sitting up in the elevator just staring into space, the assault obviously having triggered his trauma. The EMTs wanted to take Richard to the hospital, but he was having none of it. The EMT's were trying to get him on the stretcher, but he was nodding "no" even though he was unable to stand up. Going to the ER, she figured, would likely also trigger his PTSD, due to his memories from when he was twelve.

"Ken wants me to take photos," she gently told him. She took photos of his neck with her phone. "Now show me your hands."

Richard complied. "Now the back of your hands."

Karen not only took those photos, she then she shot a video of everything, including the inside of the elevator and the EMTs.

"Let me call your Dad. Maybe he can meet us at the ER."

Hearing about his Dad calmed Richard down considerably. "Okay." He handed Karen his phone. She found Kent in "favorites" under "Dad," and spoke to Kent outside the elevator.

"Your Dad agrees with the EMTs, Richard. He wants you to go to the ER. He says you need to get your hyoid bone checked out. And he wants to talk to you." She handed Richard the phone.

"Hey, sorry about this Dad," Richard said. His voice was very raspy, and Karen shot more video to capture the sound.

"Dad, I'm really fine. I don't want to go to the hospital. It's not necessary. I don't think I can handle it Dad, really I'm fine. Okay. Okay. Okay. Okay. Karen, he wants to talk to you."

Richard handed her back the phone. Kent told her that it would be extremely difficult for Richard to go to the hospital. There were four times that Richard had gone to the ER, beginning with Rachel's death, and, well, he didn't want to go into the details, but it would almost surely trigger Richard in a big way. But he was more concerned that Richard's hyoid bone might be broken or that he might have internal injuries that needed to be treated, so he had no option but to go, and that Richard had agreed. Kent said that he was at the hospital now -- he was just finishing up his patient reports -- and he would wait at the ER entrance for the ambulance so he could support Richard from the moment he arrived.

Karen texted the kids and told them that she was going to be very late, and that they should order takeout. They were used to her life, so she knew they wouldn't suspect that anything was amiss. But she added, "Please make sure the doors and windows are locked."

Some Chicago cops and state troopers strutted into the lobby, chests puffed out like they were ready for war. Karen told them that they had a conflict so the case was being handled by the FBI, but they could secure the scene if they wanted until the FBI got there in a couple of minutes. They argued and said the case was under State Police jurisdiction alone because someone had attacked the director of the State Police. She gave them Ken's number.

The first two FBI agents arrived before they could call Ken, and Karen was torn about talking to them or going to the hospital with Richard. She asked the EMTs to wait for just a moment, and she quickly told the FBI agents -- one of whom she had worked with years ago -- what had happened; that Shawn had seen the whole thing and could give them a recording; that Tim Reilly had attacked Richard, who hadn't retaliated in any way, as a part on an overall plot to intimidate Richard, probably with the purpose of stopping an investigation of child sexual abuse at certain state facilities for children; and, if Reilly were to claim that Richard had attacked him, it was a lie and the video would prove it. She carefully did not reveal that she had a copy of the video in her pocket because there was still time for someone to destroy the video. Tim had a whole lot of friends in law enforcement.

As an afterthought, she suggested to the FBI agents that Reilly undoubtedly didn't know that there was a recording, with video and audio, of everything that happened in the elevator, so they could probably pin him down on his lies and his false story if they didn't let anyone know about the recording. They nodded in agreement.

One of the FBI agents, a pretty blonde young woman, went out to her car and returned with a high-quality camera and a camera light to photograph Richard's injuries before he went to the ER. "Holy shit," she said as she focused on his neck, "the handprint is so clear we can probably measure it and get the correct size." The bruise was a classic "reverse" image of the fingers, which Karen had seen more times in sexual assault cases than she ever wanted to remember. The agent took a second set of photographs with a ruler in the picture, measuring the length and width of each finger bruise, and the area where the palm and wrist obviously had been. Then she photographed the front and back of Richard's hands, and his fingernails.

The agents also said that Richard had to meet with them every day for the next three days to re-photograph the injuries, as bruises often take a few days to fully form.

Richard's Dad met them at the ER. Richard introduced Karen to Kent as Richard was rolled into the examination room. Kent said he was relieved to see Richard talking, although his voice was still very scratchy. Karen quietly told Richard that Shawn said the whole thing was on video, and she had the USB drive with the video in her pocket.

Richard carefully repeated what happened, verbatim, to every nurse and doctor who asked him. He said he got in the elevator as he was texting his sister and noticed that someone got in behind him, but he didn't think anything of it at the time.

He realized it was Tim Reilly when Reilly started yelling at him. He knew him, because Reilly took him into custody when he was ten for no reason. When the elevator door closed, with no one else in the elevator, Reilly immediately started threatening him, telling him if he knew what was good for him, he would stop this "stupid little investigation."

Richard told him, "I'm not ten years old, anymore. You don't scare me."

Reilly flew into a rage, grabbed Richard's neck so tightly he couldn't breathe, and yelled
"You'd better be scared of me, I can lock you up for any reason or no reason, and make sure you get it in the ass every day."

Reilly went on, shouting, "Go ahead, hit me. Hit me so I can charge you with assaulting an officer. HIT ME! HIT ME or I'll keep choking until I kill you!"

Richard said that he went limp. He did not struggle, didn't hit back, didn't even try to remove Reilly's hands -- which only made Reilly grip his neck harder. He was struggling to breathe, but he was still frozen and could not move.

"Then Reilly said, 'If you don't stop this stupid little investigation, I'm going to stop by your little brother's school, Robbie, isn't that his name? And drop him off at Stern Harrison, and make sure that he has the same good time you did.'

"Finally, the elevator opened, and the security guards were there waiting. Reilly let go of my neck. I must have passed out. The last thing I remember is feeling like I was falling as he ran off."

Richard checked out fine. His hyoid bone was intact. The ER doctor took additional photos of the bruises on his neck for his medical record.

Ken Shapiro arrived with the agent who took the photos of Richard in the elevator. Ken introduced them her -- Susanna James, a new agent with a computer science degree from MIT who was going to specialize in cybercrime but was learning the basics on general investigations first. Ken let Susanna interview Richard, who repeated the identical story. She took more photos of Richard's neck and the front and back of his hands. There were no bruises on his hands, there was no redness and no swelling. If Tim Reilly were to claim that Richard had punched him, the photos would confirm what the video showed -- that Tim was lying. The agents also looked at Richard's fingernails for blood and skin in case he had scratched Reilly. There was nothing under his nails, but they did their best to take fingernail scrapings anyway in case Reilly were to claim that Richard had scratched him. Richard repeated how he hadn't even tried to pull Reilly's hands off of his neck -- he was just frozen and couldn't move.

Richard and Karen had the same thought at the same time. Richard turned to Ken.

"There's something else. The bastard is tracking me somehow. He knew I was working late in the office. He was waiting for me. And last Thursday. . . .

He turned to Karen. "Can I tell them about that?"

Karen explained to Ken and Susanna, "The night that David texted me all hysterical that Richard couldn't be around the kids and that he was going to file a motion for custody -- I spent that night at Richard's apartment, and it seems like Tim somehow knew. Richard and I have only been together twice: at my house one weekend, and then last Thursday night. And I checked with the kids -- they didn't tell their father that I was seeing Richard. Tim knew when no one else did. He must be tracking me, or Richard, or both of us. That first weekend was the weekend of the threats, and Tim showed up at my house right after I dropped Richard off. Both times we were together, Tim got involved right away."

Karen asked, "Is there any way for him to know that without getting a warrant?"

"It's easy," Susanna James responded. She was very young and pretty, about Richard's age, with blonde hair pulled back in a professional ponytail and rather striking green eyes that Karen noticed occasionally strayed appreciatively toward Richard. "Anyone can buy tracking information from the companies that sell it. They say you can't track an individual's phone, but it's actually very easy. All you need to do is start with an address where not many people live -- say, Richard's Dad's home -- and see what numbers have been there, and then follow those numbers to see where they go. And then, when the number shows up at Richard's apartment, bingo: you know that's Richard. Anyone can do it. It's ridiculously legal. It's been in the tech news for a while, and some papers are just starting to report it. They say you can't see where people are in real time -- there's some delay -- but I'm sure that's not true on the black market. It needs to be outlawed. It creates a huge risk for domestic violence victims who are trying to hide from violent partners. If you think about it, for someone like Tim Reilly, all it takes is knowing the right person at your telephone carrier who is willing to pass off that information without a warrant."

Ken laughed. "She's young and sharp and understands all this stuff." And, Karen noticed, Richard was smiling at her. Why shouldn't he, she thought with a pang of jealousy, she's young, smart and pretty, and there must be countless others out there who could turn Richard's head. Another reason a relationship with Richard was out of the question.

But that was hardly something she needed to be worrying about. Karen was terrified. Here she was making every effort to stay safe, and the people who wanted to kill her probably knew all the places she went to on a regular basis, and even knew exactly where she was standing at this very moment.

As Ken and Susanna stepped out of the room for a minute, Richard brightened up and said in a quiet voice to Karen and his Dad, "Do you realize how amazing this is? Tim Reilly specifically threatened me with jail and violence if I didn't give up the investigation. I was careful to look at the camera the whole time and to speak loudly, right at the camera, before I froze. I guess he never got trained on basic elevator etiquette. If the audio picked up our conversation, he's going down. We did it, Karen, he's going to jail for this."

Karen wasn't so sure. "I don't know. He's the Director of the State Police, and he's white. Juries almost always acquit police officers in cases like this, no matter how strong the evidence is. It gets complicated. He *should* go to jail for this -- he could have killed you. And it's all recorded, which is so important. But nothing is certain.

"The problem is that we still don't know why. Why is he breaking the laws and trying to kill you to stop the investigation? We still don't have a motive. None of the witnesses identified him as a perpetrator."

The agents came back in.

"The agents on the scene got the video from security, but we would also like your copy. Can we have it?"

Richard looked at Karen's bag. "Do you have your computer here? Can you upload the video to your computer and the cloud? No offense," he added, turning toward Susanna, "But we can't risk losing it or having something happen to it. We should copy it now before we leave the hospital."

"Of course," Susanna said as she smiled at him. Karen was starting to find her annoying.

Karen couldn't believe how brilliant Richard could be even in his present condition. She would have simply turned it over, and that could have been a critical mistake. She started up her computer, put in the USB drive, and they all watched the video together. It was exactly as Richard had described, but it was much more horrible to see it in person. She saved it to her hard drive and her cloud account, and then also saved it to the investigation file on the Firm's online storage drive.

"Let's also ask the doctor to upload it to be a part of my medical record. We want it in as many places as possible," Richard said.

"Listen, both of you," Ken made eye contact with them both. "Do not do anything with that video until we finish our interview with Tim Reilly. Don't put it on Facebook, don't tell a soul about it. If Tim lies about what happened on that video in his FBI interview, it gives us another path to convict him and put him away. And he won't lie if he has any inkling that there's a video."

"Okay."

"I'll let you know the second Tim's interview is done, and then -- it's up to you what you do with it. I'm not advising you one way or the other, but please, do not do anything that is going to prejudice this investigation." Ken turned to Karen.

"And another thing. No more investigating. You guys are obviously putting yourself and the people at the Firm who are working on this in danger. It must stop. We're in charge now, okay?"

"Yes, of course."

Richard smiled. "Who would have thought that being strangled could turn out to be a good thing? I really think we're finally going to get Tim Reilly off the street so he can no longer hurt anyone."

"Richard," Karen said, "do you know what's so amazing about this? You were just nearly killed by Tim Reilly, and you are able to talk about it."

Richard and his dad both smiled.

"Plus, the freeze response probably saved your life. If you had hit him or struggled to get away, he probably would have killed you. At a minimum, he would have come up with some bogus charge like assaulting an officer or resisting arrest. The freeze response saved you Richard, and that's really fortunate."

Chapter Thirty-Nine

Richard went home with his Dad to Evanston, and Karen went back to the office, got her car, and started to drive home.

She called Jonathan.

They'd texted and talked a few times over the weekend after that quick Friday night kiss. A kiss she had relived it in her mind a thousand times over. 20 seconds? And so nice. Sexy, easy and comfortable, with the wonderful feeling that there was likely much more to come. And talking to Jonathan on the phone was so easy and fun. They laughed, a lot.

"Hey, is this an okay time?"

"Of course. What's up?"

She breathlessly told him about Richard and the elevator, the recording, the FBI, the hospital, the hyoid bone. "Did you get a litigation partner to take on his civil case about the juvenile records?" he asked at the finish.

"Not yet. I'm sorry. I had a crazy day. But I was able to confirm that there's no conflict with us taking the case."

"Good -- because I'm going to do it myself. Email me all the relevant records you have so I can put it together for you guys to review tonight. I want to file it first thing tomorrow morning, and include the video of the assault. It will send a message if my name is on the complaint. We need to go public with this immediately after they've finished their interview with that guy -- what's his name? Tim something?"

"Yeah. Tim Reilly."

"The only way to keep Richard safe is to make this all public. Immediately. And the only way to go public is to file the lawsuit to get the facts out in a court proceeding, where they'll be immune from the defamation laws. And then I'll hold a press conference."

"Great. Except we need to hold off just long enough for the FBI to interview Reilly without his knowing about the video. I'll let you know when we hear from them."

"Okay."

"Do you want me to call Richard?"

"No, I'll call him, now. You shouldn't talk to him about the facts anymore. You're a witness. I'm his lawyer. And after I talk to Richard, I'm going to talk to Kent to make sure that he agrees this is a good idea."

"Sounds like a great plan."

"I'm going to need to talk to you as I draft the complaint through the night. How late can I call you?"

"All night. I'll start drafting the fact section now while you talk to Richard and Kent."

The three of them worked through the night. Richard did the legal research on the civil torts that Tim Reilly had committed -- assault and battery, threatening a witness and obstruction, of justice as part of a conspiracy directed at extortion, intentional infliction of emotional distress -- the list went on with a lot of creativity on Richard's part. Karen wrote the fact sections. Jonathan wrote the intro, did the editing and made it perfect. And Kent signed off on all of it.

It was important for many reasons to get the truth out to the public immediately. Tim Reilly should not be leading the State Police, where he would have enormous power to intimidate witnesses and destroy evidence. Once the complaint was filed in court -- which would make it public -- Reilly would surely be suspended while the investigation was pending. They attached the video to the complaint, knowing that the video would thereby become a "public" record that anyone could access -- which would help to get the truth out more than anything they had written in the Complaint could accomplish. And, with Reilly suspended, more witnesses might have the courage to come forward.

Ken texted Karen at 6 a.m. He, too, had been up all night. "Did she have time to talk?" Karen called Ken immediately.

The FBI had interviewed Reilly at 10 p.m. As they had hoped, he had no idea that the elevator was monitored by video, let alone with audio. The FBI videotaped the interview, and Ken had just finished working with the AUSA assigned to the case, writing up the draft for the grand jury charges. "According to Reilly, he had had a meeting with his accountant after work on the 63rd floor -- which was true, but the accountant told us that the meeting had ended 30 minutes earlier than Tim said. That's Tim's false statement to the FBI #1. Then, Tim said he hopped into the first express elevator that arrived on the 59th floor. False statement to the FBI #2. Then he said he was surprised to find himself alone with Richard, which is false statement to the FBI #3 -- since the video shows him waiting in that lobby on 59 for 30 minutes until he clearly recognizes Richard and follows him into the elevator. Then, lie #4 -- he said Richard immediately began threatening him, when the video shows that Richard was typing on his phone and didn't notice Tim at all.

"Tim said Richard then went nuts -- 'you know how he has mental health issues,'--" Ken mocked Tim's tone of voice, "and then Richard punched him in the jaw for no reason.

"Tim had a big, fresh bruise on his jaw to prove it. His jaw was red and swollen, and you could see the knuckle marks. Tim even went to Evanston Hospital to get the injury documented. Nothing was broken. Someone did punch Tim, but we know it wasn't Richard. Every second is on that video -- from when they were both in the lobby on 59 until the EMT's took Richard out of the elevator. There was no punch, and Tim's face looked fine in the video as he walked out of the elevator. He's tall -- the camera is up high -- it gave us a close up of his face. And get this, he was smiling. Grinning from ear to ear, in fact. And, of course, why would he go all the way to Evanston to go to the hospital if he was punched downtown? Someone punched him, probably in Evanston.

"I asked details about the punch, and he kept lying. Richard hit him with his right fist, which was closed and tight, and his knuckles went into Tim's jaw. He said, 'See this bruise? You can see the knuckles.'

"He said he went to the ER because he thought his jaw might be broken. And, I'm telling you, his jaw looked bad. Tim said that Richard was angry that Tim had told your ex about his juvenile records, which Tim denied doing.

"And here's the worst part. Even worse than I expected. Tim had prepared a sworn affidavit, in preparation of the arrest warrant for Richard, charging him with assaulting a police officer, disorderly conduct, and a host of other bullshit crimes. I acted like I was concerned that Richard had assaulted him, and we went over the affidavit together. I took him point by point through his affidavit. I lost count of his lies and had to go through the video of the interview a bunch of times. There were twelve material lies, which he affirmed to us, so, besides the perjured affidavit, we have 12 additional counts of making a false statement to the FBI. Plus, a host of other charges that the AUSA will figure out once it gets through legal review this morning. And that's not even the most serious of the charges, like attempted murder of a witness in a federal investigation."

"Where is Tim now?"

"He's being held downtown until we can have the probable cause hearing, and then we'll get the grand jury to issue the indictment. Hopefully the probable cause hearing will happen today or tomorrow -- we have 72 hours after the arrest to get that done. The AUSA is going to ask that he be held in jail due to his risk of harm to Richard."

"Great work! I knew you'd nail him. The firm is planning to file a civil suit on Richard's behalf and release the video at 9 a.m. this morning. Will that affect your investigation?"

"Not at all. Our work on this specific incident with Tim is done. Of course, I don't have to tell you that we don't try our cases in the press, and we won't be releasing any information beyond what's in the four corners of the indictment. But it could be problematic for you, coming in as the U.S. Attorney -- I don't know when that special ethical rule about statements to the media begins to apply to you."

"No worries. I'm not involved in the civil case at all. Jonathan Kennedy is handling it."

"Wow. Bringing out the big gun, huh? That's a powerful message. So, Richard has a thousand-lawyer law firm supporting him. Awesome. He deserves it."

Karen couldn't agree more. She let Jonathan and Richard know that Ken had said that the civil suit would not affect the FBI investigation, so they were good to go.

Chris arranged for a messenger to be at the court door when the court opened for business, so the complaint could be filed immediately after 9:00 a.m. At 9:30, Jonathan held a very well-attended press conference -- he had personally talked to his contacts at the news stations, cable networks, and the print and social media press to let them know -- on the plaza in front of the federal court building, with Richard at his side. Karen watched it on live local television because, as soon-to-be U.S. Attorney, she didn't want to participate in a civil lawsuit press conference in a case that had a related federal criminal component.

Jonathan had also, quite brilliantly, privately and "off-the-record," told his media contacts that they "might" want to view a copy of the video file which had been filed with the Complaint. Jonathan did this off-the-record so Reilly's lawyers could not claim that Richard's lawyers had done anything to intentionally taint the jury pool. By noon, the video of Tim Reilly strangling Richard had 5 million views.

While the team was still celebrating and, at the same time, finalizing the records to turn over to the FBI, Ken called Karen's cell. He needed to see her immediately -- he was on his way upstairs. He wanted to meet with the entire team, but with each person alone. He started with Karen, in her office with the door closed.

"Yesterday morning, I was thinking about the threats against you in the Willkommen case. You know, Reilly said that they checked all the CCTV at the four places where the threats were sent, but they didn't show anything?"

"Yeah, I remember."

"Well, as I thought about that, it seemed fishy. For example, how could CCTV cameras at a busy downtown donut shop, in the middle of a workday, ever show nothing? Obviously, people would have been there, and many of the people would have been on their phones. So, I decided to watch the videos myself. I tried to get the evidence logs to find out where the videos were stored, but guess what? There are no evidence logs. Either the logs -- FOUR logs -- went missing, or no officer ever went to any of those places to begin with. So, I sent agents to get the videos of your threats first thing this morning. Many businesses erase everything every 10 days, or every week, as the video gets written over with new video, but three of the four places still had the video, which we've now watched. And, get this -- all four places said that no police had ever requested the videos for that day."

"Holy shit. Tim just made that up?"

"Seems like it. And here's why. Tim Reilly is in one of those videos. He's on his phone, typing, at the precise time that the threatening email was sent from the donut shop on Wacker."

"Are you fucking kidding me?" Karen replied with shock.

Ken opened up his secure FBI computer and showed the video to Karen. Not only was it clearly Tim Reilly, he was in full uniform. How brazen.

"I don't get it. Why would he threaten me? I barely knew Richard then, and it was before I got started with the investigation."

"I don't know. We can't figure that out either. That's why I'm separately interviewing everyone on your team -- to see if anyone has any idea. But I want you to look at the videos from the other places and see if you recognize anyone."

Ken took her through the video from the coffee shop. There were two cameras, and they looked at every angle, again and again. Karen came up with nothing.

Then Ken had her look at the video from the donut shop down the block. The video was very grainy, but about 12 seconds in, Karen said, "Isn't that Judge Smith?" The man Karen had identified was ordering coffee at the counter, then another camera showed that he sat down at a table and was typing on his phone.

"I don't see how you think that's Judge Smith. The guy is wearing a MAGA hat, and Judge Smith was the head of the Chicago Democratic party. But, you know, it does look kind of like Judge Smith," he added, perplexed.

"Zoom in," Karen asked. "Look," she told him after he'd done so, "it's the glasses. I sat across the table from Judge Smith in his chambers about ten months ago on a case. His glasses are a unique shape, rectangular, but not quite. And then there's the color. His glasses have this light green undertone in the right light. And there's a slight crack in the frame in the top left that catches the eye every once in a while and makes a streak inside the frame. Like . . . right there." Karen pointed at the screen. "That is DEFINITELY Judge Smith."

"And the answer to your question about why he would wear a MAGA hat -- the obvious answer is that he was probably trying to avoid being recognized."

Ken smiled. "I worked with you long enough to know that when you remember a visual detail, you are always right. But I still can't believe that Judge Smith would have any reason to do this. He's a federal judge. He has a lot to lose and nothing to gain. Why would he send you a death threat by email in a case that he has nothing to do with?"

"Why don't you get a limited warrant on the GPS info for his devices. See if he was there. And, if he was, try to get a full warrant to get the content off his devices, the emails, all of it. By the way, I'm not suggesting this as your future boss, but as a citizen and a victim of the crime."

Ken looked concerned. "Okay, as you know, you will definitely have a conflict on this case once you take office. But I like your idea, because there's no way we'll get a warrant to look at any of the content of a federal judge's devices just based on your ID of his glasses. I'll also have someone look into those tracking services we talked about yesterday. Maybe we can verify that he was there without getting a warrant from publicly-available records.

"We have Tim's phone, work computer, work iPad, and, at this moment, the agents are finishing up the no-knock search to collect all the devices in his home. They started at 4:00 a.m. If Tim was using a geo-locator service to track you and Richard, we will hopefully find that out in a couple of days."

Karen immediately thought of Tim's wife Sally and their kids. How horrifying to have your husband not come home -- she was sure he would normally have told Sally something to make her not worry, but he probably didn't get that chance. And then to wake up to the FBI breaking in the door in the middle of the night with a search warrant and stand outside in your pajamas as they ripped your house apart in quiet, suburban Winnetka. With the kids. They wouldn't even be allowed to get in their car to leave, as the cars would be included in the search warrant. But if you politely knock at the door and wait for someone to answer, evidence, quite literally, goes down the toilet.

"I know, it's hard to believe, but I'm telling you that guy in the video is Judge Smith. I'm 100% certain of it. Also, do you think forensics can read what he's got up on his phone screen? The image looks pretty clear, maybe it can be enhanced?"

"Good idea. I'll ask. I'm going to need you to sign an affidavit about the glasses for the warrant. And one more thing," Ken paused. "I'm telling you this additional piece not as the future boss but because you and Richard Adams are identified as victims in the Tim Reilly case. Tim was about 30 minutes from having Richard arrested last night. The affidavit was signed. All he needed was a judge to sign off on the arrest warrant. Can I meet with Richard now? I want to tell him about that. The victim advocate also needs to hear your input, and Richard's too, on whether you want Tim held in jail or released pending trial. You need to give the victim advocate all the reasons why you don't feel safe with him on the outside."

Karen called Richard to let him know Ken would be coming to his office.

"Before I take you to talk to Richard," she told Ken, "there's something you need to know. He has terrible PTSD from childhood trauma."

"I know. We got a copy of the criminal referral from Judge Carroll yesterday. She wrote a pretty detailed referral for our investigation. We have to accommodate his disability and offer him the opportunity to write or text his answers in the interview. She cited Richard's articles in the law journals as authority. The referral document itself is not public, or I would give it to you. His work is very impressive, and he's breaking new ground already. We were also directed to inquire about the circumstances of Richard being taken into custody when he was ten. I should not have told you that, but I'm sure he's going to tell you when my interview is over because I'm going to ask him about it. Apparently, she pulled his juvenile file and found it very sketchy."

Karen stood up. "Come on, I'll take you to Richard's office. And thanks for everything you guys did yesterday. You really saved the day. If Tim had arrested Richard -- even a false arrest as it was -- it would have destroyed his career forever."

"I know. That's one of the reasons why we've charged Tim with so many felonies. He's facing more than 30 years just on the witness tampering charge alone. And who knows whether, when this is done. . . . He might be facing a lot more."

"Yeah, with the threat against me, and making it look like it was about the acne drug, that's unbelievably creepy. I just don't understand why. On any of it. He was one of my best friends."

"Me neither, but that's what the FBI is for. Let us do our work. You guys need to step back."

"We are, Ken. We've cancelled the interviews, and we've gotten permission from all the witnesses to give you the records we have. It's your case now. Completely."

"Thanks, Karen. You guys have done amazing work on this -- as you always do."

Karen walked Ken to Richard's office, and Richard welcomed Ken in and closed the door.

When Karen got back to her office, Chris was standing at her desk with her office phone to her ear, waiting for Karen.

"Hey, I've got someone who is adamant about talking to you. She says she cannot give me her name, but that you will know her when you talk to her. She says it is extremely important. She says she knows that Tim Reilly was arrested last night, and she has information about Tim Reilly that will help Richard Adams. Do you want to take the call?"

"Does she sound like a lunatic?" Karen asked. These high-profile cases always brought out some crazies, but Karen had found that every once in a while, one of them knew something helpful.

"Actually, no. She sounds pretty direct and smart."

"Okay, I'll pick it up in my office." Karen went into her office and closed the door. She wished she could record the call, but Illinois law required that every party on the call had to consent, and she didn't need a felony right now.

221

Chapter Forty

On the phone, to Karen's surprise, was the last person she expected -- Sanctimonious Helen Harris. To Karen's understanding, Helen spent her spare time when she wasn't on duty as a State Trooper teaching bible study, and protesting at abortion sites, transgender bathrooms and gay rights events. Why would she take time out of her busy schedule to help Richard? But Karen always had the impression that Helen didn't like Tim much -- although she also thought Helen didn't like her much either.

"I'm terrified, Karen," Helen blurted out, and then she started talking so quickly that her words barely made sense. "You and I disagree about a lot of things, but I read about Richard's lawsuit today, and I can tell you we agree about one thing: Richard. I've known him since he was a toddler. His Mom and I, although we had different views, we set up a play group when our boys were two. My son played with Richard after school and on weekends from the time Richard was two until he was taken into state custody when he was ten. Richard was over my house at least weekly. My son went to school with him in Evanston. They were in the same class when Richard's mother was killed. Richard has the right to know the truth. I'm scared to death. This isn't about losing my job -- I can go to jail over this. I'm calling from a burner phone. Please don't ever call my office number, work cell, or private cell. If you want to talk to me, you need to call me on this number from a burner phone too, okay?"

"Okay." Karen was being polite, but the truth was that she was thinking that Helen had lost her fucking mind.

"I'm teaching a bible study class tonight at the East Presby. The class should end at 8. I can text you from this phone when the last person has left. Can you meet me on the second floor? In the closet next to the woman's room? I want a room with no windows. I'll leave the side door in the alley unlocked." The more she talked, the more agitated she sounded.

"Sure. Can you tell me what this is about?"

"No. Not here. Not on the phone. Tonight. And promise me that you won't tell anyone about this. No one. Except please tell Richard. He needs to know. But don't bring him. Just come by yourself, okay?"

"Okay, but just to be clear, you're not my client so I can't withhold information on the basis of client-attorney privilege. If I were to get subpoenaed, I can't promise confidentiality. Also, the FBI is on this case now. I'm not supposed to be involved."

"I'm not talking to the FBI. I'll talk to you because I trust you. You're it. No one else."

"Okay."

"If I get subpoenaed, I will tell the truth. I've been praying about this all day. If I go to jail, it's God's will. I know I am doing what Jesus would do."

Yup, she's definitely gone off the fucking deep end, Karen thought to herself. This was the last thing she needed to be doing tonight. And she doubted if God would be involved in deciding whether to prosecute Helen Harris. But there was never a question about Helen's honesty. If Helen said she had information, there was no question that she had *something*, although Karen couldn't imagine what it might be.

Or was there? Could this be a set up? Was this how the threat was going to be implemented? Helen sounded so irrational and crazy, like she was under duress. Was someone putting her up to this? Maybe Karen shouldn't go. Pretend the call never happened.

Richard confirmed that he had known Helen and her son, but he said that his Dad moved to a different neighborhood in Evanston after he remarried, on the advice of Richard's therapist who was concerned about the old house triggering his trauma because of all of the memories. He hadn't seen either Helen or her son since he was ten. Like Karen, Richard thought the family was a bit "off," but he told Karen that, "Mrs. Harris' heart was always in the right place. She has never been anything but kind to me. I think you should go."

Chapter Forty-One

Karen got to the church around 7:30 p.m. and drove around the perimeter. There were a few cars parked there, probably for the bible study class, maybe six in total. Other than that, the area was dead for blocks in every direction. No one was walking around, no one was in a car, and Karen's car was the only one on the road. She decided to run to the pharmacy to pick up a few things, and then she drove by a second time at 7:50. Everything looked the same as before, so she parked and waited for Helen's call. Soon, people started exiting the building and leaving in their cars, and only one car was left. Karen hoped the car was Helen's and not some hitman's. Or maybe the hitman was Helen.

Helen called at 8:00. She was always fastidiously punctual. She sounded nervous but not crazy. Karen decided to go in.

Karen locked her car and walked to the side alley. There was a metal door, unlocked as Helen had promised. She entered the building into what was obviously a fire stairwell and went up to the second floor. The lights were off, so she guided her path in the stairwell with her phone screen on dim. She got to the second floor, passed the woman's room in the unlit hallway, and then found the closet next to it. Helen was inside, waiting. An easy place to kill her with no witnesses and no one to hear her scream?

It was a dimly-lit janitor's closet with a single light bulb hanging from an outlet in the ceiling, filled with mops and soap buckets, with shelves holding paper towels, toilet paper, and commercial-sized bottles of cleaning fluid. And an unmistakable bleach smell, but at least it wasn't overwhelming. Helen had put two child-sized chairs by a small cabinet against the wall. She was sitting in one and motioned for Karen to take the other.

Karen sat down as Helen started talking a mile a minute, as though the faster she said it all, the sooner she could get out of there and leave things in God's hands. So fast that Karen was completely lost within seconds. And Helen was also whispering.

"Can you back up a bit?" Karen said. "I don't understand."

"I mentioned to you. I knew Richard when he was little. I knew Rachel, his mom Rachel. I knew his Dad Kent and his sister Dennie. I still see Kent all the time around Evanston. After Rachel was shot, it was horrible, for Richard, for Dennie and Kent, and for everyone who knew them. It was beyond horrible what Richard went through. I knew all about Richard's hospitalizations after his mom died when they were happening. He was very depressed -- you could see it from across the room -- and it took him a long time to get back on track. Personally, I think he blamed himself for Rachel's death, regardless of how many times we all told him that it was God's will, and that he couldn't have stopped it.

"But then, literally, one day, and I don't know why, he was just better. And he was better for a period of years -- I don't know how many, but it was years -- before Tim took him into custody. Richard always got great grades in school and was perfectly behaved. He was the class academic star before his mom died and that never changed. He was always perfectly behaved when he was at my house. And he was at my house the day before Tim took him into custody. We had a birthday party after school for him and Billy-- their birthdays are just a couple of days apart. Not only was Richard smiling and happy the whole time, he asked if he could help me do the dishes afterward. He was a perfect kid, and he had been that way for, I don't know, I would say, four or five years at that point. There was no sign of depression. No sign of out-of-control behavior. Nothing. I mean, anyone would feel blessed to have a kid like that, you know? He was perfect.

"Then, when I heard from Billy that Tim had taken Richard into custody in the middle of the Valentine's Day party at school, I knew something wasn't right, because there was nothing wrong with Richard. I didn't know what to do. I had been a trooper for less than a year. I was still in my probationary period. I didn't feel secure enough in my job to even ask, but I got up the courage. Tim told me a few days later that Kent had called DCFS and said that he couldn't handle Richard anymore and begged the court to issue an order to take him into custody. But I knew that wasn't true. The school called Kent the moment that Tim took Richard, and Kent was calling the barracks nonstop, every five minutes, for hours. I spoke to Kent multiple times that day. He was distraught.

He and I both talked about how Richard was doing fine, and this was a mistake. That somehow the judge had confused the files of two kids or something.

"It was a holiday weekend and Tim wasn't back until Tuesday. I heard him tell Kent that the school had called DCFS, asking that Richard be taken into custody. I knew that was also a lie.

"I've been praying about this for fourteen years Karen. I didn't know what to do with this information.

"I was there when Judge Smith's order was faxed to the barracks. And I remembered that Tim was actually supposed to be off that day. Tim had called in sick. But then he came in five minutes before the order arrived. It was like he knew the order was coming. He personally picked it up off the fax machine. And then someone else offered to take Richard to Southern since Tim was sick, but Tim insisted on doing it. He said it was easy work to do when you don't feel well, so he could save the sick time.

"When things came into the fax machine at the barracks back then, they were stored in a file on the fax machine. Then, when the file got full, they got deleted. You could usually get faxes going back a couple of days. So, the next day, when I was alone in the barracks when everyone else was out on a call, I retrieved Richard's custody order from the storage file, printed it and kept it. I brought it home, and I saved the paper copy. I also scanned it and kept a digital copy. I know that order is a confidential juvenile record. and what I did is a crime. But I felt like God put me in the barracks that day for a reason.

"And then, over the next however many years, the same thing happened to thirty different boys when I was in the office. Usually on the Friday afternoon of a holiday weekend. I think maybe that was so the family couldn't reach anyone until Tuesday. The orders kept coming on a pretty regular basis, at least three or five a year -- just on the days that I was there and knew about it. I wasn't in the barracks all that often since we're supposed to be out and about in the community, you know? I think it is likely that there were a lot more orders. And then, the orders stopped coming. Looking back, they might have stopped coming when Tim went to teach at the academy. Or maybe they came on days that I wasn't at the barracks. I don't know."

Helen reached under her shirt and pulled out a folded bunch of papers. "There are over thirty orders. Every order is a custody order for a boy. I know it's a crime for me to give you these confidential juvenile records, but I believe that every one of them probably constitutes a crime against a child, and I don't know what to do. If there is any possibility of getting to the bottom of it, I know you can do it. You've already gotten Tim in jail. I believe God is telling me to give these to you.

"Every order was signed by Judge Smith. Every single one of these kids was picked up and taken to Southern or Stern Harrison by Tim Reilly, often after Tim came into the barracks five minutes before the order came in, usually on his day off or when he had called out sick. He knew the orders were coming. He stood by the fax machine waiting for the fax to start coming in. If you get his time records, you can probably prove that he put in overtime for those days because he was scheduled off or out sick. Or maybe he didn't put in time so there wouldn't be a record of what he did. But there have to be records that he transported each of those kids. And there should be a log of his time proving that he was in the barracks when the fax came in. See? The faxes all have the date and time at the top.

"I don't know these kids. I don't know if they were good kids like Richard or kids who were troubled or struggling to find their way, but I know that these orders were not done in the normal course. It's just not normal for the State Police to transport kids being taken into custody as unmanageable or depressed. Those kids are always transported by DCFS by trained social workers who know how to handle kids, never by the state police like they're criminals in the back of a squad car, unless maybe an older kid killed someone. What happened here is so wrong on so many levels.

"So, now you know everything I know and you have the records. I don't know what they prove, but I know that, if anyone can figure that out, you and Richard can.

"You and Richard are doing God's work, Karen. And God told me to give these to you. Please tell Richard that I have prayed for him every single day since his mother died, and I won't stop praying until you find a way to end this and put the people who did this to Richard and the other children in jail for what they did."

Karen was stunned. "Helen, I don't know what to say. I'm just overwhelmed. This is the piece that we were missing. To this day, Richard has no idea why he was taken into custody. It will help him to know these facts, although it's obviously upsetting to learn that there were other boys who were removed from their homes under similar circumstances. Do you have any idea about what Tim's involvement is? Is it money?" Karen was hopeful that it was money, because she did not want to believe even worse things about Tim.

"Honestly, Karen, I have no idea, other than that he knew the orders were coming and he made sure that he was the one to get the order and to transport the boy. And there might be other orders. These are the ones that came in when I was in the office."

"Helen," Karen hesitated, "I'm very nervous about just taking these papers with me in this form. Is it okay if I scan these documents right now on my phone and upload them to my secure online account?"

"They're yours, you can do whatever you want to with them. But please do let Richard know that I gave them to you."

"Absolutely. And there's another piece. The FBI has now taken over our investigation of child sexual abuse at these facilities. I need to give these records to them. Is that okay with you?"

Helen looked like she was going to throw up and faint at the same time. She gripped the cross on the necklace she was wearing.

"You do whatever you need to do. And that counts for everything I told you, too. As I said, I've done a lot of praying for many years about this, and I've prayed all day today. God did not put children on this earth to be sexually abused. What happened to Richard still makes me cry every time I think about it. It needs to stop. And God gave me access to these records for a reason."

"Is it okay if I tell the FBI your name, and tell them that you gave me these records and told me these things, and have them contact you?"

"Yes. As I think about it, yes. Because it's the right thing to do."

"Thank you, Helen. Richard will be very moved by your actions."

"I need to get out of here, Karen. I'm going to set the back door to lock behind you on your way out."

"Okay. Thanks again. I think you are going to be a hero when the full story is told."

"Thanks, but Richard is the hero, not me. I knew about this for years and did nothing -- absolutely nothing -- and that's a shame I will take to my grave. I watched for years as those orders came in and I did nothing. And the worst part is, I knew what happened to Richard was wrong, and I never said a word to anyone before now. If I had done the right thing at the time, maybe he would not have been abused. Maybe his life would have been different. I owed him that -- he was a little boy for God's sake -- and I failed."

Karen noticed Helen wiping away tears in the dark hallway as she started to walk away.

Then she turned back to face Karen. "One more thing, it's not important, but I just want you to know. I never told a soul about the condoms." Karen was speechless as Helen walked away.

Karen read the records as she scanned them to her cloud account. Unlike Richard's order, every order was very detailed and seemed to have a legitimate basis for placing each boy in residential custody. The kids were mostly either violent and/or sex offenders, or addicted to drugs and in need of long-term residential treatment. A few were arsonists; a couple had scary gun offenses. Nothing seemed out of the ordinary. All of the orders seemed appropriate.

Karen sent Ken Shapiro an email with a secure link to the records. That way, if someone killed her, the FBI would have the documents and would know that they came from Helen. As Karen stepped out into the alley, she quickly looked in every direction to check for someone lurking, but saw nothing concerning and walked toward her car. She stooped down to make sure no one was underneath her car, and circled her car looking for wires. It looked okay, so she got in and started driving home. She was glad that at least Richard's apartment was so secure. But if the police want to get you, nowhere is safe.

Ken called her instantly. "I thought you agreed today that you were off this investigation!!"

"I *am* off the case. Helen said she would only talk to me. I figured she was just nuts -- you know how she is -- and I'd save you some time. I was shocked when she handed me the papers. I convinced her to let me give the information to you. She is very concerned about potential criminal repercussions because of the juvenile records. I told her that I was sending the info to you because the FBI is heading the investigation, and I am no longer involved."

"I'm reading them now. This looks like the break we desperately needed, but I have no idea what it means or why. The orders all look legit."

"I know. I've always judged Helen for her holier-than-thou views, and I feel really bad about that now. All these years, she was getting and keeping these records. For the kids. With a huge personal risk for her. But I agree, the orders all look like they were justified."

"By the way, did you hear? Your security clearance went through and your nomination is on the Senate floor next Thursday."

Karen quickly checked her email and found an email from Shondra that was sent while she was driving to see Helen.

"Yeah, I just read it. Fingers crossed!"

Ken added, "We have a video meeting with Washington tomorrow about this case. If you're confirmed, another US Attorney's office has to supervise it. You have a conflict and can't be involved."

"I totally agree with that, of course."

"Okay. I'll let them know that you agree. Good work on this, by the way, but please direct all new witnesses to me before you talk to them."

"Thanks. Will do. Sorry about this one -- I really think it couldn't have been avoided."

"These records are scary as hell. Will Helen talk to us?"

"Maybe now. I think I talked her into it. Can you offer her some protection, and protection from prosecution for the juvenile records? I think she'll need it."

"Understood. We're very limited with protection, as you know, but I'll see what our options might be. The juvenile records are a state crime, so it will be up to the Illinois Attorney General to give her immunity. And this will all be another reason to keep Reilly in jail, but then we would have to disclose her as a witness, and we won't be ready to do that until after we've interviewed her."

Karen could not wait to talk to Richard.

Chapter Forty-Two

"Is this a good time to talk?"

"Yeah. What happened with . . . I don't want to say the name on the phone, just in case."

"You weren't the only one. She has 30 commitment orders just like yours."

Silence.

"You ok?"

Silence.

"Richard?"

"Yeah, I'm here. Hard to talk."

She could hear him crying.

"Also, I didn't get to talk to you about my meeting with Ken about the threats. It looks like the threats against me were from Tim Reilly and Judge Smith."

"What?"

"The FBI has them on video at two of the places where the threats originated, simultaneously, at the time the threats were sent, typing on their phones."

"Why? I thought Reilly was your good friend!"

"Yeah, I know. I'm at a total loss. He seemed so concerned when he met me outside the house when I got back from dropping you off that Sunday. Total bullshit. To think that the threat was from him all along. And a federal judge?"

"Maybe Reilly was already using that tracking info and knew I had been at your home for the weekend."

"Could be. I have no idea. This whole thing is so upsetting, and I don't understand it at all. Why would either of them threaten me? I barely know Judge Smith. I had a couple of cases with him, but they were nothing special."

"Judge Smith issued my custody order."

"And he issued all the orders that Helen has for the other 29 boys."

There was a knock on Karen's bedroom door. "Come in!"

Joey and Cyndi came in together. They both looked very upset. "Mom, can we talk to you?" She quickly got off the phone with Richard.

"What's up?"

Joey began, "I remembered something. I'm not sure, maybe it's not important, but it was keeping me awake, and I talked to Cyndi about it just now, and we need to talk to you about it."

"What honey?"

"You know how Mr. Reilly takes the team up to his cabin in Door County every summer?"

"Yes," Karen said, getting very concerned that Joey was about to disclose that he had been abused.

"Well, two years ago, he said that there wasn't enough room for Amir, so Amir had to share his bed. But there actually was plenty of room because we were all just sleeping in our sleeping bags on the floor."

"Okay, thank you for telling me. You did the right thing. Do you remember anything else about that?"

"No, that's all, but now I'm wondering if Amir was safe."

"This might mean nothing, or it might be very important. I'm going to let the man at the FBI who is heading the investigation know. They will probably want to interview you. But it's important that I not ask you any questions, and we don't talk about it until they interview you first. Is that okay?"

"Yeah, sure, but that sounds scary, being interviewed by the FBI. Could I get in trouble?"

"No, of course not Joey. You just have to make sure that you tell the truth. Don't exaggerate, don't talk about something unless you're sure and you really remember it. You're doing the right thing by being brave and coming forward with information that might or might not lead to something. Your information might be very important, or it might not be important at all. But it is great that you have the courage to tell. That's how the FBI solves important cases -- by people having the courage to come forward because they have information that *might* be important.

"But I do need to ask you both something." Karen looked at Joey carefully, and then Cyndi, to judge their demeanor. "Has Tim ever done anything to either of you that made you uncomfortable?"

"No, Mom, never, we actually just talked about that," Cyndi said. Joey nodded in agreement.

Joey shook his head. "I don't get how he could be so nice to me and do what he did to Richard."

"We've talked about this before. Abusers don't abuse every child they encounter. The fact that Tim has never done anything to you doesn't mean that he hasn't hurt someone else, but still, right now, other than assaulting Richard in the elevator, we don't know that Tim has ever hurt anyone, okay?"

"Sure Mom, I understand. Should I talk to Amir about it? Should you talk to his mom?"

"No, sweetie, we have to let the FBI handle it. I'll text Ken Shapiro now to tell him what you've told me."

Karen texted Ken to let him know what Joey had reported. He was still awake and responded immediately.

"Will set up forensic interview asap."

Lying in bed, too wound up to sleep, Karen realized that Shawn at the front desk had said that he knew that Reilly was a bad cop. What was that all about? Something they needed to follow up on.

She called Richard about Shawn, and told him that she was going to ask Ken to interview him.

"Actually, Karen, we need to talk to Shawn. Shawn's not going to talk to the FBI. He doesn't trust law enforcement at all."

"How do you know Shawn that well?"

"I generally leave the office at 11 p.m., which is when he usually gets off work. We walk a few blocks together until he reaches the el. He made more than a few comments about not trusting the police *before* I was assaulted by Reilly. That's why he was watching him like a hawk in the elevator. There's no way Shawn will talk to the FBI."

They decided she'd call Ken in the morning to discuss it.

Chapter Forty-Three

Karen called Ken to let him know about Shawn as soon as she got to the office. Ken said that they would follow up.

Ken told Karen that he, too, had news. They were going to interview Amir later that day at the child advocacy center. Meanwhile, the FBI had already done criminal history and background checks for all of the kids identified in the court orders. "This might just be a coincidence, but one of those kids is the younger brother of one of the four men who were convicted for sending death threats to Judge Smith."

"Wow, well that makes sense as to why he would have sent a death threat to Judge Smith."

"Well, actually, that's the piece that doesn't sit well with me. You would have expected him to say, in his confession, that he was angry with Judge Smith for sending his little brother away. But he didn't say that. He said he was angry that Judge Smith had ordered the seizure of his mother's house, and that his little brother and sister were out on the street. He never mentioned Judge Smith's custody order."

"Maybe he didn't know it was Judge Smith who ordered his brother into custody? Those aren't public proceedings, and the older brother would not have been allowed into the courtroom. I doubt that anyone in the family even knew the judge's name," Karen offered. "Or maybe the seizure was the final straw?"

"I know, but there's something that I just can't put my finger on. This just doesn't sound right, but I don't know why.

"We have four teams going to re-interview all four men today, along with the mom and sister of Jamal -- Jamal's the one whose house was seized. We cannot interview Jamal's younger brother, because he is deceased. But we are going to try to find out about his death. Maybe that too is somehow related, maybe not. Anyway, we're going to try to find out.

"Also, we reviewed the files and evidence logs on the old threats case. Reilly told me, back then that all four guys were on the CCTV videos at the four places where we know the threats were sent from, and I found his police report from setting it all out. But, again, there's something that doesn't fit. No evidence log lists those videos as ever being made a part of the evidentiary record. It was a federal case, so we should have a chain of custody log for each video, and we don't have any logs. We also don't have the videos."

"That's really odd."

"Tell me about it. Did you ever work on a case where four items of evidence, and their evidence logs, went missing? This would have been four different logs, because the videos were collected at four different locations."

"That makes no sense, although it wouldn't be the first time that the State Police accidentally messed up on an evidence log. Maybe it's in their evidence locker, and it just never made its way to you."

"That's certainly possible. A lot to think about, anyway. And, oh -- I just got an email right now. The lab's facial recognition technology agrees with you: it's Judge Smith in that video. Man, who would have guessed? That should help us get the warrant, but what the fuck, why would Judge Smith be sending you and your Wilkommen team threatening emails? Do you have any idea at all?"

"Not a clue. I'm at a total loss. I've known Tim Reilly for 20 years. He's David's best friend, and Judge Smith -- it just makes no sense. I barely know Judge Smith. I had a couple of cases before him that were just routine matters. Even if Tim or Judge Smith had a relative die from one of those Wilkommen drugs -- it makes no sense that they would threaten me. Tim, in particular, would know that the threats would do nothing to me. He knows that I get threats often, he knows that I accept them as part of my job. I mean, he knows that I get scared and constantly check my doors and windows, but he also would know that no threat would stop me from going forward with a case."

"Hmmm. Do you think that David could have put Tim up to this for some reason?" Ken asked.

"Definitely not. David was distraught that night. He was at the house. He was terrified and very upset about the threats. He was actually nice to me for five minutes. He wasn't making that up. He's not smart enough to be such a good actor. I'm confident that David did not know that the threats were from Tim."

"Karen, this is all so disturbing. I feel like those four men in jail might have the answers that we need, but I can't imagine they'll cooperate.

"Oh, and one more thing. We're interviewing Helen Harris today. Did you talk to Richard about the orders? Does he know any of the kids?"

"No, I didn't share them because they are juvenile records. You'll need to be the person to do that."

"Okay. I'll set that up. He's really remarkable, Karen. It's amazing all that he has accomplished, given what he's been through, and what he is doing now to protect kids when so many people failed to protect him."

"Yup."

Chris buzzed her to remind her that it was time to leave for federal court -- Reilly's bail hearing was in 30 minutes, and Richard was waiting.

"Are you still going to the bail hearing too?" Karen asked.

"Yeah, we'll meet you in the lobby."

Chapter Forty-Four

There were about a dozen people from the firm at the bail hearing to support Richard, including the entire team on the investigation, as well as Chris, Jonathan, Denise, and some of the summer clerks, including Richard's friend, Jackson. They pretty much filled up all the pews in the front of the courtroom.

Richard's family was also there. Kent, his stepmother Susan, and his sister Dennie. Karen got to meet them all, and they seemed very nice. She sat with Richard in the front public row, directly behind the FBI agents on the case.

Karen was somewhat relieved when she saw Tim Reilly's attorney, even though he was one of the best criminal lawyers in the city. He wasn't one of those buffoons who viewed every press contact as a client development opportunity, and who defamed witnesses in press conferences to try to bully the prosecutors into settling. Those tactics rarely worked, but witnesses would get timid and often distraught. It's difficult enough to be a crime victim and do the right thing by reporting the crime, and then get your name dragged through the press like you were at fault. She knew Tim's lawyer wouldn't do that to Richard. For one thing, he was smart enough to know that it would only piss off Richard and make things worse for his client. Victims always have some input in plea negotiations, and Richard's opposition to a plea deal could only make Tim's life harder.

The courtroom was packed. Journalists were sitting in the empty jury box, as judges generally allow them to do when the regular rows are filled with spectators. A sketch artist also was in the jury box with her easel and materials ready. Cameras are not allowed in federal court, so the artist's rendering of the proceeding would be the only image that the public would see.

Tim's wife Sally was there, but fortunately not the kids. Karen always despised the defendants who brought their kids to bail hearings to show the judge how much the children would suffer if the judge sent mom or dad to jail. Of course, the kids only suffered worse by *watching* mom or dad get carted off in shackles.

The sketch artist walked up to Richard and introduced herself. Karen knew the artist well -- her cases were often high profile, and she had bought a few portraits of herself in court that hung in her office. The artist asked Richard whether, "due to the nature of the circumstances," he would be okay if the artist sketched him.

"You mean because I was the victim of a sex crime?" Richard asked.

"Yes, and the fact that there is a lot of juvenile information that the public might figure out relates to you."

"Please feel free to sketch me and name me. I'm not ashamed of what happened to me, and I think the public should know what these people did."

Karen had never felt so proud of anyone.

Karen looked around trying to figure out who the rest of the people were and, to her surprise, she noticed Shawn in the back row. It looked like he was trying to hide his face. He was looking down at his lap, with his hand partly covering his face. He was there with a woman around his age -- mid-fifties -- who was doing the same thing. Her face looked like she had been crying for days. Shawn briefly touched her shoulder in support.

Judge Murphy, who was only in his late 30's and had only been on the bench a few years, was hearing a number of matters that morning. When Tim's case was called, the marshals brought him into the courtroom, shuffling his feet in the leg irons and chains. Wearing a prison-issued orange jumpsuit and flip flops, his hands were cuffed in front of him, and he was holding some papers -- probably the court papers for the hearing -- between his fingers, along with a pen. He hadn't shaved, and the stubble was the first thing Karen noticed. His jaw was bruised and swollen -- a Ken had described -- and he looked dirty, like he had not bathed. He probably hadn't slept much if at all. All in all, he looked a wreck.

His lawyer stood up to address the judge. "Your Honor, may Director Reilly's handcuffs be removed so he can assist with his representation by writing notes to me?"

The judge turned to the Marshals. "Has the defendant been cooperative? Does he pose a risk?"

"He's been highly cooperative, Your Honor."

"Mr. Reilly, I trust that you will continue to be cooperative."

"Yes, Your Honor."

"Okay then. Please remove the handcuffs."

The marshals unlocked his cuffs, but not his leg irons, and Reilly took a seat at the table furthest from the jury box, next to his lawyer. He looked down at the table and did not make eye contact with anyone, including Sally, who was sitting in the front row on the defense side, directly behind him by a few feet. She, too, looked like she'd been crying. Sally worked at the Winnetka Village Hall where she interacted daily with members of the community. This had to be hard for her on so many levels. Karen felt like going up to Sally. How many years had they been friends? She thought of all the Bears games they'd watched together, at the stadium and at the Reilly home. But she just couldn't acknowledge Sally. Not now.

His lawyer began his argument.

"You Honor, Timothy Reilly is the Director of the State Police who has served our State with bravery, honor and distinction, for over twenty years. But lesser known is that he is a decorated war veteran, who served in the Middle East. He witnessed terrible things there, Your Honor, and upon his return, he was diagnosed with PTSD. Since that time, Your Honor, he has been receiving regular treatment through the VA for PTSD.

"Your Honor, Director Reilly should be released from custody, as he poses no risk of flight and no risk harm to anyone. I want to outline the evidence we are prepared to present today.

"Years ago, when he first returned from the Middle East, there was an incident when then-Detective Reilly was called on patrol to a domestic dispute. The man was threatening his spouse and the officers. Detective Reilly grabbed the man in self-defense, but he grabbed him by the neck -- much in the same way the video here shows him grabbing Mr. Adams' neck.

"Director Reilly was devastated by his loss of control in that situation, and he immediately self-reported his action and loss of control to his superiors and asked to be removed from patrol. In response to his request, the State Police moved him to the police academy, and --

through his admirable and distinguished service at the academy -- he advanced through the State Police in non-patrol positions until, in a few short years, he was promoted after two decades of stellar service to his current position as the Director.

"Director Reilly wants to apologize to Mr. Adams for his conduct in the elevator, as he never intended to harm Mr. Adams and never intended to threaten him in any way. Director Reilly is as horrified as we are -- even more so -- by what he sees in the video. The conduct we see on the video was completely out of his control, Your Honor. It was an uncontrollable neurological PTSD response, brought on both by his war experiences and his experiences on the patrol, which had been triggered by events earlier in the day.

"I have a letter from Director Reilly's coordinator of services at the VA, Your Honor, and she is also here to testify today if the Court requires her testimony. She describes in the letter how Director Reilly has been fully engaged in treatment for PTSD for years, was actively engaged in treatment at the time of this incident here, and plans to continue treatment upon his release."

"Counsel, please provide the letter to the marshal," Judge Morrison said.

The lawyer gave a copy to the marshal, who gave it to the judge. The government attorneys clearly already had a copy. Karen wished she could read it as well.

"We also have affidavits, Your Honor, from twenty people who know Director Reilly, including his neighbors, and people in the State Police, who attest to the fact that they were aware of Director Reilly's PTSD, and that they have never seen him be violent in any way. What happened here, Your Honor, was really a horrible aberration, caused by a documented mental illness caused by his extraordinary service to his country and his community, in a commendable 30-year career of public service. Director Reilly poses zero risk of harm to Mr. Adams or to the community at large, and should be released."

The lawyer handed the affidavits to the marshal, who handed them to the judge.

"Your Honor, also present is the Defendant's wife, Sally Reilly, who is prepared to testify that she, on one occasion, experienced the same reaction from Director Reilly, where his PTSD was triggered and he, very briefly, grabbed her by the neck. She is prepared to testify that Director Reilly was devastated by what he had done, he broke down sobbing, and immediately called his therapist at the VA. Furthermore, he has never been violent since with her since and has never been violent with their children or anyone else she knows.

"So, reason number one for release is that Director Reilly presents no risk of harm to Richard Adams or anyone else.

"Reason number two is that, legally, Your Honor, there is no possibility that the Government will ever be able to prove the requisite criminal intent in this case. What happened here was an uncontrollable neurological response, due to PTSD, which caused Director Reilly to misperceive a threat that was not there, and to respond violently. His response was completely beyond his control. There was no intent to cause harm or injury. We will be filing a motion to dismiss the charges as soon as we collect all the necessary materials. Today, we propose that Director Reilly be released on bail, with an ankle bracelet, an order of no contact with Mr. Adams and any other witnesses in this matter, and an order that he continue to pursue counseling and treatment at the VA for his PTSD as recommended by his treatment team."

A pretty good argument, Karen thought -- but total bullshit under the circumstances. Tim Reilly did have PTSD; he did self-report his problem years before after grabbing a defendant by the neck. And she wasn't surprised to hear that he once grabbed Sally -- Tim had shared with her his fear that he might do that one day. Was it possible that his PTSD was a complete bar to prosecution here? Karen had heard of a case, years before, where a judge had thrown out a case against a defendant who had bi-polar disorder who had stolen checks out of a mailbox and cashed a dozen checks. The judge had held that spending money you don't have was a common symptom of bi-polar disorder, and that the man's conduct was controlled by his mental illness and that there was no evidence of the required criminal intent. But that wasn't at all what had happened here, and she hoped the Assistant U.S. Attorney, Patricia Noble, a seasoned prosecutor, would make that clear so the relatively inexperienced judge would not be fooled.

Assistant U.S. Attorney Noble began. "Your Honor, the PTSD defense that defense counsel has raised, even assuming for the purpose of argument that it is even legally cognizable, and we believe it is not, is completely bogus and belied by the facts. The evidence shows that this was hardly a spontaneous PTSD response, but was, in fact, a calculated decision that took place over the course of hours, if not days, for the purpose, explicitly stated by the defendant and recorded with video and audio, to threaten and intimidate Mr. Adams so he would cease an investigation of grievous police misconduct. Director Reilly got access to the building prior to 5:00 p.m. The video shows that he waited in the lobby of the 59th floor for nearly an hour until his intended target, Richard Adams, stepped off the local elevator -- alone -- and got into the express elevator -- alone. So this in no way resembles a situation where the defendant stepped into the elevator and was surprised, and supposedly had his PTSD triggered, by encountering Mr. Adams. Instead, after waiting for that extended period of time -- during which time Director Reilly could have done any number of things to calm himself, including calling his therapist or his wife, or, better yet, taking the elevator to the ground floor and leaving the building. Instead, he followed Richard Adams into the elevator, threatened Mr. Adams, explicitly told Mr. Adams to stop his investigation, attempted to engage Mr. Adams such that Mr. Adams would assault him, and when that effort failed, tried to kill Mr. Adams by strangulation.

"What Director Reilly did after that event is also telling, Your Honor. He typed out a false affidavit and had it notarized, claiming that Richard Adams had assaulted him when he knew that was not true and, appallingly, took the steps necessary to have Mr. Adams, the victim of defendant's attack that sent Mr. Adams to the hospital, arrested. I should point out that defense counsel didn't bother to mention that. Mr. Reilly's patent and intentional perjury in his arrest affidavit -- hours after the brutal assault -- could not possibly have been caused by PTSD. And Mr. Reilly subsequently compounded that by telling the same lies to the FBI. Sitting with FBI agents telling them at least a dozen lies about what had happened could not possibly be attributable to PTSD.

"Moreover, Mr. Reilly also conjured an injury to his jaw to further frame Mr. Adams. The Government does not know how Mr.

246

Reilly's face was injured that night, but the video makes clear that Mr. Reilly was never injured by Mr. Adams -- as Mr. Reilly's perjured affidavit claims -- and that Mr. Reilly's jaw was not injured when he stepped out of the elevator.

"In short, this was a carefully-calculated violent crime, Your Honor, not a PTSD sudden response, which was followed, outrageously, by the filing in court of a signed and fully-executed perjured affidavit alleging probable cause to arrest Mr. Adams, and the filing of a request for an arrest warrant. In other words, defendant took all the steps necessary to arrest Richard Adams for assaulting an officer, when he knew Richard Adams had done nothing of the kind and was in fact the victim of defendant's violent and near-fatal attack.

"Your Honor, Richard Adams is a third-year law student at Northwestern. He will be Editor-in-Chief of the Law Review in the fall. An arrest like that -- even if he had been acquitted later -- would have completely destroyed his career. Yet, Director Reilly prepared those documents and prepared to arrest him. That process undoubtedly took hours. He was hardly suffering from PTSD all that time.

"Your Honor, the only reason Director Reilly is standing here in shackles, and not a falsely-accused Richard Adams, is because the elevator assault was witnessed by live video by the security staff at the front desk of the office building, and that video was recorded. Without that, Director Reilly's scheme of assault and framing an innocent law student would have been successful. This was a crime that took hours to plan, hours of waiting, and hours after that to prepare a perjured affidavit and execute a false arrest. This was precisely the opposite of a sudden-trigger PTSD response, and the Court should disregard that defense.

"Director Reilly's course of conduct shows that he is a dangerous man who needs to be held in jail, not because he has PTSD, but because he knowingly and with the requisite intent planned an assault and a false arrest in order to harm and intimidate Richard Adams, and, if released, he poses a direct risk of harm to Mr. Adams and potentially to others.

"And that brings us to the next question, Your Honor, which is 'Why Richard Adams?' Your Honor, Mr. Adams was engaged, until this week, in a pro bono investigation with his employer this summer --

one of the most prestigious firms in the City, as the Court is aware -- of what is believed to be an extensive enterprise involving criminal acts against children. We cannot comment because the Justice Department has now taken over the investigation, and we cannot comment on pending investigations. But I can inform the Court that Richard Adams was investigating a matter in which Director Reilly's conduct in the past is now being examined by the Justice Department. That was what the assault was about, Your Honor. It was a pre-planned assault to intimidate a witness in a federal investigation, and, if Mr. Reilly was unable to intimidate Mr. Adams, as was the case, Mr. Reilly's plan was to destroy Mr. Adams' credibility by charging him with a felony crime which he did not commit -- that is, if he survived the assault."

Karen was excited to see that this woman was going to be on her staff at the U.S. Attorney's Office. Her presentation to the court was brilliant. But was it enough? The judge took a recess to read all the materials.

The judge returned half-an-hour later, and addressed the packed courtroom.

"I have read the affidavits offered by defendant, and the letter from his treatment coordinator at the VA. I will accept these documents into the record. For purposes of this hearing, it is clear that the defendant can present substantial evidence that there are many people who know him well who, if called to testify, would testify that they have never known him to be violent, and that they do not believe that he would pose a risk of harm to anyone in the community, including Richard Adams. It is also clear, although I make no finding about this, that his treatment coordinator at the VA would testify that he was diagnosed with PTSD after his second tour in the Middle East, that he served honorably in the military, and that he has been engaged in active treatment for PTSD since that time, and that his wife would testify about a similar event which she claims happened several years ago when the defendant was triggered.

"I will also note, as it is undisputed, that Director Reilly has served with distinction in the State Police for many years, and that he served with distinction on the front lines in the military during a period of war in service to our country.

"However, what we have on the video is a clear incident of what a jury could find was an unprovoked act of attempted murder. Moreover, Director Reilly, after strangling Mr. Adams, did not walk out of the elevator and call for an ambulance. Nor did he, as purportedly happened in the domestic assault incident, and the incident with his wife, report his conduct to anyone after he had 'calmed down.' Instead, there is evidence upon which a jury could find that he continued in the same course of conduct by executing a false affidavit, taking the steps necessary to facilitate a false arrest, and subsequently lying to the FBI.

"I am also mindful of the order issued yesterday in Cook County family court, in a matter related to Richard Adams, where the court made a criminal referral relating to an allegation that Director Reilly had, perhaps, unlawfully revealed Mr. Adams' confidential juvenile records. While I am loath to mention Mr. Adams' name in connection with his juvenile records because those records are forever confidential as a matter of law, I am aware that Mr. Adams filed a public lawsuit this morning, in his name, bringing civil charges against Director Reilly for the allegedly unlawful release of that information. Therefore, Mr. Adams' identity as the 'victim' named as "Individual One" in the family court order has been made public by Mr. Adams. I make no finding, obviously, as to whether or not the Director actually released Mr. Adams' confidential juvenile records. However, it is concerning that Director Reilly's attack on Richard Adams allegedly began days before this assault, with the allegedly unlawful release of Mr. Adams' confidential juvenile information.

"For these reasons, I see no conditions of release which can adequately guaranty Mr. Adams' safety, and I will order that the defendant be held without bail. The defendant is also ordered to have no contact, either directly or through a third party other than his lawyer, with Mr. Adams or any of the identified witnesses.

"I recognize that there are safety risks, in any prison facility, for someone with Director Reilly's position with the state police. Therefore, I will also suggest to the prison, if Director Reilly or his counsel so request, to consider whether to place Director Reilly in a particularly secure setting, including solitary confinement. Of course, the prison facility is always in the best position to determine where an inmate should be housed and has the authority to make the final decision regardless of any suggestion from the Court, but I am adding this provision in the event that Director Reilly requests solitary confinement for his security. We will take a short break before the next case."

"All rise!"

Karen had hoped to speak to Shawn on the way out, but he and the woman were gone.

Many journalists tried to talk to Richard in the hallway, and in the front of the building. There were multiple camera crews from all the networks. Richard had now been identified both as the person Tim Reilly had assaulted, and as conducting an investigation regarding sexual abuse at youth facilities in Illinois. Richard handled the requests with respect, but he declined to comment. One of the journalists noted the fact that the indictment had indicated that Richard was investigating sexual abuse at certain boys' facilities, and she asked Richard how he had gotten involved in the investigation. Richard paused, and with the cameras rolling, said, "I wanted to investigate because I was a victim of sexual abuse at the Southern facility twelve years ago, and I wanted to make sure that children placed at similar facilities today are safe."

"Sir," the reporter said, "We have a policy of never reporting the name of a sexual assault or child sex abuse victim, but the court just named you. Are you willing to go on the record with your name, or should we not identify you?"

Richard looked directly at the cameras. "My name is Richard Adams. I was sexually abused, on a regular basis, at the Southern facility for two years, from the time I was ten years old, until I was twelve years old, and I was injured so severely that I had to have emergency surgery. I started this investigation after I learned that two of the men who had been abusing me sexually when I was twelve are still working today at Stern Harrison, twelve years after I reported their conduct at Southern. I believe that Tim Reilly assaulted me in the elevator because he wanted to silence me, but I will not be silenced."

All of the reporters started asking Richard questions at once. He declined any further comment.

There was a mob scene of reporters and spectators in front of the federal building, so Karen and Richard got in a cab to go back to the office. She held his hand, "You spoke."

"I know. Pretty cool, don't you think? I think it's because, for the first time, maybe I feel safe."

Chapter Forty-Five

Ken Shapiro called the next morning. Amir had corroborated Joey's story that he had slept in the bed with Tim Reilly at the cabin; that Tim told the kids that it was because there were not enough room; and that it was not true. But he said that it was because he had a bedwetting problem back then, and that Tim let him sleep in the bed with him on a special pad so his friends wouldn't find out about his bedwetting. He had nothing but positive things to say about Tim, and he was adamant that Tim never abused him, never touched him and never did anything inappropriate.

Amir's mom corroborated the story about the bedwetting, and that sleeping in the bed with Tim was pre-arranged. Molly Klein -- the best child forensic interviewer in the district -- did the interviews.

Molly felt that Amir was telling the truth. While it is well-known that boys routinely do not disclose sexual abuse, there were no signs that he was anything other than 100% truthful. She reported that he had shown no change in demeanor, no indication of trauma -- basically nothing to indicate that he was withholding traumatic information.

"I'm glad to hear that," Karen said, truthfully. She was honestly relieved that Tim -- the man her kids had probably spent more time with than anyone other than their parents -- might not be a child sex offender. He clearly was not the man she thought he was, but she was still holding out hope that he wasn't *that*.

Ken continued, "We interviewed Helen Harris, and she was very helpful. She told us the same things she told you. But other than that, we're striking out. The four guys in jail all refused to meet with us. Jamal's mother and sister both hung up on us and slammed the door of their apartment. Shawn Jeffries, the security guard, was very polite, but said he wouldn't talk to us either.

"The thing is, not one of them said, 'I don't know anything' or 'I don't remember.' We think they all know something but are afraid or reluctant to talk to us. So, I'm wondering. . . . Richard is all over the news. He's a hero to so many people. Do you think he would be willing to interview these people? He would have to strictly follow our guidelines and the law because this is at our request, so the rules would apply the same as though we sent an FBI agent. But maybe they would feel comfortable talking to him."

"I'll ask him. Richard wants this case solved more than anyone. I just don't know if he can do interviews. He's been terrific at interviewing witnesses so far in the investigation, but, you know, he has great difficulty speaking about these things."

"I know, but did you see him on tv? He was amazing."

"Yeah, he was. I'll have him give you a call if he's up to it."

Karen walked down the hall to Richard's office.

Chapter Forty-Six

"No way. I can't. You know I can't."

"Actually, I think you can. You did an amazing job on the witness interviews."

"That's different."

"Why?"

"Those interviews weren't about me. This is about me."

"You were able to speak to a whole gaggle of reporters yesterday. You're much stronger than you realize, stronger still with Reilly in jail. He can't hurt you anymore, and you're the person who was strong enough to put him there. You don't need to talk to these witnesses about what happened to you -- they all know from watching the tv reports that are now all over the internet."

"Maybe."

"You just have to be yourself and explain that you want to protect today's kids in those facilities by finding evidence of what happened in the past. And you can tell them that you don't believe that the four men in jail made those threats against Judge Smith, and you want to get the evidence to prove it, because you have a hunch that somehow those threats might be related to your investigation."

"Why do you think those threats are related to the investigation? The Judge Smith threats happened years before you ever met me."

"I don't know, it might be a long shot. But one of those Judge Smith custody orders that we got from Helen was for a boy who was the younger brother of one of the four guys in jail for threatening Judge Smith. That can't be just a coincidence."

"But the police had all that evidence about Judge Smith ordering the seizure of the guy's mother's house, etc. Isn't that what you said?"

"Yeah, but Ken thought at the time that it didn't make sense. The guy who supposedly was the ringleader, Jamal Johnson, was living a clean life. He had had significant problems in his youth, but he was working and going to school and supporting his mother and his little brother and sister."

"Did you say Jamal Johnson?"

"Yeah, why? Do you know him?"

"I don't know, maybe. It's a common name, but I knew someone at Southern with that name. I haven't thought about him for years. He's in jail now? Do you know if this Jamal Johnson was at Southern?"

"I don't know. Please call Ken. If you know Jamal, and he trusts you, he and everyone else might talk to you."

"I just can't do that."

"Think about it, Richard. I can go with you and support you if it would help."

"Maybe. I'll call Ken to see what I can find out. I'll come by your office after."

Twenty minutes later, Richard called Karen. "Do you mind coming to my office?"

"Sure, is everything okay?" He didn't sound okay.

"I'll tell you when you get here."

Karen knocked on Richard's closed office door as she let herself in. With tears streaming down his face, he dabbed at them with a tissue while also wiping his nose.

"What happened?"

"It's really bad. I don't know if I can talk about it, but I'll try. Jamal Johnson was the supposed ringleader in the Judge Smith threat. This is what Ken told me: Jamal's 25, spent time at Southern when I was there, he's from the south side. I know him. I know Jamal. And I know that he's innocent. There is no way that Jamal would have threatened anyone. He's the kindest person I've ever known -- except for maybe you. He was my best friend, my only friend really, at Southern. We were inseparable. We supported each other through all the abuse. We talked about it. He held me together, and I held him together. He's also a genius. He taught me how to play chess, we played all the time. I was playing chess with him when. . . .

"When I was called up to the director's office that day. That was the last time I ever saw Jamal or spoke to him. I wrote to him several times after I got out of the hospital, but my letters were all returned with a note that he didn't live there anymore, and then the place closed and I had no idea how to reach him."

"Jamal's family couldn't afford to visit because they didn't have gas money. His mom, sister and little brother tried really hard to come at Christmas time. When I told my Dad that my friend Jamal's family couldn't afford to visit him, Dad drove Jamal's family down when his mom could get time off from work. Dad bought a Chevy Suburban to fit them all. He brought Jamal candy and presents just like me. Jamal was like a brother and a best friend, all in one."

Richard pulled his knees up to his chest and wrapped his arms around his legs as tears kept streaming down his face. "I know that whatever supposed reason he's in jail, it's an injustice. I don't know how, and I don't know why, but the Jamal Johnson I know would never do anything bad."

"But Richard, you might be looking at this from the perspective of a ten-year-old boy," Karen said gently. "Ken told me that Jamal was sent away when he was ten for felony murder of an elderly woman."

"That's true, but you don't know the facts. Jamal was with a group of boys in the neighborhood when one of them decided to be tough and steal an old lady's purse. They were little boys who were poor, and they did something stupid. Jamal blamed himself because he went along. The woman broke her hip and later died from complications. Jamal had just turned ten and was the only one old enough to be charged with felony murder. The other boys were nine. None of them ever intended to hurt her, it was really just the one kid, and all he wanted to do was grab her purse. It was a stupid thing -- kids do stupid things all the time. But Jamal paid the ultimate price for doing something stupid when he was ten-years-old. The judge who convicted him ordered that he be held in juvenile custody until he turned eighteen. And I'm sure that if a group of my white ten-year-old friends in Evanston had done the same thing, they never would have been sent anywhere. Their parents would have grounded them, they would have written apology letters, and no one would have dared send them away.

"The fact that Jamal is in jail today is an injustice. I don't know how I'm possibly going to do this, but I need to speak to him. I need to fix this, because I know it's wrong." Richard was now sitting upright in his chair and speaking forcefully.

"Did you explain this to Ken?"

257

"No, as soon as I realized that we were talking about my friend Jamal, I was too upset to talk at all, and I told him I had to go and hung up."

"Richard, Ken gave me the names of all of the men who are in jail for threatening Judge Smith. I have it here, somewhere on my phone," Karen said as she fumbled with her phone. "Here it is," she said as she handed Richard the list.

"I knew all these guys, Karen. They were at Southern. One of them was kind of an angry and troubled kid, but the other two, like Jamal, they were squeaky clean. Good kids, from loving families. They were poor, and their families couldn't afford to visit them much, but they were good kids. I don't think any of them got in trouble at Southern when I was there."

"Okay. Let's call Ken, together," Karen said. Richard picked up his phone and made the call.

Chapter Forty-Seven

Ken had Jamal's "worker" at the prison arrange a time for Jamal to call Richard. Unlike most inmate calls, this was going to receive the special treatment that an inmate's call with their lawyer was given -- the call would not be recorded by the prison and would be conducted from the worker's office with no one listening in. Jamal would be told that it was being treated as an attorney call.

But then Richard got cold feet. He wouldn't be able to talk on the phone. It would have to be in person, face-to-face. The arrangements were changed, and he drove out to the prison. The idea was to meet and, if Jamal agreed, they would set up a time for a full interview.

Richard broke out into a sweat as he pulled in the front gate of the prison and parked his car. As required, he had his license with him, but he left everything else in the car except his keys, which he would have to turn in at the desk. He walked through security monitors and was patted down. And then he went through multiple electric gates where guards, sitting in a glass booth, controlled all the doors. As soon as Richard walked through the first metal gate, he heard it close and then electronically lock behind him. He started to sweat. He felt like he was back at Southern, with doors that you cannot open from the inside. Richard moved forward through the locked gates in a daze and eventually reached the worker's office. Jamal was sitting in a chair by the desk.

"Hey man," Jamal stood up to greet him, and Richard instinctively went up to hug Jamal, as tears streamed down Richard's face.

"Whoa," the worker intervened. "No physical contact allowed!"

"Yeah, I'm sorry, totally my fault. We just haven't seen each other in a long time," Richard said. He saw that Jamal, too, was wiping tears from his face.

"I'll leave you two alone, as I've been instructed to do by the FBI. But no physical contact. No handing nothing back and forth between you two. I'll be sitting right outside this glass window watching to make sure. Just knock on the glass when you're done."

Richard's meeting with Jamal was going to be in full view of the worker as well as anyone who walked by.

Jamal started, "Hey, the last time I saw you I was about to destroy you in chess.'"

Richard smiled. "Yeah, you always beat me, pretty badly. You were a master."

"I waited for you to come back. I memorized where all the pieces were. I was four moves away from check mate. I think about that board all the time in here, like if I could go back and finish that game. Like if everything that followed never happened."

"I thought about that game, too, for so long. It kind of held me together, somehow. I was definitely losing, but I kept trying to think of some way out."

"Richard, I would do anything for you, but I can't talk to you about anything, and we need to make this meeting as short as possible so that everyone knows that I didn't talk."

"Why? Tim Reilly is in jail, we're so close to figuring out everything that happened. Did you know that Judge Smith issued over thirty custody orders for no reason? We have the orders."

Jamal looked very uncomfortable. "I trust you. You're like my brother. That hasn't changed. But I just can't. These guys, they have all the power, you know?"

"I know, that's how I've felt my whole life. But our truth is stronger than their power. I have to believe that."

"Maybe for you. But not for me. Look where I am man. I have six months to go, and maybe then I'll get out if they don't pin something new on me. And as bad as it is for me, it was way worse for my little brother -- in the cemetery now because of what they did to him."

Jamal had been very close to his little brother. Richard remembered Ricky well from the visits. Richard had been devastated to hear this week that Ricky had passed -- so young. But he hadn't realized that Ricky's death was a part of all this.

"That's so horrible. I'm so sorry to hear that. I had heard that he had passed" -- Ken had told him -- "but I didn't know the circumstances."

"Suicide. Because of Reilly and Judge Smith. All because I knew too much. So, I can't talk. I've already said way too much. I've got to go." Jamal knocked on the glass to get the worker's attention.

"I think the FBI is going to be honest with this investigation, Jamal. Ken Shapiro at the FBI is a good guy. He wants to do the right thing."

"Yeah, well, he didn't do the right thing by putting me in here," Jamal said as he left the room.
"I'll be back for you in a minute," the worker said to Richard, as the worker and Jamal started back toward the series of locked electric doors.

Chapter Forty-Eight

Richard stopped to get something to eat on the way home, then decided to go back to the office instead. He wanted to write up the conversation with Jamal while his memory was fresh, so there would be an accurate record of what had been said. Richard got back to the office around eight p.m. The lobby was empty except for security. He waived hello to Shawn at the front desk.

"Mr. Adams," Shawn called to him. "Do you have a minute?"

Richard walked over to the desk. "Sure Shawn, what's up?" He hated that Shawn called him "Mr. Adams," but he knew Shawn had no choice. There were rules about that. Shawn called him by his first name when they were outside of the building. But, in the lobby, he had to be "Mr. Adams."

"I got a call from my sister, who got a call from my nephew after you left the prison. Apparently, you went to see him today."

"You're Jamal's uncle?" Richard was shocked. "Small world. How is Mrs. Johnson? She was always so nice to me."

"She's okay, but this situation is difficult. You need to understand that there are important reasons why Jamal feels that he can't speak to you or to the FBI. Very important reasons."

Richard wasn't sure how to respond, but he did his best. "Okay, I know Tim Reilly is a monster and he's covering up something terrible, but if we don't stand up to stuff like that, it's never going to get better."

"For you, maybe," Shawn said. "But, you know, it's not like that for us. Believe me. But my sister and I think that if anyone has a possibility of breaking this story wide open and getting justice, it's you. She and I talked a long time. You know, my nephew -- Jamal's little brother --died because of this."

"Yeah, Jamal told me. I'm still really upset about that."

"My sister and I -- we don't want any more boys to be harmed. Jamal is going to call her back at 9 p.m. tonight, on a recorded inmate call. She wants to tell him that he needs to talk to you, but they can't talk about it on the recorded line. So, we're not sure how to tell him that before we can visit, which won't be until the weekend. How urgent is it that you speak to him?"

"It's extremely urgent."

"Okay, but it has to happen in a room with no windows. No one watching. And we don't know how to communicate all of this to him when he calls tonight."

Richard thought hard. "I can take care of the windows part. Please have his mom tell him that he should not talk to anyone in law enforcement, but that you and she have decided that he needs to play more chess. He'll understand."

"Okay. One more thing, please promise me, and I mean, really promise, that you and Ms. Harding are going to do everything you can to keep him safe?"

"I promise. With all my heart. I love Jamal like a brother. I looked for him for years when I got out."

Richard went up to his office and wrote memos about his conversations with Jamal and Shawn, and then emailed the memos to himself so he would later be able to prove the timing. And then he called Ken to leave a message. To Richard's surprise, Ken answered his phone at 10 p.m. They planned Jamal's interview for 10 a.m. the next morning. Ken said he would work with the prison to make sure it would be in a room with no windows so no one could see.

Richard texted Karen that the interview might be on after all. He was heading to the apartment now, but they needed to prepare for the interview. Once he got home, they spent hours on Facetime lining up the questions and the documents for Jamal to sign and calling Ken to make sure Richard would cover everything Ken needed -- the release of his juvenile records, permission to share the interview with the FBI, and an oath that everything that he said in the interview was true and correct to the best of his knowledge, information and belief.

Richard and Karen arrived at the prison the next morning at 9 a.m. to allow ample time to get through security. Ken met them there, but stayed outside. His presence inside would do a lot more harm than good, but he wanted to be nearby in case he was needed. After Richard and Karen were searched multiple times, they were directed to the warden's office, where the interview would be conducted.

The warden introduced himself and said he was honored to meet Richard and Karen after reading about their work. He said that he'd seen the stories on television and the internet, and that someone needed to be protecting the boys in juvenile facilities. "So many of them end up here, because they are damaged beyond repair in those places. I'm glad that you are working to change that."

Jamal was brought in. Jamal and the warden clearly already knew each other, and it appeared that their relationship was positive. "Jamal's always been a model inmate, here," the warden said. "Frankly, I'd be happy if you get him the hell out." Richard introduced Jamal to Karen, as "my friend and a really brilliant lawyer," and he asked if it would be okay if she stayed nearby if any legal issues came up or if Richard needed help. Jamal agreed.

Karen and the Warden stepped out, leaving Richard alone with Jamal. Richard explained that the interview would just be the two of them, but that he had asked Karen to come because he wasn't sure if he could do it on his own. "You know, man, some of this stuff is still really, really hard for me to deal with." Richard also asked if it was okay if he recorded the interview, so that no one later would be able to change anything that was said and put words in Jamal's mouth. Jamal agreed.

Richard began. "So, in a normal interview, I would go through your background and everything, but I know you already, and this situation is stressful enough for both of us as it is. So, I'll just ask a really open-ended question: Do you have a story you want to tell?"

"Yes. I know that Tim Reilly and Judge Smith were paid cash for kids."

Chapter Forty-Nine

Richard's jaw dropped. "Okay, let's start at the beginning. What do you know, and when and how did you find out?"

"Well," Jamal began, "after you left and the Director got fired, things were really in chaos. Some guy who was on the board of directors, I don't know his name, he was an old white guy, came in to oversee things for a few weeks. The acting director was, I think, someone from DCFS who was just there for a few weeks before they closed the place down, and the board director was really running the place.

"I got called into the office because I was your friend, and some DCFS person wanted to interview me, along with law enforcement. But when I got to the office, the acting director wasn't there yet, and the board member was in the director's office, and the cop who was going to try to interview me hadn't arrived. They had me take a seat in the secretary's office, right outside the director's door. It was a kind of weird set up. You had to walk through her office to get to the director's office, and when you opened the door to her office, it totally blocked off the chair where I was sitting.

"So, I'm sitting there, and this is maybe a week after you left, maybe? The secretary, Mary -- remember her? She wasn't there. Someone told me that she had just gone to the bank, but she would be back in a few minutes, so I should just sit there, be quiet, and wait. Which I did.

"She came back in and sat down at her desk. She didn't see me when she came in, because I was kind of hidden from view, behind the door and she wasn't looking in my direction, which was kind of to her back. But I saw her real well. At that point, the guy on the board peeked his head in -- he couldn't see me either from where he was standing, but I recognized his voice because he'd spoken to all of us at a meeting after the Director was arrested. He said to Mary, 'Did you get the cash? Tim just called -- he should be here any minute to drop off the boy and make the delivery to Judge Smith.'

267

"Mary said that she had just gotten back from the bank and was about to count it. He said, 'great' and left. Mary then took a manila envelope out of her purse, and two white envelopes out of her desk. She pulled a lot of cash out of the manila envelope, and she started counting. She was counting out loud, but quietly, one hundred, two hundred. . . like that. She got to five thousand and put that money in one of the white envelopes. Then she counted the remaining money. There was fifteen thousand total -- which was shocking to me, I had never heard of anyone having that much cash, you know? But I figured that this was a business, and what did I know. She put the ten thousand in the other white envelope, and she wrote something on each of the envelopes. I thought it was a name or something.

"Within a few minutes, Tim Reilly came in. I knew who he was because you had warned me about him, and you had pointed him out from your window, remember?"

"Yes, I remember that."

" I remember he was in uniform," Jamal continued. "So, Reilly said to Mary, 'do you have my envelopes?' and she said, 'yes,' and handed them to him.

"Then, Reilly turned around to go out the door, and, for the first time, he saw me. His whole face and neck turned red. I could see his veins pumping in his neck. I thought he was going to kill me.

"He came over to me, grabbed me by the neck, and lifted me out of my chair by my neck. He said, 'if you ever tell a soul what you just saw I will lock your family up for the rest of their lives.'

"I was so scared, man," Jamal said as his eyes teared up, "I couldn't breathe. I thought I was going to die, and I literally shit my pants."

Richard interrupted, "Well, I know now what it feels like to have his hands on my neck, but he did it to me as an adult. I can't imagine how terrifying that must have been when you were a kid. How old were you?"

"Twelve. This was right after you left."

"So, what happened next?"

"Reilly dropped me back into my chair and left. Mary was quite angry too -- she said that I should have let her know I was in the room."

"And what happened after that?"

"Well, I thought to myself, there must be something really wrong with the cash and the two envelopes, or Reilly wouldn't have threatened me, and Mary would not be so angry. Honestly, if Reilly hadn't done that, I don't think I would even remember anything about that day. I was just waiting in the office, you know? But when he lifted me by my throat and I couldn't breathe, it was like every second that I was in that room was burned permanently into my memory."

"What happened next?"

"Nothing at first. But then I thought about how you told me and others about Reilly, to be wary of him, and I thought that I should tell kids about what I had seen. You know, I'm sure you remember, how we were all good at keeping secrets. So, over the next year, I told three friends. And the three of us, we kept it among ourselves until we each graduated at eighteen. They were a little younger than I was, so we reconnected after we all got out.

"When we were out, I got a job and I was taking classes at the community college -- I was studying criminal justice because I wanted to be a public defender one day for kids charged with crimes, and this whole thing really started to bug me. After a while, I learned that businesses don't do legitimate transactions of $15,000 in cash. I was lying awake at night, thinking about you and how Tim transported you and lied to you, saying that your Dad didn't want you anymore when that clearly wasn't true. I didn't remember the name of your judge at the time. So, I started talking to my three friends about it, and they started talking to others.

Reilly must have found about about it, somehow, because the next thing that happened was that he showed up at the house for my brother. Ricky was 15 at the time, and he took him to Stern Harrison. For no reason. Ricky was a good kid who had never done anything wrong -- not like me. Ricky was an honor student."

"Ricky was awesome. I remember him from the visits."

Jamal started crying. "They took him to Stern Harrison. Judge Smith issued the order. The reasons in the order were all lies. They said I had caught Ricky threatening to kill people with a gun. They had a fake affidavit that I never signed but contained my signature.

"Ricky couldn't handle it there. He didn't say, but we know what happens at those places to the kids. Ricky changed. I think he must have blamed me. We were really worried about him. He wasn't the same anymore. He refused to see me or Mom when we went to visit. And then he was gone."

Now, Richard and Jamal were both crying.

"It's not your fault man, you know that. These guys are just evil."

"I know that, on some level, but the truth is that it would never have happened if I kept my mouth shut."

"What happened next?"

"I was really pissed and I didn't care if I lived or died anymore, so I started telling everyone I knew the story. Then, about three years ago, I was at work, and Reilly came in. He said that he needed to talk to me down at the station. I was scared shitless, you know? But I didn't know what else to do, so I went. He drove me to the police station at Michigan Avenue and 35th. In the back of a cruiser. I hadn't been in a cruiser since I was ten.

"At the station, he took my phone, my wallet and my keys. He was gone for a long time -- like maybe forty minutes -- while I sat in a room. Then he came back in, and he told me that he wanted to 'remind me' that if I ever told anyone what I had seen in Mary's office that day, that he would put my entire family in jail. He said that I obviously had not gotten the point from what happened to Ricky, and I needed a reminder to keep my mouth shut.

"I was so scared, but I tried not to show it. I lied, and I told him that I had no idea what he was talking about, that I didn't remember anything in Mary's office. He said, 'Well, that's good,' and he handed me back my stuff and let me leave.

"I was supposed to meet my friends for wings that night, so I told them all about it over dinner. They wanted me to call the FBI, to do something about the threat, but I was too scared. Meanwhile, the state cops raided my Mom's house. My mom's boyfriend smoked a little bit of weed, we all did, you know? But there was probably less than ten joints worth of stuff in the house. My mom's boyfriend admitted that it was his pot, and they arrested him.

"And then one day as I left the house for class, Reilly was waiting in an unmarked car out front. He called me up to the car, and he said, 'You lied to me. You're not keeping your mouth shut, and now, you're really going to pay. I hope you learn your lesson.'

"He knew I was talking to the guys about it, but I had no idea how he knew. Within a couple of days, Judge Smith issued an order seizing my Mom's house. It was just about paid off. She had a 30-year mortgage and only had six payments left. We were homeless, just like that, and she lost all that money she had in the house.

"After we were homeless, Reilly came into McDonald's, where I was working. He picked the line where I was the cashier. When he came up to the register, he placed his order, and then he said, 'Have you learned your lesson yet, Jamal?'

"'Yes sir,' I said. But really, when he said that, it just made me want to tell the world. So, I immediately texted my three friends. I texted his exact words. I told them I wasn't scared of him. They all texted me back, saying that he and Judge Smith were obviously on someone's payroll. That Reilly and Judge Smith were selling kids.

"And then, all four of us got arrested. Reilly came to the barracks when I was being processed, and he made the trooper leave the room so he could talk to me alone. He told me that, if we all pleaded guilty to threatening Judge Smith, that would be the end of it. But if we ever told a soul about the payments, he would put my mother in jail and he would do to all my friends what he did to me -- take their brothers and sisters away.

"The four of us, we were in separate facilities and we couldn't communicate with each other. I signed a confession, and my lawyer told me that my friends all signed confessions the same day, with everyone saying the same thing: that we had threatened Judge Smith because we were angry that Judge Smith had ordered the seizure of my mom's house.

"Richard, we never threatened Judge Smith."

"I believe you, Jamal," Richard said, very earnestly.

"And I figured out how Reilly knew that I had told people."

"How's that?"

"I think the day when Reilly took my phone, my wallet and my keys, that he installed some kind of malware on my phone so he could read my texts."

Richard's heart started pounding as he remembered that Reilly had asked Karen to let him install an app on her phone and computer.

"What happened to your phone?"

"That's the good part of the story. My phone was really old, and it basically only worked if it was plugged in. The cops came and arrested me at work, and my phone was turned off and plugged in back in the kitchen. The cops never asked me about my phone when they processed me -- they just took the stuff in my pockets, which was my wallet, my keys and my asthma inhaler. But one of my co-workers, who knew that I would never do something wrong, she unplugged my phone and gave it to my mother.

"My Mom is really smart about internet privacy stuff, and she immediately figured out that Reilly must have found out about our texts by monitoring my phone. So, Mom never plugged it in again, and she gave it to my uncle the moment she got it.

"Shawn?"

"Yes, Uncle Shawn has been like a dad to me my whole life after my Dad died when I was little. Shawn has it in a safe deposit box somewhere. If you get the phone, it probably still has the malware on it, sending stuff to Reilly's phone, or at least, the phone he had at the time.

"Two days later, the police went nuts about my phone. They interviewed me in the prison, even though I had a lawyer and they were not supposed to talk to me without my lawyer being present. I know that they were wrong to question me, but I was so scared. I told them I did not know where the phone was, which was true at the time. Then the police got a search warrant for my mom's car because she and my sister were living in the car at the time, but of course, the phone wasn't there. They yelled at my mom and my sister and demanded that they tell them where my phone was. My mom and my sister were real quiet. They were careful not to lie. My mom said, 'Didn't you get his phone when you arrested him?' and put the blame back on them. They got frustrated and left them alone."

"Do you think those texts are still on the phone?"

"They should be, because I don't think Reilly could have done anything to my phone when it was turned off and charging, or afterwards, when it was dead. That's why Shawn keeps it in a safe deposit box. So, when the FBI gets the phone, make sure that they use some technology to save the messages before whatever Reilly put on the phone erases it, okay? And they have to turn it on in a safe room where there's no internet access.

"But even more important -- the malware will still be on the phone. Maybe they can link that directly to Reilly. Maybe it was forwarding my texts to his cell or something."

"That's brilliant. I'll make sure the FBI knows," Richard said.

"So, Richard, I trust you -- and only you -- to get that phone from Uncle Shawn, okay?"

"Sure, man. For sure. I'll get the phone and turn it over to Ken Shapiro."

"Are you sure you can trust him? I mean, look what happened last time, and how I got here."

"Yes, I am pretty sure we can trust Ken. I've talked to him a lot about our investigation generally, and his heart is in the right place. I think he'll work hard to try to undo the damage here. I can't promise, but that's what I think." Richard was actually much more confident about Ken's character than his words might lead Jamal to think.

"Yeah well, nothing's going to bring my brother back."

"No, but at least maybe Reilly and Judge Smith will pay for that, and they'll be in jail so they can't do it to anyone else."

"One more thing I forgot to mention, my three friends, when they got their phones back, their families looked for the text messages, and they had all been erased."

"Wow. So, it is incredibly important to get them off your phone. Did you have a cloud account or anything? Do you think Tim might have been able to access that and erase them?"

"I don't think so. My phone was so unreliable that I used my mom's phone for two-step authentication. I don't think he would have ever been able to get into my cloud account, but I don't know. I can give you my account number and password now, if you want."

Richard wrote the information down. "I'm wondering, what about GPS monitoring, through your apps or Google? Do you think your phone will show that you were never at any of those places where the threats were sent from?"

"It should. Between tuition and supporting my family, I never had the money to go out for a coffee or a donut."

"I have another question. You said that Tim Reilly and Judge Smith were paid cash for kids. How do you know that Reilly and Judge Smith actually got the money? I mean, Reilly got the envelopes, but how do we know what happened with that money?" Richard looked pensive, like he was trying to figure it out.

"It was obvious to me that first day in Mary's office that Reilly was on the take, because there was no other reason that would explain him threatening me. But I wondered about the fact that there were two envelopes for years. But I got the answer when Judge Smith wrote the orders to take my brother into custody for no reason and to seize my mom's house. He had to be getting some huge benefit from keeping me quiet in order to risk his career like that. Of course, no one would ever believe me because I was a black kid who was convicted of felony murder when I was ten, but obviously, that wasn't enough for Judge Smith. He had to destroy me to make sure that I would never tell."

"This is all so overwhelming. You're incredibly strong and brave to tell me this now."

"You were brave when you warned me about Tim Reilly. It's all about keeping other kids safe, you know?"

"Amen to that. Is there anything else you want to tell me? Anything we've missed?" Richard wanted to get the story about Jamal's brother's suicide, but it didn't seem like the time to bring it up.

"Oh, yeah, one more thing. My time here is almost up, I should get out soon. But, all of a sudden, out of the blue, I was interviewed again this month by the state police for some threats that were sent to Karen Harding. I know nothing about that, and it's crazy because I have no access to the internet here. I don't know anything about those threats, but the state police said that they had the same pattern as the threats that I'm in jail for. I refused to speak to the state police about it, but it seemed like it was a message from Tim Reilly. It was his way of saying, 'You're about to get out of jail Jamal, but I still control you.' That's what I think, anyway. I just want it to stop. I don't want them to keep doing this to my family, but, maybe even more important, I don't want them to ever again do it to someone else."

When Richard had no more questions and Jamal had nothing more to say, they stood up and held each other tightly in a long embrace. "I missed you man. Can I come to see you? Can I bring a chess board? We need to finish that game and start a new one."

"That would be great," Jamal said. "We have some chess boards here. I'll ask if I can bring one to the visit."

Chapter Fifty

Ken, Karen and Richard listened to the recording of Jamal's interview in their car in the prison parking lot. Ken was devastated. "We failed this kid, and worse, we allowed Tim to destroy him, his family and his friends. I failed him. I failed all of them."

"Don't beat yourself up Ken. You were one of Tim's victims, too," Karen said.

"How do we prove that Jamal's telling the truth?" Richard asked.

"There are pieces of his story -- the most material piece, about the money -- that we have already corroborated," Ken began.

"The number one rule in law enforcement is to follow the money. The Southern facility doesn't exist anymore, but its bank still maintains its records -- as required by law. We got those records, which were so fruitful that we used them as a basis to get a warrant for the bank records at Stern Harrison. For every one of the thirty Judge Smith custody orders, we have a check written for $15,000 from the Southern or Stern Harrison account to a charity called 'Better Days for Children.' All of the checks were written on the same day as a Judge Smith custody order."

"Oh my God," Richard said.

"It gets better," Ken said. "The secretary he identified, Mary Kaminski, she signed each of those checks. Kaminski was also a signatory on the Better Days account, so we got those records as well. The facility checks were never deposited in the Better Days account. Instead, the checks were all cashed, in person at the bank, by Kaminski, on the same day that the checks were written. She's on the security video, cashing the checks, on behalf of Better Days. She signed the checks on the facility account, and then she endorsed them and cashed them on the charity account without ever depositing the funds. The charity was a fraud-- it was a shell that they used to launder the money to essentially purchase the children from Judge Smith.

"And it looks like there are way more than thirty transactions like that. The total amount in checks made payable to Better Days was over $150,000 per year, for eighteen years, but we haven't traced each of those checks to a Judge Smith order. After Southern closed, Kaminski moved to Stern Harrison and it continued. On the books of Southern and Stern Harrison, it looks like those entities donated over $150,000 to Better Days every year, but the foundation never saw a penny of that money. The last check corresponds with the last order, which was Judge Smith's order for Jamal's brother. After that point, Judge Smith was no longer a juvenile court judge, so he had no authority to take custody of the kids. It looks like Tim got $5,000 per kid and Judge Smith got $10,000. And we suspect that a new juvenile judge started issuing orders after Judge Smith was elevated to the federal bench, because the checks to Better Days, which were cashed without ever being deposited, started up again a few months later.

"Tracking cash is really hard," Ken continued. "We're going to have to look at Tim's and Judge Smith's financial records with a fine-toothed comb to prove that they were spending more than they were making through legitimate means. But Mary Kaminski might be our ace in the hole. If we can get her to flip and cooperate, we'll be golden."

Karen jumped in, "I think it will be easy to make her flip if you first accuse her of stealing the money. She'll want to convince you that she didn't steal the money, and she'll be more likely to tell you where the money went."

"Brilliant idea, Karen." Ken was impressed. "And then there is always the possibility that Tim or Judge Smith will cooperate, but we'll have to see where the evidence is at that point. You don't want to give a sweet deal to the monsters of the world, and those two are at the top of my list for sick behavior. They were literally selling kids."

"I don't understand," Richard said. "Was this a sex ring? Were all these kids sent there so they could be abused?"

"It doesn't look like that's the case. It was just simply about money. The average cost around the country of housing a kid in facilities like these is $150,000 per year. Southern and Stern Harrison are privately-owned facilities. Whenever there were empty beds, that was money that wasn't being made. For every kid Judge Smith wrongly sent there, or kept there pursuant to one of his court orders, the owners profited. This was a money-making venture where kids were for sale to keep the facilities full so the owners made as much money as possible."

"That's really disgusting," Richard said. "But, there's still one thing I don't know -- why me? Why did they pick me?"

"We have a lead on that, too," Ken said. "We are now working with the Illinois Attorney General's Office to get all of Judge Smith's custody orders, and the Assistant AG on the case told me that, when she contacted Judge Smith's former clerk, the clerk asked her if it had to do with 'that Richard Adams investigation.' The AAG told her that she couldn't talk about it, and the clerk responded -- without any questioning -- that 'Judge Smith despises Richard Adams.'"

"Did she say why?" Richard asked. "No one hates me, except I guess Tim Reilly."

"The clerk said that Judge Smith is Officer Michael Connolly's brother-in-law, and that Judge Smith has said many times that you destroyed his sister's life. Our agents then went back and screened all the old video and newspaper clippings, and the video court records from Connolly's two trials, and we used facial recognition technology. Judge Smith was at both trials. He attended every day of the murder trial when you were five, and every day of the weapons case when you were ten. Judge Smith must have seen you and your father during the weapons trial, and it re-fueled his anger. He issued your custody order within 24 hours after Connolly was sentenced. And Karen, of course you were the one who tried the weapons case, so we can assume Judge Smith doesn't like you much either."

Ken continued, "And here's the best part. While Tim deleted all of his emails and texts with Judge Smith, Judge Smith was too stupid to do the same. He stored his emails on his email account and his texts on his cloud account forever, so we have them going to back more than fifteen years. Although there are no messages that directly refer to money, Judge Smith was constantly texting Tim about what time Tim would be bringing his envelope. And we can tie those texts to the dates of his orders and the dates that Tim dropped the kids off at Southern and Stern Harrison."

"I still have so many questions, Ken," Karen said. "Like why did they threaten me? And how did Tim know that Richard was investigating this?"

"We don't have all the answers yet, Karen. We might never have them. Maybe if Tim cooperates, we'll know more. But there's a text exchange from Judge Smith to Tim the day before your threats." Ken read from his phone, "Did you hear that Richard Adams is spending the summer working at the bitch's firm? I think he's up to something."

"Why does Judge Smith hate me? He's never shown been anything but professional in the cases of mine where he was the judge." Karen said.

"You put his brother-in-law in jail, and destroyed his sister's life." Ken turned to Richard. "I also have a question for you Richard. Do you remember what time Tim dropped you off that day at Southern?"

"I believe it was around 5, because the kids were all heading up to dinner when we got there, and that happened at 5."

"Interesting. The reason I asked is because one of Judge Smith's texts to Tim is dated on February 14th, fourteen years ago. Judge Smith was inquiring about what time his envelope would be delivered, and Tim responded, and I quote, 'dropping kid off at 5 pm, should get to your house by 10.'"

Richard slumped into a chair and started crying. They all tried to console him, but there are some things that words just can't fix. Ken said that they had agents who were going to stop Mary Kaminski on her way home, after she left her office at 5, and bring her in for questioning. That helped a little.

Chapter Fifty-One

Richard went with Shawn and Susanna to retrieve Jamal's phone from the safe deposit box, along with the charger. Having Susanna there was awkward, and she didn't say much, but Ken said she had to be there to establish the chain of custody of the phone.

Ken called Karen two hours later to tell her that the phone was a gold mine. Susanna had run Jamal's phone through the latest cellphone-cracking system. All of the texts Jamal had discussed were still there; there was malware on the phone that tracked the phone's location; and additional malware that forwarded all the texts to an online drive maintained by the State Police. Susanna was working with the Illinois Attorney General's office to determine who in the State Police had accessed the file and when. All bets were on Tim Reilly.

Meanwhile, Karen was confirmed by the Senate, and she was going to be sworn in at 9 a.m. on Friday. She was relieved about the timing because she'd made an appointment with her gynecologist to get an IUD later that morning. Things seemed to be progressing with Jonathan, and she didn't want to have to use condoms once things got to that point.

News about her confirmation was spreading and everyone started calling her to congratulate her. Jonathan stopped by, closed the door, and walked over to kiss her to congratulate her. It was a passionate kiss, and wonderful, but it ended abruptly when Chris buzzed her, "The U.S. Attorney from the Northern District of Indiana is on the line."

The call was from the U.S. Attorney who was overseeing the Tim Reilly-Judge Smith investigations. She pushed the button to put him on speaker.

"Hey, Karen, congrats about your swearing in on Friday. Great news. I'm calling because, while you obviously can't be involved in this investigation, I need to let you know what is happening on Friday. You're being sworn in at 9, right?"

"Yes, do I need to move that?"

"No, not at all. That works fine. The issue -- this is completely confidential, I'm sure you understand. . . ."

Jonathan motioned toward the door, and Karen nodded as he stepped outside.

"Yes, of course, I won't tell anyone," Karen said. She turned off the speaker.

"We're arresting Judge Smith on Friday morning, and, if everything goes according to plan, we'll have a press conference at 2 p.m. You and Richard Adams are welcome to attend, as victims in the case.

"The secretary at Southern, Mary Kaminski, gave a detailed, credible statement under oath about the payments to Judge Smith and Tim Reilly. They're going to be charged with a long list very serious charges. Kaminski has entered into a cooperation agreement; she'll plead guilty to a lesser charge. Reilly is obviously already in custody, so getting him to court is not an issue, but Judge Smith is presenting some complications."

"What's up?"

"Judge Smith is a hunter, as am I, but the word is that he is really obsessed with guns. According to the registry, he owns 27 operable weapons, from handguns to various rifles. He has an open-carry permit, and one of our agents who was a former clerk of his told us that Judge Smith wears his gun every day, even to the office, strapped to his ankle. But the clerk swears that Judge Smith takes the gun off before he goes into the courtroom, and that he locks the gun in a safe in his office."

"That's terrifying."

Karen was well aware that men and women in law enforcement put their lives at risk every day from unknown terrors, but some of their tasks are more dangerous than others. Responding to a domestic violence call or a live shooter are at the top of the danger list, but arresting someone can always be treacherous, so the agents put a lot of thought into how to arrest someone safely. When they know someone has guns at home, for example, they will likely plan the arrest for outside the home. When the person has a license to carry, it becomes even trickier.

A lot of people go nuts when they get arrested. Some attempt "suicide by cop" by pointing the gun at the police, hoping to get shot. Others just try to kill the cops and get away. Some take hostages. There are countless things that can go very wrong when you arrest someone who has a loaded gun. Knowing that Judge Smith had a license to carry *and* that he carried his gun everywhere was complicating his arrest.

"Based on what his former clerk is telling us, we think the safest place to arrest him is in the courtroom. That's obviously very unconventional, and it poses a risk of harm if we are wrong to everyone in the courtroom. But, if we arrest him anywhere else when we know he'll have his gun, we're definitely putting other people at risk. It's a tough, tough, decision, and we've run it by Washington. We're going to arrest him Friday morning, in the middle of his jury trial. When he's on the bench, we're going to go in his chambers and confirm that his gun is in the safe, and then we're going to take him down in the courtroom."

"Wow, that's so scary. I assume your guys are all going to be wearing vests and helmets?" Karen always got worried when her officers were planning dangerous activities like this, and she knew she really didn't need to ask about the obvious precautions, but the answers somehow always made her feel slightly better. "Is there anything I can do to help?"

"Yes, on the vests and helmets, of course, and thanks for the offer, but we're all set. I just wanted to let you know the arrangements. And, um, well, the FBI agents working the case wanted me to tell you for another reason.

"Jury trials are public, you know? We could get in quite a bit of trouble for this, but some people thought that Richard Adams might want to be there. Normally, we don't warn victims about the details of the arrest, but this is a special case. Richard would have to be subtle so as to not cause Judge Smith to notice him and think something was up, but jury trials are public and he has the same right as anyone else to attend Judge Smith's jury trial. Friday at around 10:30, when the judge usually brings the jury back from his mid-morning break, would be a good time, if you get my drift."

"Are you sure that won't affect your case? And what about the jury trial?"

"We don't think having Richard there will affect anything. Apparently, it's a high-profile case, so the courtroom will be packed. If Richard sits in the back, Judge Smith won't see him, and Richard can quietly leave afterward. No one will notice that he's there. And, in terms of the jury trial, it's going to be null and void, a mistrial, the moment Judge Smith is arrested anyway.

"Then, if all goes according to plan, we'll hold the press conference. We definitely want you and Richard at the press conference, Richard especially. The official statement that is going to be released discusses Richard's efforts, and the efforts that you and the firm have made. Our staff is going to go over the statement with Richard directly to make sure that he is comfortable with it in terms of whether we reveal private information relating to his childhood or not. I mean, obviously, it will be in the indictment, but it's up to him whether it's in the press release."

"Okay. I'll let Richard know. Please let everyone know how grateful we are for the extraordinary work that the FBI has done on this case, and that we will be praying that everything goes well and no one gets hurt during the arrest." Although she was not a religious person, it was always her practice to pray for the agents when they were doing arrests like this. Whether there was a God or not, the prayers couldn't hurt, and the agents needed all the help they could get to stay safe.

Richard said that there was no way he would miss this for the world. Although the whole team wanted to go with him to support him and watch the arrest, they decided that only one summer clerk would go with Richard -- his friend Jackson. Jackson also checked the rules on videotaping court proceedings from your cell phone and decided that it was better to check their phones with security downstairs than get arrested.

Richard and Jackson went to the courthouse at 10 a.m., wearing jeans and sneakers so as to not stand out, and they hung out in the hallway outside the courtroom until Judge Smith announced the mid-morning recess at 10:15. When everyone went back in shortly before 10:30, Richard and Jackson shuffled back into the courtroom with the crowd and took a seat in the very last row, where they wouldn't be noticed, with Richard sitting on the aisle, by the door.

"All rise!" the court crier announced.

Everyone stood. Judge Smith came in and sat down in his seat at the bench. And then all the doors opened at once. Agents rushed into the courtroom in full protective gear, with vests and helmets with "FBI" in large white letters, and face protectors to keep them safe from spit and who knows what else. They rushed from the two doors in the rear of the courtroom that flanked the bench where Judge Smith was sitting, and agents rushed in from the public access door in the front. Judge Smith yelled at them to get the hell out of his courtroom, and then, when he realized they were there to arrest him, he began to run. Of course, a middle-aged judge wasn't about to outrun in-shape FBI agents, and he was quickly tackled to the floor. No shots were fired. They searched him for weapons, finding only the empty gun sling by his ankle, stood him up, in handcuffs, attached leg irons, and started to march him down the aisle through the courtroom, toward the front door.

Richard took a half-step into the aisle so he could get a better look. He stood straight and tall, staring at Judge Smith, directly into his eyes, as the agents lead him, now a prisoner, down the aisle toward the door. Judge Smith was struggling with the agents, futilely trying to somehow pull his arms out of their firm grasp, while yelling, "How dare you arrest a federal judge! You have no right to do for this! You will go to jail for this!" He was too agitated to notice Richard.

Tears started streaming down Richard's face, and then he noticed that the two agents who were holding onto Judge Smith were fighting back tears as well. As they got closer, Richard made eye contact with then. Through all of their protective gear, he recognized Ken Shapiro and Susanna James.

Chapter Fifty-Two

Karen was sworn in at 9:00 a.m. as the United States Attorney for the Northern District of Illinois. Karen brought the kids, and Jonathan and Richard both came to watch, along with Denise, Chris, and other friends from the Firm. The whole thing took fifteen minutes, and that included some nice remarks by Senator Williams and the Chief Judge of the District. Karen and Jonathan were going to have a celebratory dinner with Cindy, Joey and Kyle. Not a "coming out" event, not just yet. Just friends for a little longer, until Jonathan thought Kyle would be more comfortable with the idea. But it was an encouraging step in the right direction.

At 1:00 p.m. sharp, the U.S. Attorney for the Northern District of Indiana began the press conference on the arrests to a packed crowd of reporters, both local and national, in the press room at the federal building. The national press was already covering the story of the Director of State Police who was caught on video attempting to murder a young lawyer, so every network and every major paper and internet news site was there.

The U.S. Attorney explained that his office would be overseeing these cases, because the new U.S. Attorney, Karen Harding, had a conflict. And then he said the following:

"We are here this afternoon to announce indictments brought by the grand jury and the arrests of United States District Court Judge Harold Smith, Circuit Court Judge Angela Henry, Former Director of the State Police Timothy Reilly, and others. Before I begin, however, I must caution that, in our criminal justice system, everyone is presumed innocent until proven guilty, and found guilty by a jury. The fact that charges have been brought does not mean that a person is guilty. At this point, this discussion involves allegations of fact found by the grand jury, but those allegations are merely allegations and the individuals named in the indictment are presumed to be innocent.

"Fifteen years ago, a ten-year-old boy was taken into state's custody for no apparent reason, and that little boy is standing here today, as a 24-year-old law student at Northwestern, Richard Adams. Mr.

Adams was determined to get answers about what happened to him and whether there were other children who were harmed in the same way. Today, due entirely to the outstanding work of Richard Adams, with the support of Karen Harding and the distinguished law firm of Christian and Johnson, we are announcing the arrests of Judges Smith and Henry, who, together, over the course of 15 years, ordered dozens and dozens of boys into state custody in exchange for hundreds of thousands of dollars from the institutions that profited from those placements. The former Director of the Illinois State Police, Timothy Reilly, has been indicted with multiple crimes for his participation in this scheme, including for the unlawful receipt of illegal payments in exchange for delivering the children to the facilities, for attempted murder of a witness in a federal investigation, obstruction of justice, mail and wire fraud, income tax evasion, perjury, and making multiple false statements to the FBI in an investigation. Also indicted today is the former bookkeeper of both the Southern and Stern Harrison facilities, Mary Kaminski, and the Chairman of the Board of Directors of Stern Harrison, Andrew Thomas. The charges filed against these defendants include obstruction of justice, conspiracy, mail and wire fraud, money laundering, human trafficking, and income tax evasion. The full indictment is available on our website and we have copies here for the press.

"When Judge Smith was promoted to the federal bench, the indictment alleges that he passed off his side job of taking cash for kids to his cousin, Judge Henry, who had been elected to replace Judge Smith. By that point, Mr. Reilly had become the Director of the State Police, and, as far as our investigation has determined, Mr. Reilly was no longer taking cash for kids at that time.

"Judge Smith and Mr. Reilly have also been indicted by the grand jury for threatening attorney Karen Harding, and criminal conspiracy.

"Again, I must reiterate that these charges are merely allegations, and that all defendants are presumed innocent until proven guilty."

The U.S. Attorney continued: "We also want to report today that we have filed emergency motions with the court to vacate the convictions of four young men who were wrongfully prosecuted for having made threats to Judge Smith. We know now that they are innocent of those crimes, and the grand jury has determined that they were framed by Director Reilly and Judge Smith in order to coerce these young men to remain silent about what they knew about the "cash for kids" illegal scheme. We have filed an emergency motion in federal court requesting the immediate release of these four individuals from prison, and that their convictions be vacated. The Department of Justice apologizes publicly to these men and their families for their wrongful convictions, incarceration, and other harm that was done to them and their families as a result of these false arrests. Former Director Reilly and Judge Smith have been indicted by the grand jury for additional charges regarding these four young men, including extortion, criminal conspiracy, making false statements to the FBI in the course of an investigation, and obstruction of justice.

"In addition, as a result of this investigation, the Attorney General of Illinois will be announcing additional state charges against five individuals who, until today, worked at the Stern Harrison facility, for the alleged sexual abuse of children. These men will be charged for their conduct in an ongoing child sexual trafficking scheme, and of aggravated sexual abuse of multiple boys, over a period of many years, involving dozens of victims, at both Stern Harrison and Southern."

He then named the men that Karen and Richard's witnesses had identified, including John Stone. "Again, I remind you that individuals are presumed innocent of these charges until proven guilty."

"Finally," the U.S. Attorney continued, "we want to announce that there is an ongoing investigation regarding the sexual abuse of children at the Illinois facilities for children, including at Southern and Stern Harrison. If anyone was a victim of abuse at either of those facilities, or any other facility in the State of Illinois, or has evidence that might assist us in our investigation of child sexual and/or physical abuse at state facilities, we urge you to contact the Attorney General's office.

"Mr. Adams and Ms. Harding will not be taking any questions, as they have advised us that, as a lawyer and a law student, they are obliged by the rules of ethics to not make any extrajudicial statements about a pending criminal case."

CHAPTER FIFTY-THREE

Afterward, Richard joined Karen in her new office, and they closed the door.

"Congratulations! Nice space! And thank you!" he said as he hugged her, then hesitantly pulled away.

"Best day of my career, that's for sure," Karen said.

"Best day of my life."

"Um, I have some news, too."

"Do tell," Richard said as he sat down in the government-issued chair in her office.

"I'm glad you're sitting down. Well, after I got sworn in this morning, I went to my gynecologist to get an IUD, but I can't get it."

"Why are you telling me this, when you've made it clear that we have no future?" Richard seemed irritated, but then concerned. "How come? Is everything okay?"

"I can't get it because, um, well, I'm pregnant."

Author's Note

Although this novel is a work of fiction, the idea that juvenile facilities can pay kickbacks to judges to place children at those facilities for profit is all too real.

In 2007, the Juvenile Law Center in Philadelphia received a frantic call from a parent. The investigations that followed, conducted first by the Juvenile Law Center, and ultimately by the FBI and the United States Attorney's Office, determined that two Pennsylvania judges, Mark Ciavarella, Jr. and Michael Conahan, had accepted nearly $2.6 million in alleged kickbacks from two privately-run juvenile facilities. In 2011, Judge Ciavarella was found guilty following a jury trial, and was sentenced to 28 years in prison. Others pleaded guilty. Judge Conahan was sentenced to 17.5 years in prison; the former co-owner of the privately-run facilities, Robert Powell, was sentenced to 18 months; and developer Robert Mericle was sentenced to a year in prison.

In 2009, the Pennsylvania Supreme Court, after first denying requests for relief on behalf of the children, finally vacated all of the juvenile decisions for youth who had appeared before Judge Ciavarella during a five-year period, dismissed the cases with prejudice, and ordered the children's records expunged. It has been estimated that this order affected more than 2,500 children and more than 6,000 cases. According to the Juvenile Law Center, over 50% of the children who appeared before Judge Ciavarella lacked legal representation, and over 60% of those children were removed from their homes. You can read more about the tragic scandal here: https://jlc.org/luzerne-kids-cash-scandal

In the civil cases brought on behalf of the children against Judges Ciavarella and Conahan, the United States District Court held, in case after case, that the judges had absolute immunity for their "judicial acts" of ordering the children into custody, and thus, they could not be sued by the children or their families for their court orders -- even though those orders were allegedly issued as a part of the overall kickback scheme.

Today, states can pay upward of $150,000 or more per child, per year, to place a child at a residential juvenile facility. As the costs get more and more prohibitive, many states are turning to privately-run facilities to save money. The temptation to keep these privately-run facilities full and make the most money possible puts children (and their families) at risk of such potential schemes.

Unfortunately, the very procedures designed to protect children in juvenile proceedings can have the opposite effect. Across the United States, juvenile detention hearings are confidential court proceedings, where no one other than the participants to the hearing have access to the record. There is no way for a family to ever know, for example, whether other children who commit similar acts are sentenced to a facility, much less whether other children of the same race or different races are treated equally. There is also no way for the press to access the court records. The purpose behind the confidential nature of the proceedings is to protect the children who are involved, as it can ruin a person's life if misdeeds and crimes committed as a child become part of the public record. But that well-intended purpose of secrecy can also increase the risk of undetectable abuse, of which the Pennsylvania case is perhaps an extreme example, but the reality is that all children are at risk.

Furthermore, once a child is placed at a facility, the judge's decision about whether to keep the child there is typically based on recommendations of the employees at the facility. Even absent a heinous scheme like the one uncovered in Pennsylvania, employees in a private facility may well have a conflict of interest in keeping the child housed there since the profitability of the institution in which they work is dependent on maximizing the number of residents/inmates. While private prisons of all types have come under recent criticism, the issues are particularly profound with regard to juvenile institutions given the closed and confidential nature of juvenile proceedings.

In addition, the entire juvenile justice system needs to be scrutinized. The ACLU has committed to challenging the "school-to-prison pipeline," which the ACLU describes as "a disturbing national trend wherein children are funneled out of public schools and into the juvenile and criminal justice systems." The ACLU has found that,

"Many of these children have learning disabilities or histories of poverty, abuse, or neglect, and would benefit from additional educational and counseling services. Instead, they are isolated, punished, and pushed out." In the end, "the ACLU believes that children should be educated, not incarcerated."

You can read more about the ACLU's work here: https://www.aclu.org/issues/juvenile-justice/school-prison-pipeline.